CRYSTAL FALLS A WITCH'S REVENGE

MARK SPEARS

Copyright © 2023 Mark Spears
Crystal Falls is a work of fiction. All names, characters, locations, and incidents are the products of the author's imagination or are used fictitiously. Any resemblance to actual events, locales, or persons, living or dead, is entirely coincidental.

CRYSTAL FALLS
Copyright © 2023 by Mark Spears
Cover by Amy Spears
All rights reserved.

The uploading, scanning, and distribution of this book in any form or by any means—including but not limited to electronic, mechanical, photocopying, recording, or otherwise—without the copyright holder's permission is illegal and punishable by law. Please purchase only authorized editions of this work and do not participate in or encourage electronic piracy of copyrighted materials. Your support of the author's rights is appreciated.

For Amy, Cory, Kayla, and Apollo.

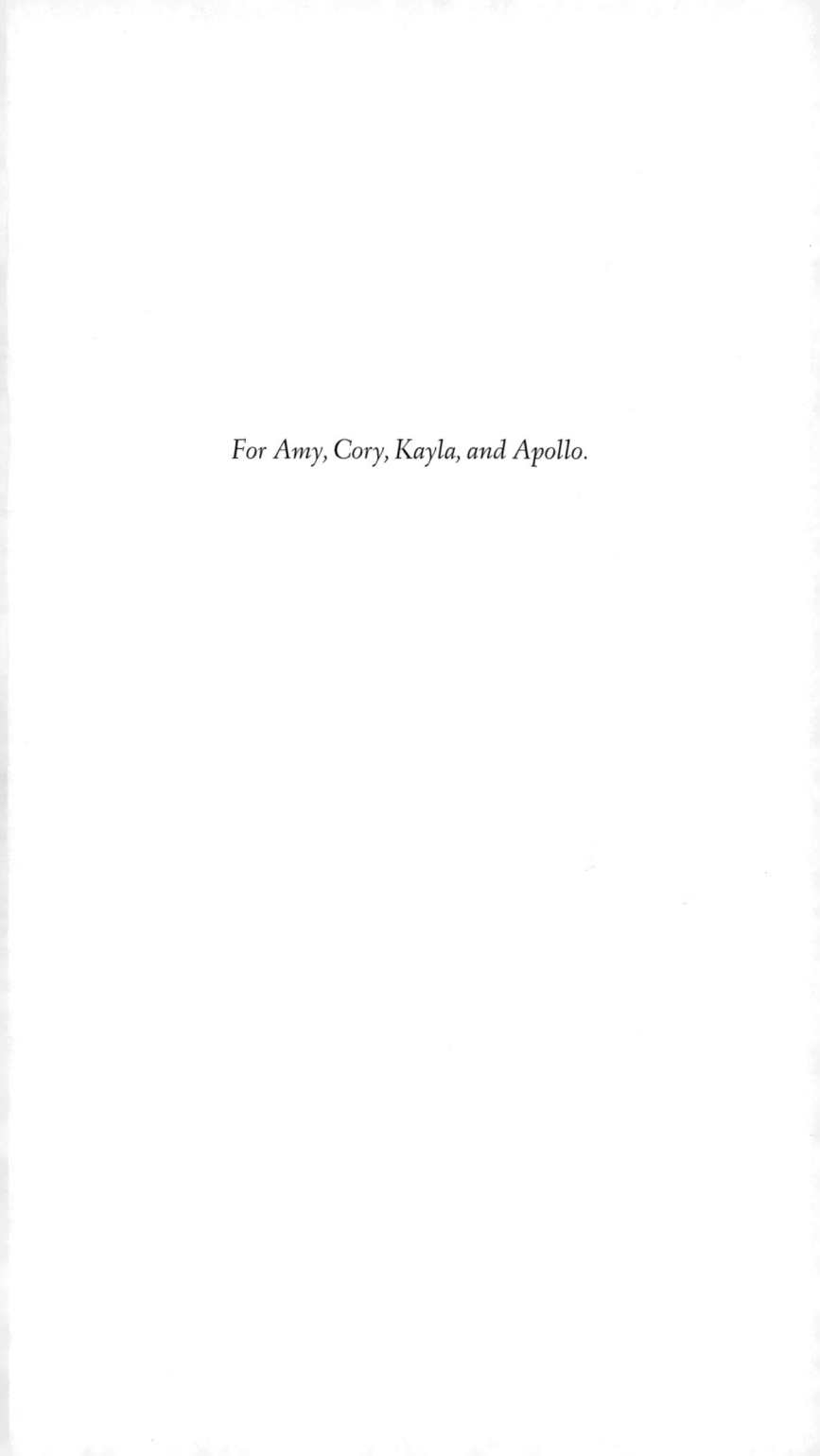

1

Crystal Falls
Kentucky
1891

The cancerous gloom wafting from the cave's entrance rode a cool breeze scented with death. There was no sneaking up on a demon. The men were sure Isabella Rhodes already knew they were waiting outside. How could she not? Witch, succubus, demon, it didn't matter what they called her. Any name connecting her to the devil down below would be appropriate.

"Come on out, Isabella," Cornelius Miles ordered, not foolish enough to enter the demon's lair. Isabella could only lose outside the cave. He listened intently, picking up the sound of what he thought were teeth tearing at flesh and the *smack, smack, smack* of wet lips. "Do not let her escape!"

Isabella Rhodes crawled from the darkness and sat on her haunches. Naked and blood-covered, she hissed at the five men from the town of Crystal Falls, who'd decided to surround the cave's entrance. She cackled at their bravado.

She licked the sinew hanging from her fingers and stood. Dried blood dropped from her skin like bark dropping from a tree. She knew these men and why they had come. It was only a matter of time before they arrived, so she was prepared, her plans for the future in motion.

"Cornelius Miles." Isabella hissed the man's name as if he were a sore between fetid toes.

Cornelius Miles lurched forward a step, leaving the other five men behind. He methodically released the rope attached to his belt, his eyes remaining trained on Isabella and her demon eyes. He dared not look up at the two men above the cave but sensed Isabella knew they were there.

"Two ways of doing this," Miles said. "You stand there nicely, and let us tie your hands behind your back while we go in there and see what you've been up to." He rubbed his chin. "Or we force you to do it."

Isabella bent her head to the side, red eyes on Miles. She closed her blood-caked mouth, hiding bloody, ravenous teeth. Her hands relaxed, and so did the men around her. Perfect. The glow in her eyes disappeared. "Okay, Cornelius. Have it your way."

Miles waved a man forward. "Shackles around her feet first. Don't want her running off."

The man didn't like it one bit. He froze and looked at Isabella, trying to figure out if she was bluffing. Creatures like her bluffed. It's how they lured you in. If all the rumors were true, she could tear him apart before he had the shackles around her bare ankles. But Miles would make sure the town knew what kind of coward he was if he didn't do it. He knelt before Isabella, avoiding eye contact and her putrid breath. He prayed like all good men did.

"Get back!"

Miles' order came a second too late. Isabella already had a clawed hand in the air, coming down at the man, taking his head off in one rapid swing, splattering the other men with blood. She grabbed the head and bit a chunk out of the cheek.

Isabella formed two fists and screamed. Where her eyes should have been white, they were blood-filled. As she charged, her fingernails, still dripping blood and flesh, glimmered beneath the full moon. As her feet left the muddy ground to tear apart the next man, a net from above sent her sprawling to the ground, rolling head over heels, stopping at Miles's feet. She slashed at the netting with her blade-like nails and hissed.

"She's cutting through!" Miles yelled. He hit her with a club, and she stopped moving.

The four men behind him charged forward, the first two meeting the balls of Isabella's feet. They flailed backward but recovered quickly and joined the other two men, who managed to force Isabella onto her stomach. Miles reached through the netting and pulled Isabella's hands behind her back, where he tied them tight enough to draw blood. Miles pushed to his feet while the other four men caught their breath.

"Didn't have to be like that," Miles said. He removed his hat and wiped ripples of sweat from his forehead. It had been too easy, he was sure. "Get her up." He turned to the two men who were above the cave's entrance. "You two grab the lanterns."

"The netting?" one of the men said.

Miles nodded. "Remove it, but watch yourself. Her teeth are as bad as her nails." With the netting off, Miles grabbed the three feet of rope hanging from Isabella's bound hands. He grabbed the back of her neck with his free hand. "Walk," he ordered. "Templeton," he called to one of the men who had been standing above the cave. "Go back to town. Isabella's daughter is visiting the Dells. We need her in case she's like her mother. The rest of you follow me."

They entered the cave, Miles guiding Isabella with the rope. His hand clenched around the back of her neck. The lanterns illuminated bloody, art-covered walls. Miles guided Isabella to the wall on his right. The other five men stopped.

"So what do we have here?" Miles asked. "You're worse than any witch."

"Back there," one of the men said, raising the lantern but refusing to step forward. The lantern illuminated the small bodies, and he and the other four men backed away.

"You've been busy, demon." Miles pulled Isabella back. "Ring the church bell. I want everyone in town at the church. I also want volunteers to seal off this abomination." Miles was sure there would be no volunteers, and he'd have to do it himself.

Cornelius Miles slammed the gavel against the table and looked around the small church and at the people anxiously awaiting the demon and her demon child. The hundred or so people called the woman a witch, but Miles knew her as something far worse, far more dangerous. She and her offspring needed to die as soon as possible.

Miles steadied his eyes on the demon woman, shackled, her chains rattling, scraping the floor as she entered the church. Free of restraints, her daughter followed closely behind, unaware of what was happening.

"You'll both be put to death at sunset tomorrow evening." Miles moved around the table. The four councilmen who had unanimously joined him in sentencing the woman and child remained in their seats, terrified.

The accused, Isabella Rhodes, glared at the town's Mayor and raised her hand. "You," she glanced around the room, "and all your followers will pay a price so great and for so long." She cackled, pleased with herself.

Catherine Rhodes held a flimsy doll in her lap, unaware she and her mother were about to die. Of course, she knew something was wrong—her mother had never acted like this. And these people, the ones looking at them so angrily, their friends, had never been so mean to them.

Miles approached the shackled Isabella. He grabbed her jaw and held her stare. Their eyes met, and Miles flinched, seeing an abyss so dark and so fiery that he was sure it was a sight he would never forget. "Time to send you back to the hell you came from."

Isabella screamed again, raising half a dozen heads who had refused to look at her. She pulled on the chains, struggling purposefully. They wanted a good show, and a good show is what she would give them. Put her to death? The fools had no idea what she was capable of.

Miles motioned to several men in the congregation. "Take her away. Confine them to their home until morning."

"You can't do this," Isabella screamed as she was dragged from the church. Her nails splintered and cracked like eggshells as she tried clinging to wooden planks. "I never hurt any of you! Never!" A rotten tomato glanced off

Isabella's head and landed with a splatter at Miles's feet. A young boy charged forward and viciously spat at Isabella.

Isabella turned to the young boy and scowled. "You," she said to the boy, "will die in your mother's arms this evening." The child's father pulled him away and landed a hard blow to Isabella's chin. "This town will never forget Isabella Rhodes," she howled, the blow to her chin stinging but not deterring her spew of vengeance. "I promise you'll never forget." She looked around the room. "All of you will suffer."

Catherine walked behind her mother, holding the hand of a large, unshaven man who was to escort her home. Catherine tugged at the man's hand until he looked down into her emerald eyes. "What's wrong with my mother?"

The man, Thomas Templeton, gently squeezed Catherine's hand, unsure what to say. He moved his attention to the screaming woman. He had seen Isabella running naked through the forest, chanting nonsense. They had momentarily shared eye contact, and what Thomas saw had no explanation. He only told the Council that Isabella's eyes were shining with madness. Although he was too far away to be sure, he thought blood covered her breasts and stomach. That night, Thomas immediately returned home and gathered his family in the prayer room. Together, they prayed for God's protection from the evil that ran rampant through their town. So far, his God had protected his family.

Thomas glanced down at Catherine. The little girl had no control over her mother's actions. No child asked to be born into such evilness. He wished he could help her and decided he would, somehow.

The five men, Isabella and Catherine, arrived at Isabella's cabin shortly after sunset. The forest was dreadfully silent on a night when cicadas should have been singing. The men stared at each other, none wanting to acknowledge the shadowy darkness creeping across the cabin's front porch. One of them had to go first. One of them had to open the front door. One of them had to enter the awaiting darkness. There were no volunteers.

"Do it, Templeton," one of the men ordered.

Thomas studied the darkness. He'd been here once before. Arthur Rhodes, Isabella's husband, had offered to fix a rip in his saddle. No charge. He was just being kind. Rhodes didn't invite him inside, which Thomas found odd. Crystal Falls was a community of good, righteous people who always invited neighbors into their homes. Instead, the two stayed in the shed, well away from the cabin. Thomas remembered that Rhodes never even mentioned Isabella or Catherine, at least not while on his property. Now Thomas understood why. There was always a darkness about the place, which had only now become apparent. He let go of Catherine's hand and finally addressed the others. "Why me?"

"Cause you're the biggest, that's why. Nothing's going to bother you," one of the men replied, his hand firmly wrapped around Isabella's thick, black hair. "The sooner we get this over with, the sooner we can get the tree and ropes ready." He tugged on Isabella's hair and guffawed.

Thomas glanced at Catherine, who was teaching her doll how to dance. "Let's go, honey," he said. He led Catherine up the three rickety steps and pushed the door open, ignoring the layer of darkness that seemed to be tapping his shoulder. What he saw was no different than his own home. He knew not to cross the doorway; you didn't invite yourself into the house of the devil. No, you stood there, not tempting the darkness.

Seeing that Templeton had made it safely up the steps, the other men followed and tossed Isabella through the doorway. They laughed and pointed at Isabella.

Isabella landed like a cat and arched her back. The glare she shared with the five men brought the front door to a resounding close.

Catherine screamed and ran to her mother. "What's wrong, Mommy?"

Isabella pushed to her feet and guided Catherine to a chair by the fireplace. "Stay here, sweetie," she said. Isabella retrieved two black sheets from the bedroom and hung them across the two windows flanking the front door. She pushed back one of the sheets to see Templeton leaning against a porch support. The others had already hurried to their next set of chores. She stared past Thomas, considering how she would get her revenge not just on the men who had brought them back to the cabin but also on the entire village. Death, she considered, would be too good for them. No, they would all have to suffer. Maybe not tonight or tomorrow, but certainly somewhere along their lineage.

"What're they going to do to us, Mommy? Catherine asked. "Why were those men mean to you?"

Isabella went to Catherine, running her long, bloodied fingers along Catherine's cheek. "I won't allow them to hurt you. I promise. You stay here and play with your doll while mommy works in the kitchen."

Catherine nodded and returned to her doll, a look-a-like her mother had made nearly two months ago. Her mother was good at making and fixing things . . . much better than all the other mothers.

A witch? Isabella thought to herself. *How eighteenth-century of these people.* Isabella turned away from

Catherine and laughed to herself. She'd show these foolish people.

"Mother," Catherine said and motioned toward the front door.

Isabella turned. Thomas stood in the doorway. Isabella stepped in front of Catherine. Catherine peeked around her mother. Isabella looked around Thomas. "You're alone."

Thomas held his large hands out, palms facing the mother and daughter. "I'm here to help," he said. "Help Catherine." He stole a glance toward the tree line. If anyone came back now and saw what he was doing, he'd burn with Isabella and Catherine, his family right along with them.

Eyes narrowed, Isabella approached Thomas. If he crossed the threshold, she would rip his throat out. She wanted no help. Her plan was already in motion. Then she reconsidered. Maybe she could use this man. "What is it that you think you can do for her?"

Thomas took a step back and lowered his large hands to his sides. He took a deep breath. He'd lost his mind. He shouldn't be here. But that girl needed his help. "Let me take her away from here. I promise I'll keep her safe. It's you they really want."

Isabella moved forward, her toes skirting the doorway. "They'll follow you. They'll find her and kill both of you. Miles will never quit until he finds you."

"No," Templeton said. "There's a boat waiting at the river, ready to take her to safety." Flames from the fireplace flickered in Thomas's scared eyes. "It'll be okay." He wanted to move forward, walk in there, get Catherine, and be gone. But he couldn't. Isabella would make him pay for what the town had done.

"Mommy?" Catherine said, moving to her mother's side.

Isabella moved to her knees and brushed a few stray locks from her daughter's face. She believed Thomas would keep Catherine safe. "You need to go with Mr. Templeton," she said. "He will keep you safe." She looked up at Templeton. "You're a good man, Thomas. Nothing will become of you or your family." *At least not right now*.

Thomas felt his knees weaken. He was partially to blame for this whole mess. He'd told the Council about Isabella and the crazy things she had done. He nodded.

Catherine hesitated but then remembered the protection Thomas had offered earlier. He'd treated her with care, the way he treated his daughter Rachel, one of her best friends. "Will I see you again?" she asked her mother.

"Of course, sweetie," Isabella replied. She held Catherine's face in her hands and kissed her forehead. And the next time they saw each other, they would finish what Isabella had started together.

Thomas caught a glimpse of Isabella's hands. All ten fingernails had returned. He swallowed hard. "We need to go now," Thomas interrupted. "We need to put distance between us and them." His voice cracked. He glanced back again and thought he saw movement in the trees. He looked down and noticed his foot had crossed the threshold.

Isabella stood and gently nudged Catherine forward, aware that she could end Thomas's life at that moment. But she trusted him and her change in plans. Catherine took his hand. "Take care of her, Thomas Templeton," Isabella said.

Thomas nodded and then took Catherine down the porch. He turned back and steadied his voice. "Arthur," he said, referring to Isabella's husband.

Isabella stepped out onto the porch, her black hair rising with a sudden gust of wind. She could go away with them and stay on the run, but she had other plans. "When he returns and finds us missing, there'll be no hiding from him. He'll make this town suffer ten times what I suffered." Only Isabella's revenge would be much different.

Thomas lifted Catherine from her feet and rushed into the forest, not bothering to look back to see if Isabella had changed her mind.

Isabella returned to the cabin. She walked to the chair by the fireplace and sat down. She smiled and closed her eyes. Crystal Falls was just the beginning.

***

Six men, including Cornelius Miles, barged into Isabella's cabin the following morning. Four men wrestled Isabella to the floor and bound her hands and feet in chains. Isabella fought like a gazelle hunted by a pack of lions, but it was all part of the game. She could have easily killed them all. Could have ripped heads from shoulders and cooked them for dinner. Her master had other plans for her and Crystal Falls.

Miles lifted her from the floor and then threw her against the wall. "Where's the girl?" He sent two men to the back room, both returning empty-handed. Ragingly, he grabbed the kettle from the fireplace and slung it across the room. "Where is she?"

Isabella blew shards of hair out of her face. She stared at Miles, then let loose a laugh that echoed throughout Crystal Falls. "How foolish the great Cornelius Miles looks," she said. "Arthur will make you pay . . . until I return."

Miles clenched his fists, and his right temple began to hurt. Yes, Arthur Rhodes would have to be dealt with. But

Rhodes was also smart and would understand why the town had to do this. "Where is she?"

Isabella shuffled forward and spat in Miles's face. She struggled against the chains, if only for show.

Miles wiped away the foul-smelling saliva. "Ernst," he hollered to the man who was supposed to have stood watch through most of the night. Ernst pushed past the four men restraining Isabella. "The girl is gone," Miles said.

Ernst shrugged, not comprehending what exactly the problem was. "No one ever left the cabin. I kept my spot all night."

"There's only one way out," Miles said.

Ernst raised his hands. "I'm telling you, Cornelius, no one left the house after I took over for Templeton."

Miles understood. "Damn it, where's Templeton?" he asked.

"He was standing on the porch last night when I got here. I asked if he wanted some of the cornbread the Missus made. He said he was in a hurry and had something to do." Ernst shrugged again. "He ran off toward the river."

Miles shoved Ernst aside. Put idiots in charge of something, and this is what happens. He grabbed Isabella by the chin. "I'll find her," he said. "And then she'll burn just like her mama." He motioned to the men. "Take her to the tree by the river. Tie her up and wait for me. She'll burn."

2

Crystal Falls
June 2004

Jake Simon ogled Laura Reeder from the other side of the bonfire's dancing flames. He and Landon Ziehm had planned perfectly. Give the girls a little scare in the woods; before you know it, they're huddled in your arms for protection. Now, they just needed Clark to scream for help.

Landon inched toward the river. "Clark," he whispered into the darkness. "Clark, you in there?" Just as the last word slipped from his mouth, Trish Marcum stepped up next to him.

Jake, seeing Trish hanging on Landon, made his move toward Laura. She, no doubt, would need *his* protection. Raven Templeton moved to Jake's other side, not wanting to be left out. Raven had no interest in Jake, the line of girls swooning over him a mile long at school.

Laura, strawberry-blonde with a freckled nose and cheeks, had gorgeous green eyes that mesmerized every boy in school, especially Jake. Raven, on the other hand—black fishnet stockings, shiny-black leather shorts, and a black leather bikini—could have been the cover girl for Goth Chick magazine. Her black hair draped to her shoulders, and a pair of black, crow-like eyes stared forward when it wasn't hanging in her face.

Though neither Raven nor Clark knew the arrangement, Raven had been a gift for Clark. She wrapped her arms around her shoulders, cold despite the large fire behind them. "Is someone going in after him?" Raven questioned as she watched the black water head toward the Ohio River.

"She's right," Trish said. "We've gotta do something." She let go of Landon's hand and took two steps toward the water. Small waves sucked at her toes. A long chill shot up her spine to the base of her neck. A recent transport from California with her father, Trish found the small-town atmosphere of Crystal Falls a breath of fresh air.

Jake shook his head. "Okay, okay. Just give me some space." He waded into the black, steady-flowing water, the cringing stench making his stomach turn. Something caressed his ankles, and he jumped back toward the bank. He reached into the water. His hand brushed against something slick. He tentatively retrieved the flimsy piece of rubber tubing from the murk. "Clark? You jackass, get back here."

Landon whispered into the fog moving in from the north, "Clark, that's enough. Now come on." Something was wrong. Clark was only supposed to be gone a few minutes. Just long enough to scare the girls. Maybe his clothes caught onto something under the water, and he couldn't get free. "Come on, Clark!"

"Listen," Laura said. She wrapped her arms around her shoulders, scared. She felt hidden eyes boring into her. The brambles lining the trees moved. Laura turned and watched, no longer concerned about the missing Clark Hanson. "Who's there?"

The others turned from the water, refocusing on the wooden centurions. The saplings just past the fire rustled. Branches snapped under heavy footsteps. The moon played hide and seek behind puffy, gray clouds and did little to reveal what was moving toward them.

"Okay, Clark, the joke's over!" Jake yelled.

Laura turned, eyes wide. "Joke?" She was beginning to understand. She thought she had overheard Jake and Landon talking at school about some prank. She shook her head at Jake.

Jake's eyes met Landon's. This had gone too far. But before either could explain, something stepped from the shadows of the trees.

"Oh shit," Jake said.

The man walked toward them, his large, left-booted foot dragging along the ground. "Oh shits about right, boy. You got no business being on my land."

"I told you this was a bad idea, Jake," Laura said, emphasizing Jake's name. Her plans after graduation were simple: Harvard, backpacking Europe, and settling into a comfortable lifestyle. She studied the man moving toward her, her stomach twisting with every struggling footstep he made. She could make it back to the car without being caught. That was no problem. But the gun across the man's left arm suggested she wouldn't make it two steps before he shot her in the back.

The stranger moved closer to the fire. As he walked, one side of his overalls flapped like it was waving to a crowd. He chucked a meteor-sized ball of black spit into the fire. The fire sizzled and flickered. He rubbed his pepper-colored beard, eyeing the five trespassers, his thoughts squarely on Laura's pink bikini bottoms. A small stream of saliva rolled from the corner of his mouth in anticipation. As he moved toward Laura, Landon moved to block the way. The man squinted at Landon through drunken, blood-shot eyes while lifting the gun barrel to Landon's head. "Move." The man's rotted, tobacco-stained teeth appeared to move as he rolled his chaw from one side of his mouth to the other.

"Hank McCoy," Landon said. "You helped my father with his baler."

Hank squinted at the young man and nodded. "You still need to move." He cocked the gun, and Landon stepped away.

Hank moved to within reaching distance of Laura. Laura stood her ground. Unimpressed at her bravado, Hank gently ran his hand along her cheek. Laura's skin felt soft, like the underbelly of a newborn pig.

Laura knocked the grimy hand away from her face, and Hank cackled. She stared at the man, almost daring him to touch her again. He could shoot her, beat her to death even, but if he tried to rape her, she would fight back until one of them was dead. When McCoy turned to spit again, she swung her right fist, finding Hank's jaw. The others stood and watched, shocked, waiting for the next move.

Hank rubbed his cheek. So that's how it was going to be? "You shouldn't have done that, Little Lady," he said. "You're on my land, making you my property."

Laura looked down at her reddening hand. Dirt had come off the man's face when she landed the useless punch.

"We don't want any trouble, Mister," Laura said, taking a few steps back. The agony in her stomach felt like a rampant forest fire. The sulfuric smell of the river made her feel queasy like she could pass out. *Keep your senses, and stay alert. Think positive. There is a way out of this.* But what had she been thinking, hitting a man twice her size? Maybe the karate lessons her parents had suggested for her as a child weren't so bad after all—except she never followed through. She quit after the first lesson. Maybe a swift, well-placed kick between the legs and a knee to the chin?

Hank studied the newly graduated high school seniors and then pulled a dirty, red bandana from the front of his coveralls. He wiped the sweat—caused by the eighty-five-degree heat, ninety percent humidity that normally filled July nights in rural Kentucky—from his forehead. Nights like this—when not even air-conditioning could cool a man down—made a man do strange things he might never have done before.

Laura was the first to see Clark approaching Hank from behind. She needed to keep McCoy distracted. "Sir, we didn't mean to trespass." Laura swallowed hard. Her muscles tensed, beginning to ache. *After Clark throws him to the ground, be ready to wrestle the gun out of the man's hands.* Once she had the gun, she would toss it in the river, and they could return to their cars. They'd be gone before the man got his senses back.

However, Clark had different ideas. He had no intentions of wrestling the man and risking a bullet. He bent over, grabbed a large piece of granite rock, and steadied it above McCoy's head.

When Landon suddenly noticed Clark, his eyes alerted Hank that someone was approaching. The man turned just in time to see the rock, back-dropped by a partially shrouded moon, coming down against his forehead. The sound of rock splitting skull spliced the darkness. Hank dropped to the ground with a loud thud. The gun bounced away into the shadows.

Clark stared down at the lifeless body, at Hank's face lit in terror against the raging bonfire. "Did I kill him?" Clark strained to speak, his dry mouth like a bag of cotton swabs. He pushed the envelope in school and stayed on the edge of trouble. Clark, the senior class clown who would do almost anything for attention, never had difficulty finding trouble.

They surrounded McCoy, gawking at him. No one spoke. They watched the crimson spilling from the man's head. All of them participated in some way. The man was right. They were trespassing. But *all* Crystal Falls seniors made at least one trip out here. They had to stay with tradition.

Laura glanced at the others. "Now what?" Calling the Sheriff was at the top of her list.

Landon looked at Clark. "We didn't kill him, Clark did."

"Fuck you, man!" Clark said. "I wasn't going to let him shoot you guys." Well, that wasn't exactly true. He wasn't going to let Hank shoot the *girls*.

"We don't know he was going to do that, Clark," Raven said. "Maybe he was trying to scare us!"

"Oh yeah, blame Clark! I probably saved your damned lives. And you think I'm going take the rap on my own just because you guys thought you could get laid tonight?" He motioned toward Jake and Landon. The truth was out of the bag and wouldn't set anyone free. Clark wasn't going down alone.

"Get laid?" Trish understood now. "You guys thought you could bring us out here, in the middle of nowhere, scare us to death, and then get some?" There was the possibility. But not now. Not with a dead guy at their heels.

Jake's face turned hard. Yeah, that was pretty much the plan. And other than the dead guy lying on the ground, he thought things were progressing reasonably well. "Right now, we need to figure out what to do with the body." Jake motioned toward McCoy as if McCoy were a dead animal on the side of the road.

"We tell the police it was an accident," Laura said. Miss Goodie-two-shoes. No matter how bad things got, Laura was sure to do the right thing. And when she couldn't decide in a split-second what that was, she counted to a hundred, which gave her mind time to process things.

"Yeah, and the rock that smashed him in the face just happened to fall out of the sky," Clark said. He was scared. It would be him that did life-to-twenty in prison, not them. At five feet eight inches tall and on the chubby side, prison would be a real hoot. He had no plans of being a convict's boyfriend. "We need to get rid of the body."

"No way," Raven replied. An ocean of sweat made her stringy hair cling to her forehead.

"Yeah, toss him in the river," Landon said.

"No, we can't do that. He'd get stuck somewhere, and we'd really be in trouble. We need to find a permanent place. Somewhere he won't be found." Clark's eyes were wild, his mind working in a different reality. "I passed a tall tree trunk when I circled around. Get your stuff together, and we'll carry him over there."

Laura grabbed her backpack while the others tossed their beer bottles into the water. She took several empty bottles to the river. "We need to put the fire out." She poured water over the flames as the others stood in the darkness, embers watching them like glowing eyes. Crickets chirped, and water silently flowed northward. An animal scampered across the ground somewhere close, hidden among the trees. She considered hightailing it with the animal.

Trish flicked on a flashlight, training it on the lifeless body. Clark grabbed McCoy's feet; Landon held one limp hand, Jake the other. The stench from McCoy, mixed with the smell of the river, was enough to make them all vomit. Like a pig carried to slaughter, they hauled McCoy through the trees. No one spoke as brambles and branches swashed back and forth across bodies.

The tree trunk stood nearly ten feet tall, four feet wide, and hollow. Not what any of them had expected, but even in the darkness, with the moonlight seeping through trees, they could see the scorched scars that marred the trunk. Larger trees surrounded it. The cover around and above blocked any view from the air. Its remoteness was a safe bet that no one would happen by.

"How will we get a 250-pound man into that tree?" Landon asked.

"Nice move, Clark," Raven snapped. "Any other bright ideas?"

Clark raised his middle finger. When he reached into his backpack, the others froze. Laughing, Clark pulled out a battery-operated lantern. He turned the lantern on and held it close to his face. His eyes were wild, his face hard and unfamiliar to the others. "You're with me or against me," he said.

For a moment, Laura thought about what Clark had said. His mind, scattered, worked differently now, like a criminal. However, he couldn't be more right. The whole group would make him take the blame. She didn't pick up the rock. She didn't smash it into Hank's head. Laura looked at the others. They were bug-eyed. Even the two guys stood frozen. Men turned to boys. "I'm not sure we have much of a choice, do we, Clark?"

Raven crossed her arms. "What's that supposed to mean?"

Laura felt Clark's glare. But there was nothing to lose by speaking her mind. She wasn't afraid of Clark, but she was afraid of losing her future once the news spread that she was involved in a murder. "It means we're also dead if we don't help him. Right, Clark?"

Clark's jaw moved back and forth. "You two idiots got me into this." He felt emboldened, no longer afraid of the two toughest guys in school. "So yeah, like I said, with or against me."

"We need a rope to hoist him up to the top of the trunk," Laura suggested. If they weren't going to the police, someone with half a brain had to make damned sure no one ever found the body.

Clark stood over the man like a slaughterhouse worker sizing up a cow. "Feet or head first?"

"I can't believe we're discussing this," Trish interrupted. Her life was more complicated than those around her. Six years ago, at age twelve, she killed her mother. After a short stay in the hospital, she was released into her father's care. They moved from California to Crystal Falls shortly after. The child psychologist back in Los Angeles suggested a small, unassuming town. No one in Crystal Falls knew Trish's past. Caught up in the murder of Hank McCoy would place her front and center, especially when the press in California caught wind of her involvement. Everyone in town would know her dirty little secret.

Laura turned from the group, drawing a glare from Clark.

"Where do you think you're going?"

"Someone needs to return to get the rope we were swinging from." As senior class president, Laura was used to being a leader. But she had never expected her leadership skills to help cover up a murder.

Clark nodded, his attention quickly returning to the body before him. He lit a cigarette and took a long, lung-filled drag. The end of the tar stick gave his face an eerie glow, the face of a lunatic. He intentionally scowled. The more scared the others were, the more likely they would follow his lead.

Laura stepped into the surrounding woods, disappearing into the darkness. She still couldn't believe what was happening. How did a Valedictorian allow herself to get into this kind of situation? She continued on the path they had made earlier while carrying McCoy, suddenly aware she'd not changed out of her bikini bottoms. She pictured herself on a movie screen, walking through the woods as a deranged killer chased after her in the dead of night. *The dead of night? Stop that.* This couldn't be happening to her. As she struggled down the makeshift path, she decided trying to be a rebellious teenager had been a bad idea. "Don't go out there," her parents lectured. "I'm eighteen now, a future Harvard graduate. I know what I'm doing," she matter-of-factly told them. Her parents let her go. Next time, she'll listen. Assuming, of course, she gets out of this predicament.

When Laura arrived at the river, she found the fire had rekindled. The old man's shotgun glistened only a few feet away. She picked it up, surprised at its heaviness. A thought crossed her mind. Clark couldn't stop a gun. She could hang out in the trees and wait for a good shot. She could claim self-defense. Then, they could blame Clark for killing

McCoy. But could she shoot another person if she had to? Being a leader didn't make you a killer. She dropped the gun and walked to the tree hundreds of Crystal Falls seniors had used as a swing.

Laura climbed old Betsy with little effort, the rekindled fire now a friend. The rope came free much easier than she thought it should have. Maybe it was a sign. Maybe everything from here on out would be easy. She stopped momentarily, gazing up at the stars seeping between parting clouds. No one would ever know. Sure, people would miss the man, but who would find that tree? The idea was original. Not even the police would think of looking inside a tree. She climbed down and quickly ran back through the forest, the flashlight beam bouncing around like a disco light. When her light finally caught a glimpse of the others, they parted from the circle they had been standing in. Sitting in the middle of the circle—Hank. Beaten and battered, he sat bigger than life. Then she noticed the grapefruit-sized rock in Clark's left hand. She should have stayed at the river, should have run for help.

"Don't do it, Clark," Laura demanded, too late.

Clark hit the man again. Blood spurted from McCoy's nose like water from a spigot, running in two streams over his lips and down his chin. "That should do it," Clark said. "Now throw me the rope, Laura."

Laura realized the others froze in the chaos. Landon, Mr. Football, couldn't seem to move, a splattering of blood marking his left ear—the man's blood. Jake had tears in his eyes. Trish and Raven were still trying to recover from the first rock smashing. Laura tossed the rope to Clark.

While holding one end of the rope, Clark threw the other end over a tree limb shadowing the tree trunk. When the free end of the rope finally touched the ground, Landon, who had not said a word in nearly an hour, grabbed the free end of the rope. He kneeled in front of Hank. The smell of blood and alcohol was enough to make him wretch. As he held his breath, he fixed the rope into a noose and placed it around the man's neck. Blood seeped onto the rope, the fibers glistening in the odd, yellow glow of moonlight.

"This is bullshit," Raven snapped.

"Turn around if you can't watch," Clark ordered. His face was hard, his brown eyes the size of golf balls. He brushed the sweaty, brown hair from his forehead. The only movement on his face was a vein pulsating down his forehead.

Laura stood next to Raven. They watched Hank hoisted into the air. As the noose around his neck tightened, more blood flowed from his nose. Laura watched unnervingly. The images of Hank McCoy firmly burned into her mind.

Raven turned away and vomited into the shadows of the surrounding trees. A rodent darted in front of them, vomit covering its head.

Trish watched trance-like. She had not seen this much blood since she shot her mother. She wondered how many times in a person's life they might witness a murder, much less two. This was not the kind of luck she had been hoping for.

Once hoisted above the tree trunk, Jake shimmied up the trunk and guided Hank's feet into the top while Landon and Clark slowly gave the rope slack.

When Hank's head was just about to disappear into the tree, he grunted. "She's watching you, boy."

Jake panicked and lost his grip on the tree as his hands and feet went numb. He fell to the ground with a thud that echoed into the night. "Holy shit, he's still alive!"

Clark and Landon let go of the rope. The rope's end

whipped over the tree limb as the old man's weight pulled him into the tree trunk. The one murderer and five conspirators stood silent for several minutes, all eyes on the tree—Hank a tight fit. Even if Hank was still alive, there was no way he could climb out. Laura moved forward, listening for sounds from inside the tree. All quiet.

"One last thing," Clark said. He retrieved a hunting knife from his backpack and pointed it at his accomplices. "We need to seal the deal."

Jake moved in front of Laura. Falling from the tree trunk had brought him back to his senses. He flexed his bare chest as if daring Clark to touch Laura. "We did what you wanted. Now back off."

Clark, unimpressed, walked to the tree trunk. "So now you want to be a hero," he said. "You didn't bother stopping Hank back at the swing, but you think you can take me?" Clark etched a large C-H into the tree's bark using the knife's point. "Now you," he said, tossing the knife at Jake's feet.

Jake picked up the knife, his eyes falling onto Clark's as he held the twelve-inch blade. Maybe two could fit inside the tree trunk. The night couldn't get any worse. He looked at his watch. Yes, it could. It was after midnight, so his parents would ask what he had been up to. *Nothing, Mom, nothing, Dad. I ran into a little misfortune down at the river. Had to kill a man to stay out of trouble. How was your evening?*

Seeing the look in Jake's eyes, Clark reached into his backpack again, retrieving a small handgun. "Don't fuck with me, Jake."

"I always knew you were an idiot, Clark. I don't know why we brought your ass out here in the first place." Jake was telling the truth. Clark was one beer short of a six-pack.

But they had befriended him anyway, hoping he and Raven might hit it off.

Each of them carved their initials into the tree. It was as if they had just signed a statement of guilt.

"If just one of you goes to the police, I'll track each of you down and slice you from ear to ear. Now get the fuck out of here!"

Trish tossed the knife to the ground. She looked at the initials, T-M, and silently made up names. Tom Mackey. Tina Mallory. Todd Moore. But it didn't matter. She knew the initials stood for Trish Marcum.

As the six seniors parted ways, she watched from the shadows. The time was close. She only needed her daughter.

3

Nashville, Tennessee
Present Day

Laura listened to her husband's gentle breathing while staring at the ceiling, contemplating the phone call she had received earlier in the afternoon. Two things bothered her about the call: How did the caller get her cell number, and who was the caller? At first, she suspected some kids who didn't have enough to do to keep them busy. But then her mind began questioning the caller's only five words: *This is your old buddy.*

Nothing more.

She rested her hand behind her head and glanced at the devilish red numbers of the alarm clock . . . after midnight. The smell of lavender coursed through the room, a new scent she had added—right before climbing into bed—to the oil lamp plugged into the socket next to her nightstand. Her doctor prescribed valium, but Laura refused to put drugs into her body, opting for a holistic approach to settle her anxiety attacks. The attacks had progressed from one every couple of months over the last twenty years to a wave of attacks every month for the past year. And she knew when one was coming, like right now. She opened the nightstand drawer and looked at the bottle of valium—unopened, unused.

"You okay?" Richard asked as he rolled toward her. He put his hand on her leg and squeezed gently.

She rolled to her side, facing him. She nodded but didn't care to share her worries, at least not the current one. She placed her hand against his cheek and watched him close his eyes, thankful he was too tired to press her for more. She'd been lucky to find him. A good man, he kept her mind off the past and focused on the future. Although, he didn't know what she and the others had done that night.

She played the caller's voice back through her head, unable to place it. She tried to recall past boyfriends' voices and people she had worked with. When the phone rang, her husband Richard had been in the garage working on another of his bookshelf projects, so it couldn't have been him. He wasn't much of a prankster anyway. The call worried her. It was as if someone from a dark corner of her life had suddenly reappeared. Her thoughts traveled backward, before her marriage to Richard Knox, to her days at Harvard. She and Richard had met and dated steadily since their sophomore year, marrying during their senior year. Before that, there were only a few other guys she was interested in. They were normal men, at least while she dated them. Sure, each tried to get into her pants at one time or another, but that's what made them normal.

She went further back in time and then stopped. The answer was obvious. She just didn't want to admit it. Clark

Hanson. It had to be. He was the only sicko she knew. She tossed the covers to the side and put on her slippers. She passed the kids' room and then snuck into the den. Her dusty and seldom viewed high school yearbooks were on the bottom shelf of Richard's first bookshelf project. She chose her senior edition and snuggled on one of the black, oversized recliners she used for reading. Memories flooded her head and, at least momentarily, pushed away the latest anxiety attack. Most of the memories were good; high school had been a blast. She made the honor roll four consecutive years and led the debate team, and if it weren't for her eleventh-grade science teacher, Mr. Flanders, she would have finished high school with a perfect GPA. But then, the one bad moment overshadowed everything in her life. It was the one where she witnessed a murder. The one where she had helped hide the body. She thought of something her mother had once said: "No bad deed ever goes unpunished." The deed had gone unpunished for twenty years.

Laura shook her head at Clark Hanson's senior picture. She wiped away the tears building in the corner of her eyes. The invitation for her twenty-year high school reunion lay on the oak desk in the corner of the room. The desk was another one of Richard's creations.

Flipping through the pages of seniors, she found Raven's picture, Jake's, Landon's, and Trish's. She lived out most of her high school dreams, backpacking in Europe during the summer of her college sophomore year and graduating from Harvard with honors. She had a beautiful family, two wonderful kids, and a caring husband—the husband whom she never told the story about Hank McCoy. She thought about Jake and the short time they had dated before that night—about prom night when they lost their virginity together. Jake had it all planned. He had managed to get his older brother's apartment for the night, opting for it rather than Max and Erma's shanty motel on the edge of town. He respected her enough to avoid Max and Erma's, at least. They hung around prom just long enough to be seen. When Jake opened the apartment door, a dozen red roses with Laura's name on the card were in a shiny crystal vase on the kitchen table. She was impressed. What girl wouldn't be? He fixed her a rum and coke—to take the edge off—before leading her back to his brother's room. His brother had put new sheets on the bed because that's what brothers did for one another.

But no matter how many great things there were in her life, there was still the murder and guilt. After the murder, she never spoke to Jake or the others again. When they left the forest that night, Laura rode with Jake, Landon, Trish, and Raven. Clark would be late getting home, so he drove alone—not that they wanted to ride with him. The silence in the car was unbearable. She tried talking, but no one was interested in conversation. She was the last one Jake dropped off. Usually, he got out of the car and opened her door. But that night, he pulled into her driveway and waited for her to leave. Not one word. No goodbye. No, "Don't worry, everything will be okay."

The high school reunion was less than a week away. Richard would be out of town on business, so she would have to attend alone. She scrolled through the contacts on her cell phone and found Julie White, her next-door neighbor and best friend for the last ten years. She looked at the time—Julie should still be awake, working on that great American novel she was trying to write.

"Hey, Sis," Laura said when Julie answered. Since both

were an only child, they always referred to each other as sisters.

"Attack?" Julie asked.

"When isn't there one? Listen, I've got this class reunion next week that I've been thinking about attending. Richard'll be out of town, and I'll need a sitter for a few days."

"Gonna go see an old flame, are you? Don't get yourself into any trouble."

Lord, if you only knew the trouble I could get into. "Trust me, no one from high school I am interested in being that intimate with." *Liar, what about Jake? No, he's probably old, fat, and bald, with a dozen kids and one on the way.* "Could you tear yourself away from writing that book for a few days?"

"Anything for you, Sis."

Laura said goodbye and placed her cell phone on the table next to the recliner. She walked back through the house and stopped at the girls' room. They were both sound asleep. She had managed, for the most part, to keep that part of her life away from the family, but now her past was rearing its ugly head.

She closed the door and returned to her bedroom, where she walked to the window to close the shade.

A man stood in the middle of the street, watching her. She turned to Richard but thought better of waking him. When she turned back, the man was gone. She crawled into bed and lay wide-eyed. She had to make sure that Crystal Falls stayed in Crystal Falls and away from her family.

4

Columbus, Ohio
Present Day

Landon Ziehm woke to a throbbing headache, road kill breath, and next to a woman whose name he'd already forgotten. He remembered picking her up at Charlie's Bar last night and even buying her drinks. She was good in bed, and that's all that counted. But damn it, what was her name?

The red lights on his alarm clock blinked at 4 A.M. He nudged the woman beside him. She shifted in the bed and pulled the covers over her head. He rubbed the back of his neck, promising himself no more one-night stands. He needed to get his life straightened out. Make better decisions. Stay with one job long enough to learn his boss's name. Then he glanced down at the woman's behind, which was sticking out of the covers, and remembered why he had brought her home in the first place.

He removed the covers and sat up on the edge of the bed, wasted. Liquor and women had been his mantra since his debilitating injury on the football field some twenty years ago. The ACL and MCL of his left knee shredded, ending his football career during his first game as a freshman at Ohio State University. That's all Landon Ziehm knew—football. Now, he was working the assembly line, putting together toasters for twelve bucks an hour, sleeping with any ho that would have him, and scratching his crotch, wondering if the woman beside him had given him crabs. Life was one big fucking bowl of cherries. He rubbed his scarred left knee and pushed to his feet.

Courtney. The girl's name in my bed is Courtney. She's from New Hampshire, or one of those "New" states. He stood and wobbled toward the bathroom to take a leak, leaving the light off to avoid seeing himself in the mirror. The mirror reminded him of his failures, of his need to shave once in a while. Luckily, the women he hooked up with cared about neither.

He leaned over the toilet and waited. "Gotta get that checked," he said. "Before the damn thing falls off." The woman on the bed moaned. "Shit."

In the kitchen, Landon grabbed the left over pizza in the refrigerator and put three pieces onto a dirty plate sitting in the sink since last week. *No worries*, he thought, *the microwave will kill the germs*. A large pizza served as breakfast, lunch, and dinner on some days, especially Saturdays and Sundays, when he was either hung over or was coming in late from a night on the town, like tonight or this morning. Whatever the time of day was. Morning. Definitely morning.

Just as he opened the microwave door, he noticed a

message scrolling across his cell phone. He had missed a call while in the strip club. "Now what?" he said.

No one ever called him unless it was someone collecting on his many debts or one of those places wanting to sell him a home security system (he had nothing worth stealing, so why the fuck were they always calling him?). But he had changed his number two months ago after the last asshole threatened to repo his car. He had no family. His parents were killed five years ago in a car accident, a five-hundred-foot drop, and two closed caskets. There was a marriage when he was twenty-four or twenty-five. He couldn't remember which. But it didn't matter because it only lasted three months. The second marriage happened at some point, as did *that* divorce (there were also the nightmares, which ended with him sitting up in bed, screaming, sweating like a marathon runner. In the dreams, he found himself running around trees shaped like people from his past: Laura, Jake, Trish, Raven, and, of course, Clark. Twenty years couldn't wash away what he had done. At least one of his marriages, maybe both, had ended because of the nightmares. It was as if he had fought in Vietnam and come home with all that war trauma those guys had).

He pressed play and leaned against the kitchen counter, ready for a financial lecture from someone out west who had no idea what Landon's life was like in the east. He often wondered how much debt the debt collector had and if the collector ever really felt bad—cause the man was keeping everyone down, not just Landon.

"Landon, it's your old buddy."

And that was it, nothing else. He replayed the message. Maybe he'd missed something.

Old buddy? He was as anti-social as a cat in a pen full of dogs. Everyone he had known had screwed him over at least once, some twice. Maybe that's why he went through women like a Chinese buffet. His friends consisted of Marv, the bartender at Charlie's Bar, and Edsel, the pharmacist down at the Pharmacy who ordered him the special glow-in-the-dark condoms. He had no buddies unless the dozens of one-nighters counted—though he never gave any of them his phone number. "Asshole," he said, sliding the phone across the kitchen table. The phone stopped at the opposite edge, dangling, like his life.

He returned to his cold bed with the message still echoing in his head. The woman, Susan, or something like that, was now a caterpillar in a cocoon of bedding. He lay next to her, his eyes seeking out the small plaster specks on the ceiling. "Old buddy," he said aloud. Susan or something groaned and rolled toward him. He thought about picking up the phone, calling Jake to see if he was going to the twenty-year reunion—they had both skipped the ten-year reunion for apparent reasons. The invitation sat on his nightstand, waiting for a reply. The reunion would be more than just going back to see old friends. When he left Crystal Falls a week after the murder, he never went back and never heard from Clark, Laura, Raven, or Trish. He had spoken to Jake last month, but Hank McCoy never came up. It was an unspoken agreement between the two: don't talk about what happened; maybe it will continue to stay in the past.

Landon slipped the sheet and comforter over his body and considered what would happen if he went back. They had avoided the rap for twenty years—why would it be pinned on them now? The man was dead and gone. He was surprised that none of the six who were there that night ever caved and went to the authorities. He had considered it for days after the murder. But he gave up the notion when it looked like nobody had a clue. Besides, this was all on Clark

Hanson—he made things much worse than they should have been.

"What's wrong?"

Landon looked at the woman next to him, seeing Trish's face. His tongue seemed to roll back into his throat, choking him. He flopped from the bed and crawled across the floor, his hands grabbing at his own throat. He looked back at the bed, the woman's original face returning. He gagged once more and vomited pizza.

"I'm not cleaning that up," the woman said. "I don't do that." She grabbed her clothes, dressed as she walked through the apartment, and left.

"Sayonara," Landon said and waved.

No, they hadn't been caught, but going back was going to be the hardest thing he had ever tried to do.

He crawled across the room to the window. Like a good gentleman, he wanted to make sure Christy, or whatever her name was, made it safely to her car.

The man watched him from the parking lot. Not moving, not mouthing a word. Only stared, his hands clasped behind his back, his face cold. He was familiar, but who was he?

"You're not doing this," Landon said to himself. He grabbed a shirt and shorts from the floor and raced through the apartment. He dressed haphazardly and shot from the building.

The man was gone.

5

Richmond, Virginia
Present Day

Raven Armstrong sat in her chair and glanced around her six-by-six-foot cubicle at work. She checked her hair in the mirror on her cubicle wall and pushed a renegade strand behind her ear. She stared at the 5x7 picture on her desk. Sitting beside her in the photo was her twelve-year-old son Mathew, standing behind her, Reverend Daniel Armstrong, her husband. Six months after that night, her night from hell, as she liked to call it, she found God and kicked the Goth thing to the curb.

The guilt she had felt from hiding the old man in the tree trunk had been washed away. She was a born-again Christian and asked forgiveness for all her sins, including the "big one." God was a good God, wasn't he? She couldn't have changed things. She had no power to undo what had been done. So, she pushed the event from her mind.

But the twenty-year class reunion invitation she pulled from her purse reminded her that even forgiveness did little to hide the past. She read the front of the invitation:

You Are Cordially Invited
To The 20th Reunion
Of The Crystal Falls High School
Class Of 1994

June 5, 2014
6:00 pm-11 pm
Crystal Falls Gymnasium

"I'll only be a couple of days," she told Daniel, who had wanted to attend the reunion with his *wife*. But she had shot down the idea as quickly as it had come up. The last thing she wanted was for someone to get drunk and start spouting off about her or anything else. Daniel finally relented after a dozen or so assurances by her that everything would be okay.

Raven put away her purse and powered on the computer, dreading the day because her mind would stay on the reunion.

An accounting assistant, Raven thought to herself while taking a peek at the invitation on her desk. The Goth thing had seemed so much more exciting. But then something made her conform and become an ordinary person experiencing a normal life. Of course, she loved her son and husband, but the desire to be herself ate away at her every day. What kind of example was she setting for Mathew by not being herself?

When the login screen appeared on her computer, she stuffed the invitation into her purse and logged in. She clicked on the email icon, and her email opened with a long string of unread emails. Then, her instant messenger icon began to blink. She clicked it open.

"Raven Templeton?"

Raven squinted at the message, not because she couldn't see but because no one had used her maiden name in twenty years. She moved her hands over her keyboard. A sick feeling lurched up her spine. "Raven Armstrong," she typed.

"I don't think so."

"Who are you?"

"You know who I am."

She stood in her cubicle and looked over the walls. She was always the first in the building. She returned to her chair and keyboard. "I don't know who you are, but if you don't leave me alone, I will call security!"

"This is an old buddy, Raven Templeton."

The messenger screen closed.

Raven stared at the monitor, frightened.

She quickly stood, peering over her cubicle wall. But she knew the message hadn't come from inside the office. She sat down, took a deep breath, and closed her eyes. *You're either with me or against me.* Those were Clark Hanson's exact words, which means someone had fessed-up. They were all in trouble.

"Raven, you okay?" A hand on her shoulder followed the voice, causing her to turn in terror. It was David Novak, the office computer geek. "Sorry, I didn't mean to startle you," he said.

She looked at him, through him. She saw Clark Hanson's face. He and David even looked alike, built the same, even the same height. She backed away, but he stepped forward. It's Clark Hanson. No, it's David Novak!

"Get away from me!" Raven screamed. Clark Hanson. It had to be Clark Hanson.

David stepped back, lowering his hands to his sides. "Raven, let me get some help."

"Stay away from me, you murderer," Raven screamed.

David's eyes grew wide. "Murderer? I didn't kill anyone. What're you talking about?"

"He was only trying to scare us. He wouldn't have done anything to hurt us!"

"Who? What're you saying?"

Raven took another step back and then saw the room spinning.

Raven opened her eyes to a dark room and a familiar face. "What're you doing here?" she asked.

Daniel scowled. "Your boss called and said you passed out."

"I'm fine. You didn't have to come down here."

"Why're you always like this? Always starting a fight with me."

"Because I never signed up to be your personal assistant, Daniel," Raven shot back. She moved to her feet and felt a bit shaky. "I need to go back to work."

Daniel grabbed her arm. "Wait a minute." He let go when Raven's face turned cold, her eyes piercing.

"You let go of my arm and leave." When Daniel released her arm, Raven walked away and returned to her six-by-six. She then laid the picture of her family face down. She no longer wanted to be that Raven. She wanted to be the Raven of old.

6

Crystal Falls
Present Day

Clark Hanson sharpened his hunting knife just like he had done daily for the past twenty years. A hunter took good care of his tools. You never knew when a worthy hunt might reach your front door. He stopped working the blade and glanced at the high school reunion invitation on his kitchen table. "You are cordially invited..."

He had been one of the few Crystal Falls seniors to remain in Crystal Falls. As he saw it, he had no choice but to stay. As soon as he left, someone would find Hank McCoy's bones. But there was also something else keeping him in the falls because it just seemed like when an opportunity presented itself to possibly jet, he always found himself staying. It was as though something didn't want him to leave.

He thought about the others, his conspirators, as he liked to call them. He also thought about the obnoxious, chubby kid he'd once been. But now he was lean, cut like an athlete. His job at the refrigerator plant paid for two things: his monthly gym fee and living expenses. There wasn't much left after that, but he didn't require much either. If he did have anything left, he would take it down to Tina's Strip Club just off Highway 65 and use it to get laid.

But Clark's muscular body did little to make up for his looks. He had a big nose, forehead, and chin the size of Abraham Lincoln's. All reasons why he still found himself single.

He grabbed the invitation from the table and chewed the corner of his mouth. The paper was fine, grained. Someone had spent a pretty penny on it. No need to go and waste it, he supposed. Then he wondered if any of the others would show up. He knew Landon Zeihm didn't have anything better to do, with a blown-out knee and all. The paper covered the story for a full month following the mishap. "Landon Ziehm, Crystal Falls's very own, has a career-ending knee catastrophe." That's what they called it: A "catastrophe." That wasn't a catastrophe. It was karma righting a wrong.

Then he thought about Trish Marcum, wondering if she would show. Why wouldn't she? She was still living in Crystal Falls, serving breakfast down at Fast Eddie's. Clark stuffed the invitation in his back pocket and decided he would ask her himself.

Clark entered Fast Eddie's and looked around for an empty seat. Fast Eddie's was where the townspeople frequented to fill up on cholesterol and gossip. It wasn't the place to be if you were on the tail-end of a rumor. More than five miles outside the county line, no one seemed to mind the drive to Fast Eddie's. Constructed from two railroad cars that sat back to back, Fast Eddie, the owner, had painted the outside fire engine red, the inside a dull, piss-yellow. The walls badly needed a paint job and smelled like greasy hamburgers. The white tiled floor resembled a busy, slush-covered road. If you could get past the stench of the place, the food wasn't bad at all. Breakfast and sandwiches were a permanent part of the daily menu—the customer favorite Fast Eddie's gravy and biscuits. Fast Eddie claimed the gravy was a secret family recipe, but everyone knew the gravy was ten parts bacon grease, one part flour.

As soon as Clark moved toward the only empty table, Trish Marcum spotted him. The two spoke once a month when Clark wanted greasy food. But they never talked about Hank McCoy. Some things were best left off limits.

Trish began working at Fast Eddie's shortly after graduation. She had heard the rumors circulating in the restaurant about Hank McCoy's disappearance. With no trace of a body and the subsequent torrential downpour the night following his death, the townspeople thought Hank had fallen into the river, washed over the Falls, and floated downstream, where the river met up with the Ohio River. For all they knew, Hank could have floated down the Mississippi, past New Orleans, and his body eventually dumping into the Gulf of Mexico. But then some said nothing. Those were the ones that Trish was most concerned about.

Clark sat and opened the grease-smeared menu, looking over the edge at Trish, who was fast approaching, thoroughly pissed about something. He couldn't help but admire her hips.

"What're you doing here?" she questioned, drawing Clark's surprised, bug-eyed stare.

"Damn, Trish, a man's gotta eat!"

"Haven't you heard?" she asked.

"I just came down to see if you were attending the high school reunion on Friday." Clark thought for a moment and squinted. "Heard what?"

Trish looked around before she sat. Fast Eddie didn't appreciate his employees taking unscheduled breaks. "They found another body, Clark." Her tone was more serious now.

Clark's eyes bounced around the small diner, watching the people whisper among themselves. "Was it another Crystal Falls High School senior?"

"Yeah," Trish said, "and he hung himself." She wiped off the table and moved the salt and pepper shakers next to the ketchup bottle. She stole a glance at Fast Eddie.

Clark leaned back against the booth wall and stretched his legs across the mustard-colored seat cushion. With all the yellow on the inside and the red on the outside, he thought maybe Fast Eddie had a condiment fetish. "Who was it this time?"

Trish swallowed hard, looking around for Fast Eddie, finding him when the pick-up bell rang. "Be right back," she said.

Clark watched Trish glide across the diner, admiring her nicely kept figure. So far, she had shown no interest in him, still holding Hank McCoy against him. She lived alone in a small house down by the river. She had never been married. He hadn't even heard of her screwing around with anyone in town. He straightened up in the seat as she returned. Taking a long draw on her toned legs, he sighed. He wondered how she stayed so fit or why she stayed so fit. *A lesbian*, he thought. *That had to be it.*

Trish looked over her shoulder, ensuring none of the townspeople were eavesdropping. "It was the class Valedictorian."

Clark pushed back against the wall. A smirk crept into the corner of his mouth. "So maybe they aren't so smart after all." He laughed at his joke, disappointed that Trish had not found the same humor.

"Don't be an asshole, Clark." She slid onto the opposite seat, put her elbows on the table, and leaned forward. "So, are you going?"

Clark raised an eyebrow. Trish had changed the subject without so much as taking a breath. He studied her face, not losing sight of the cleavage in his peripheral vision. She was the hottest thing going in an otherwise dead town. And it wasn't just her body or her beauty. She had a mysterious side. Like high school, so much about her was still unknown. He wanted nothing more than to find out what she was hiding. "No, I'm not going," he finally said. "Why should I give those fools my money?" he said, intentionally looking down at Trish's half-exposed breasts. He smiled.

Trish shook her head and sat back against the booth. She crossed her arms. "It'll be fun. And I don't want to go alone, but if you would like, we could go together."

Clark's head jerked back. Was she asking him on a date? His birthday? An early Christmas present? He didn't want to attend the class reunion; he didn't want people to know he had become what they had expected—nothing. But maybe this was his chance to get into Trish's panties. He pretended to study the menu. Best he could figure, Trish had just been playing hard to get. Despite his looks, he was the only option in town. He had all his teeth and owned his own home—it wasn't a trailer, neither. He even had a car instead of a pickup. Maybe this really would work out.

"Come on, don't make me beg," she said

Beg, he thought. Was she serious? Maybe she needed to be laid as bad as him. "Okay," he said. "I'll do it. But don't go asking me to wear no tuxedo or the like. If I want to wear my Wranglers, that's what I'll do. "

"Thanks, it's a deal," Trish replied, patting his hand before returning to her table.

Clark plopped down the menu. He watched her lips as she talked to the other customers and watched her hips as she moved. He'd been waiting twenty years for a piece of that action. Another couple of nights would be okay.

Clark sat down at his kitchen table with his knife in one hand and his sharpening stone in the other. Man, how he enjoyed working on his blade. It had been a gift from his father—birthday or Christmas, he couldn't remember. Neither Jake nor Landon had been able to land Trish. Now, here he was, taking her to the class reunion. He grabbed the invitation and went into his bedroom to get stamps and a checkbook, stuffing the envelope into his mailbox moments later. It could be the best fifty dollars he had ever spent.

But then it occurred to him. What if the five of them were coming back for him? What if twenty years of constant worry had finally brought them together to put those worries to an end? Trish wasn't that stupid. But, just in case, he needed to take precautions. He stuck the knife in the sheath attached to his belt and headed to the basement, where his small armament was locked away in a steel cabinet. Better to be prepared than to be dead.

7

New York City
Present Day

Jake Simon closed his senior yearbook and stared out at the city lights. Twenty years. That's how long it had been since he had last seen Laura.

The invitation to the twentieth class reunion rested on the table in his living room, waiting for a reply. He held onto that reply for two reasons. The first obvious: he didn't want the stark reminder of why he left in the first place. Secondly, he didn't want to know that Laura had grown up, chased her dreams, and found someone other than himself to make those dreams come true. If he had a nickel for every time he had picked up the phone over the last twenty years to call Laura and say he was sorry, he would be a much richer man.

He wondered where she was tonight and if she would attend the reunion. He looked around his penthouse apartment at the expensive furniture, thousand-dollar paintings, and statues from around the world. Unmarried, six-foot-two, tanned, the face of a male magazine model. Jake Simon was one of the most successful stock brokers in New York City. He had attended NYU, received his undergrad in business, and was hired immediately following a backpacking trip through Europe—two years after Laura's. Now a millionaire, he was missing two things: a wife and kids. When you made as much money as he did, you had to watch out for gold-diggers, women who wanted to marry badly and then divorce with a seven-figure alimony settlement.

Could she be married? Maybe she had held out hope. He was her first. He imagined her working as a big-time lawyer somewhere, maybe in Hollywood, representing movie stars. What else would someone do with a Harvard law degree? She probably lived on a mountainside looking down over L.A. So what if they ran into each other at the reunion? He had brokered million-dollar deals and eaten with billionaires at New York's finest restaurants. But he still didn't have Laura. He had already mailed his invitation, booked a flight, and made a reservation at a bed and breakfast about thirty minutes outside Crystal Falls. He had tried to find something closer, but the Internet offered little about Crystal Falls information—population stats, a map, and a few tidbits about its origin—nothing concerning hotels, restaurants, or other businesses.

Jake opened the yearbook again, flipping through pages, stopping at Clark Hanson. What fools they had been to get involved with such a low-life. Loser was Clark's real name—always had been. Memories of Clark also brought back memories of the old man, memories of the tree trunk. Part of Jake wished someone would find the body so that Clark could spend the rest of his life behind bars. For all Jake knew, Clark could be in jail now. The other part of him knew that it would mean jail time for himself. The trade-off wasn't worth it. He never tried to forget that night, always letting it stir in his mind. The minute he let it float into oblivion, it would sneak up like a rabid wolverine.

"Anything else this evening, Mr. Simon?"

Jake turned and closed the yearbook. Sam Mueller, Jake's butler—though Jake never referred to him as a butler—stood in the kitchen and living room doorway. "I'm going to be returning to my hometown next week," Jake said, moving away from the apartment windows. "A twenty-year class reunion."

"Sounds like it might be an enjoyable time, Mr. Simon."

Jake shook his head. "I'm doubting that possibility. Can you work with Linda to ensure my calendar is cleared?"

"Of course." Sam started to walk away.

"Sam," Jake said.

"Sir?"

"Did I ever tell you about my parents? About where I was raised? About the death of my parents?" Jake had a trust in Sam that he had in very few people. He checked his watch and realized it was time for Sam to leave. "Can you spare a few minutes?" He motioned to the chair opposite the couch. Sam took a seat, and then Jake sat in the middle of the couch, his elbows resting on his knees.

"You mentioned you wouldn't return, but that's about it," Sam replied.

Jake nodded. "Yeah, but there's more." He leaned back on the couch and put his left ankle on his right knee. He took a deep breath. "As soon as I graduated from high school, my parents moved us out of Crystal Falls and to Cincinnati, where they died a day later in a car accident.

My parents specifically outlined in their will that they not be buried in Crystal Falls and that the funeral ceremonies be private. I was the only one at my parents' funeral." He rubbed his face and blinked away the weariness.

"With no one to turn to, I left everything to the attorney and left for NYU immediately after my parents' funeral. There was no way I was going back to either place." He nervously leaned forward. "They never really told me why we left the Falls. Originally, I thought it was a last-minute decision. Dad mentioned a job offer came out of the blue." He paused and stared across the room. "The attorney shipped some of their belongings to me—the important ones, I was told. I started going through some old paperwork. Dad had lined up the job while I was a junior in high school. I found something else." He pushed from the couch and left the room, returning moments later with a shoebox. He unfolded a large sheet of paper and laid it out on the coffee table.

"This is my family tree."

Sam moved to the edge of his seat and spun the paper around to read what was on the page. He shook his head as he read and then looked up. "You're the last in a line from the Miles family."

"What else?" Jake asked. He tapped the paper with his index finger.

Sam picked up the sheet of paper and read through it again. "I'm not sure what you're asking, Jake. Everyone but you has passed."

Jake motioned for the sheet of paper.

Sam gladly passed it along, confused.

"Everyone who left Crystal Falls died in some sort of accident the day after they left, including my parents."

"Why not you?" Sam asked.

Why not me was something he had questioned since the attorneys had sent him the papers. But then, shortly after receiving the reunion invitation, he figured it out, at least part of it, the part he couldn't tell Sam.

He moved to his feet and paced the room, Sam still confused. "I need a favor," Jake finally said.

"Sure, you name it," Sam replied.

"If I don't make it back…"

"Come on, Jake, you can't be serious."

"Very. I will have the attorneys draw up the papers in the morning. If I don't return, I need you to do two things." Jake felt his heart beating in his ears. There was a pull, something forcing him back to the Falls. "I want you to be the executor of my estate, keeping it all for yourself."

"Seriously, you're freaking me out with this nonsense." Sam pushed to his feet and approached Jake. He had never talked to his boss like this, but his boss had never suggested such craziness.

"Just do it."

"If you say so. Anything else?"

Jake nodded. "There's a box of stuff in my closet. It's marked Crystal Falls. I want you to burn the box and the contents."

"If that's what you want, Jake."

Jake nodded. He shook Sam's hand and returned to his bedroom that looked toward the southwest, to Kentucky and Crystal Falls.

8

Crystal Falls
Present Day

"After we talked yesterday," Clark replied. He didn't think she would agree but decided it was worth a shot.

Trish laughed and folded her arms across her stomach. "You want to go back out there? Do you have any idea how terrifying that'll be? And what if someone finds us out there? They'd nail us for what *you* did."

Clark nodded as he picked through the runny eggs on his plate. "First, the land has been for sale for almost twenty years. No one ever goes out there anymore. I think the seniors have even stopped their little pilgrimage. We'll be fine."

"And you think I'm that stupid? To go out there with you so you can do whatever you want to me? I haven't trusted you in twenty years. I'm not about to start now."

"Come on, Trish, aren't you even a little curious?" Clark scooped up a pile of runny eggs and dished them into his mouth. "And I promise, I won't touch you." A lie, of course. He knew exactly what he would do if he got her out there. She had no one to tell where she was going. No one would miss her except for Fast Eddie.

Trish glanced around the restaurant for Fast Eddie. He was chatting with a couple of redneck customers. She pondered the possibility of having Clark out in the woods alone. He was a mouse to her, a termite in the throes of being snuffed out by an overzealous anteater. When opportunity knocked . . . you opened the door.

"Shit, Trish, nothing's going to happen to us. If it makes you feel any better, I'll take us some protection." Clark put his spoon down and wiped his mouth with his sleeve, a stack of napkins in front of him. *She'll go*, he thought to himself. *I can see it in her eyes.*

"I don't need you to protect me. I have my own protection."

"You sound like my kind of woman."

"Don't hold your breath," Trish said, giving Clark the once over, noticing the dirt under his fingernails. And didn't he ever wash his hair?

"I'm not good enough for you, am I?" Clark questioned. Why did he always have to take a backseat to every other man in this armpit of a town?

Trish frowned. "Let's just say you're not my type." She grabbed his plate and started away, satisfied she had the last laugh.

"And what is your type, Jake Simon?" Clark watched the expression on Trish's face grow pale. "That's what I thought," he said, turning away from her. He took a sip of his soda and leaned back. He smiled. Yes, he had just dug under her skin and laid root.

"You know, don't you?" Trish's expression changed from a frown to an angry stare. She imagined picking up Clark's fork and stabbing him in the neck, twisting it from side to side until she had his juggler skewered, then she would pull it out and snack on it.

"Know what? That you had a crush on Jake or that he was screwing Laura?" Clark subconsciously patted himself on the back. Score one for Clark. Clark, who had no date for the prom, saw Laura and Jake heading over to Jake's brother's place on prom night. With nothing else to do, he followed. He listened to them giggle like two school girls sharing secrets from their diaries. He watched them kiss and grope each other. He heard them both whisper the three little words. Then, he spent the rest of the night spying on Jake and Laura. Most of the time, it was a good laugh, but occasionally, he saw some decent action.

Trish smiled at first but then grew angry again. "That little Valedictorian bitch knew I liked him! She knew it!" She grabbed the fork from the plate and held it at Clark's throat. *Stab, turn, pull.* She felt the other customers watching her. She was sure that Fast Eddie was frozen in his greasy apron. *Stab, turn, pull.* She saw fear in Clark's eyes—precisely what she wanted to see. *Stab, turn, pull.* She put the fork back on the plate.

"Trish, I'm not paying you to socialize with the town's white trash," Fast Eddie yelled from behind the counter.

Trish turned and held up her index finger, knowing that Fast Eddie wouldn't wait too much longer. "Okay, Clark, pick me up at nine tonight. You know where my place is?"

Clark forced a smile. "Of course. What's your cell number?"

"Not a chance." Trish left the table, straightening her uniform as she returned to the counter. She glanced back over her shoulder. Who had just played who? He thought he had won—mistake.

Clark tossed a couple of dollars on the table, sipping his last bit of soda before getting up.

"I don't appreciate you coming in here bothering my employee of the month, son." Fast Eddie's breath smelled like stale cigars; his teeth were just as dark. "Eat and leave. That's what you need to do."

"Don't screw with me, old man."

"People are talkin'. Everyone's thinkin' you had something to do with Hank goin' missin' way back when." Fast Eddie leaned away from the cash register. "Watch your step, boy."

Clark backed away from Fast Eddie, terror in his eyes, terror that turned to anger when he got outside into the cool breeze. That would be the last time that old man spoke to him like that. But first, someone had ragged on him, broken their vow. He remembered the words as clearly as if he had just spoken them . . . *with him or against me*. Someone had chosen the low road. Trish couldn't be that stupid, could she? He looked back at Trish, who was behind the counter pouring coffee. Maybe it had been her. Maybe tonight, after he got a piece of her, he would toss her in the river—after he killed her. As Clark started his car, he knew what he needed to do next . . . go home and sharpen his hunting knife.

Sheriff K.C. Buford contemplated the photos on his desk, his police nose telling him something wasn't right. "Of course, they aren't," he said to Mountain, his 200-pound St. Bernard lying in one of the empty cells.

The photos were of six young men, four young women who had all committed suicide at some point during the last twenty years: hangings, slit wrists, self-inflicted gunshots, a little bit of everything. The latest was eighteen-year-old Casey Franklin, Valedictorian at the high school. Being smart either caused an allergic reaction, resulting in suicide, or someone hated smart people. Buford was betting on the latter. His county hadn't had a single incident of suicide in nearly thirty years until this student epidemic. And then there was the disappearance of Hank McCoy, which just so happened to be right before these suicides began.

Buford retrieved the McCoy file from his bottom desk drawer and opened it on the desk next to the other files. He tipped his hat back and then leaned forward in his chair. Sure, he was a small-town sheriff with no resources to help him figure this all out, so he had to put two and two together. A dark history of witch burnings, Hank's disappearance, and annual suicides. They were connected; he just couldn't get any help out of the townspeople to make that connection. When it came to the town's past, it was like someone had removed the tongues of every person in the community.

As he thought back to his interview for the job—too many years ago to remember what year that was he had felt the town elders to be peculiar. They asked a bunch of strange questions, questions that would get you sued today. He answered the best he could, promising to control outsiders and keep the town's integrity intact. Staring down at the pictures, he realized something else. All those high school seniors had plans to move away and go on to something better. And he didn't blame them. There was nothing helpful in this town in the middle of nowhere- Kentucky. Only one outside industry had been allowed in—that was only agreed upon because they were required to hire someone from town to manage the place.

And then they treated him cold and distant. Don't bother us, and we won't bother you. He rubbed his chin and glanced over at Mountain. The dog snored like a sailor and drooled like a baby cutting teeth.

Buford returned his attention to Hank's file. The file stated that Hank stopped by Herman's General Store at 8:15 P.M. the Friday evening before he went missing. When Elmer Miles stopped by Hank's at seven the following morning for a fishing trip, Hank was nowhere to be found. After searching Hank's house and property, Elmer called the Sheriff's office four hours later. Hank's car, billfold, money, and clothes were all still at home. However, with no body, or signs of a struggle, foul play was ruled out.

It was hard to pin Hank's disappearance on anyone in particular. For as long as Sheriff Buford could remember, Crystal Falls High School kids had been sneaking onto Hank's property to swing from the two-hundred-year-old oak tree by the river. It was the senior tradition to do so the week following graduation. Of course, they could only do it when the river was low enough to wade across. They parked on the opposite side of the river just below Steadman's pass, behind a thick grouping of trees that created a natural wall between them screwing in their cars and passersby. Buford never bothered the kids. There was no need because they could always find somewhere else to do their business.

Buford still remembered questioning all the seniors,

including the six who failed to graduate. No one knew anything about Hank's disappearance or admitted to being on Hank's property that Friday night. There was one kid who made him uneasy and made his police instincts stir: Clark Hanson. The same Clark Hanson that never left town after graduation, still living in that old Victorian his parents left him years ago. Clark had been a graduation mistake. Days after receiving his diploma, his English teacher, who had heard his name called to come up and accept his certificate, told school officials that Clark had failed English. It was later learned that Clark had broken into the school and changed his English grade. Unfortunately, Buford couldn't bust a man without proof that he committed murder. No, but he could do some follow-up questioning years later if he wanted.

Hank returned the files to his desk and found the high school's class reunion flyer lying beneath. He shook his head at Mountain. "There's something brewing, Big Boy."

Buford idled in Clark Hanson's driveway and switched off the cruiser's engine. Clark's house stood on the edge of town, surrounded on three sides by broad trees. It was the oldest Victorian in Crystal Falls and needed a makeover. Buford rubbed Mountain's chin and ordered him to watch the car.

He ascended the three porch steps, each squealing like a suffering cat. The setting sun behind Buford set the windows aglow: orange, yellow, and red. He knocked several times with no answer and then rang the doorbell.

The doorbell sounded as if it were ringing in a well full of water. This was official law business, so he would treat it like that. Curtains covered the first-floor windows. Police intuition told him something wasn't right. Clark Hanson was hiding something. His parents had been good, law-abiding folks. His dad made pretty good money farming, and his mother kept records at the elementary school. Like the rest of the town, they never said much to Buford. Then they both up and got cancer, both dying within a week of each other. *Got to be hard on a boy*, Buford thought.

He backed away from the windows and stepped off the porch, looking to each side. The sun descended behind the trees. Night had come a little quicker than Buford had anticipated. For a moment, he considered calling in his deputies. But then he remembered giving them both the day off. On most nights, three lawmen were overkill in a town the size of Crystal Falls.

Buford released his holster's flap. He was the law, but Hanson knew the house much better than he did. The windows on the side of the house were covered. He took several steps back, looking up at the second-floor windows. Not a single light on in the whole place. Using his flashlight, Buford continued around the house, stopping at the closed cellar doors. He had no warrants to enter the premises. However, he had reasonable suspicion; there was no answer at the front door, Clark's car was in the driveway, the windows were covered, and Hank's disappearance and the gatherings on Hank's property by the river. Clark was the only psychopath, as far as Buford was concerned, in Crystal Falls. It was his duty as the county lawman to protect and serve.

Buford knocked on the cellar doors. Still no answer. "Clark Hanson," he called out. "It's Sheriff Buford. I need a word with you." Hearing a noise behind him, Buford shone his light into the trees. A man watched him. Buford raised his hands to his eyes and rubbed them. When he lowered his hand, the man was gone.

"Shit, gonna have to go on in," he said. He considered turning back and should have. Instead, he retrieved a fist-sized rock beside the cellar and hit the lock. The small, rusted lock shattered. Buford pulled the doors open and turned his light beam to the steps descending into a black hole. The steps creaked as loud as the front porch. Darkness crowded around him, the evening sky behind him starless, moonless. Cicadas, once noisy and overbearing, stopped singing.

"Clark, if you're in here, we need to talk." A sheet of dark silence met Buford's words. Something moved in the darkness. He banged his flashlight against his hand, bringing the dimming light to full power. He would order some new batteries when he returned to the station. *I should've retired last year when I had the chance. Me and Rita could be RVing around the country right now instead of me pussy-footin' around in the dark,* he thought.

"Sheriff, nice of you to visit."

Buford turned around, too late. The cellar doors slammed shut. His flashlight danced a quick disco before dying out altogether. He and Clark Hanson talked in darkness. "We need to figure this out, Clark."

"Well, then talk, Sheriff."

Buford strummed his fingers against his holster, then removed the gun, pointing it mindlessly. "Where were you the night of the latest hanging?"

"Sheriff, I do believe you are accusing me of murder."

"Murders," Buford replied. "And something tells me you were involved with Hank McCoy's disappearance." He closed his eyes and listened to the room. Clark had the advantage.

"And I'm guessing you're here to do something about it?"

Buford remained silent as he listened to Clark's voice, aiming in the direction he thought Clark might be standing. The gun exploded in the darkness. In a split-second, Buford saw Clark's face to his left. He turned and fired again. This time, the bullet slammed into one of the concrete walls, ricocheting whizzing past the Sheriff's right ear.

"You're in my world now, Sheriff," Clark said before returning the room to silence. "But as long as we're having a man-to-man, I'll own up to killing Hank McCoy, although he was still alive when we ditched him. But the others? I'd say you have yourself a serial killer on the loose."

In his twenty-one years as Sheriff of Crystal Falls, Buford had never fired his weapon. He had fired it twice in one night, missing both times. Clark's upper hand was Buford's death if he didn't do something. Buford steadied his gun. "Time to die, Clark. Time to pay for what you did to Hank." He had six shots left. The flashes from the gun discharging lit up the room for only a blink of an eye. After the last blink, Sheriff K.C. Buford's twenty-one years as Crystal Falls' Sheriff ended abruptly. His body fell in the opposite direction of his head.

Clark dropped the axe to the ground and felt along the cellar wall until he found the light switch. When the light came on, he lit a cigarette and sat back on his haunches. Part of the sheriff lay next to a spilled can of red paint, and another part lay sideways on the bottom shelf next to a box of Clark's old baseball cards. Clark checked his watch. "Oh shit, it's almost nine."

9

Crystal Falls
Present Day

Clark blew his horn and patiently waited for Trish to appear through the front door. He was too nervous to get out of the car, not sure how long it would take authorities to miss Sheriff Buford.

The car had sunk quickly in the rain-swelled waters of Crystal Falls River, taking less than a minute to submerge. Of course, the damned dog gave him a fight and got away. How many other law enforcement officers chauffeured their dogs around with them? He was sure the car wouldn't be found in the next day or so. The mud-laden water would take care of that. But what about after? The axe blade had done a number on the sheriff. Murder would be obvious, assuming the body turned up. But that's why Clark had thought to dump the car and the body on the other side of the falls. The car would get stuck, no doubt. The body could float for days, the current taking Buford's headless body straight to the Big Easy.

"Nice car, Clark," Trish said, causing Clark to jump in his seat. "Geez, why so jumpy? You just kill someone?"

Clark turned his head toward Trish, wishing he still had the axe. He checked his nerves. "Want a cigarette?" He removed a cigarette and stuck it between his lips.

"Do I look like I smoke?"

Of course, she didn't. Clark eyed her body. *Delicious*, he thought. "Nice house," he finally said. Two stories, freshly painted, all brick. It had a rustic look like it still belonged, even though it was new. Every blade of grass appeared manicured. No landscapers were in town, so she had to do everything herself.

"Whatever . . . let's just go and get this over with." She buckled her seat belt and worked to suppress a smile. *You're such an asshole, Clark*, she thought to herself.

Clark put the car in gear and pulled from Trish's driveway, watching his mirrors for trouble. His face, which turned pale after murdering Sheriff Buford, appeared normal. When he let his eyes wander over to Trish, he thought about her mood swings. One minute, she's asking him to the reunion. The next, she's biting his head off. *Must be on her period*, he thought. "So, in all these years, you've never explained why you stayed here. Especially when everyone else left the first chance they got."

Trish rolled her eyes and stared out the window at the blackness streaking by. She couldn't see the leaves on the trees, but they were there, just like Crystal Falls. It's there, but no one outside the town ever sees it. It was still small-town Kentucky, where everyone knew your business or at least tried to know it. She kept her business close. She was a good little girl as far as everyone else in town was concerned. She did leave Crystal Falls, if only briefly. She high-tailed it out of town the week after the Hank McCoy debacle. She enrolled at the University of Louisville and had a successful semester. After finals week, she received a call that her father had died of a massive heart attack. She returned home to bury her father. The trees had dropped their leaves by then. It was Christmas break. She remembered every detail. School tuition was due in three weeks, so she went through her father's finances. He was broke, bone-dry. He had promised to pay her way through college, "Just take care of your other expenses," he told her. And that's what she had worked all semester to do. The house was paid for, but who wanted to move to Crystal Falls? She put the house up for sale and had zero interest, so she decided to stay. The forty hours she worked at Fast Eddie's barely supported her.

"Yo, Trish, you in there?" Clark's eyes darted between the road and Trish's face. "Can you believe nobody ever figured it out? They must've combed that old man's property a dozen times." Clark laughed and patted the steering wheel.

"Yeah, well, I wouldn't buy a one-way ticket out of town if I were you. I heard the city's council members were ready to sell McCoy's property. Put up some strip mall."

Clark continued watching the road, his Ford Mustang straddling the yellow dividing line as he listened to Trish.

Trish rolled down her window, allowing the cigarette smoke to clear. Clark was still dumb as a coal bucket. "The entire area will be stripped and cleared. I can see that old man's bones dropping from that tree as it's leveled. The cracked skull will give it away. The Sheriff will open the case again; he'll want answers."

Clark looked over at Trish again. A small bead of sweat

raced down her temple. What the hell was wrong with her? "Yeah, but don't forget, you five were just as guilty." But she was right. Some construction workers would plow over the tree, and Hank's bones would be found. But it still didn't matter. Who would they pen it on? Everyone denied being out there. His thoughts returned to Sheriff Buford. Murder seemed so easy. Clark didn't need to worry as long as no one knew where Buford was going.

Trish turned in her seat and stared at Clark.

"What?"

"Let's go by the swing first," Trish said. "If we're going to be shit-faced scared, we might as well get our money's worth."

Clark shook his head. "Have you always been this fucked up?" he asked. "You're about one more messed up comment from *me* being scared of *you*."

Trish placed her elbow on the door, studied Clark briefly, and then said, "You knew all those kids who committed suicide, right?"

"Yeah, so."

"And you even know some of the parents." She paused while he took a drag from the cigarette burning to the filter. "Who did it?"

"Did what?

"Killed those kids."

Clark frowned. "No one. They were all suicides." Damn, she was acting weird. Did he really want to go messing with a crazy woman? "You sound like one of those conspiracy theorists. Bet you think Kennedy's still alive."

"That many kids don't off themselves." Trish straightened in the seat, her eyes following the yellow center line, ignoring Clark's sarcasm. "There's a murderer in the town. That's what I think."

"You keep thinking that. But I think I'm the only one in this town crazy enough to do anything like that, and I sure as hell didn't kill anyone." Clark tossed the cigarette out the window and watched through the side mirror at the small fireworks show as the lit filter hit the pavement.

"Except Hank McCoy," Trish added.

Clark dumped another cigarette from the pack. Trish grabbed the lighter and lit the end of the cigarette. Clark took a long drag. "What's your real story?" he asked. "You're an attractive woman, partially educated, and could probably find a big city man to care for you. But here you sit, in my car, with me, one of the most disliked people in Crystal Falls. Either Fast Eddie offers one hell of a 401k, or you're hiding something." Clark took the next exit, a dirt road that led to a makeshift parking area where all the kids venture to lose their virginity. Luckily, no one would be losing it tonight. He glanced over at Trish, at her long, tanned legs. *Man, I bet she's good in bed or my backseat. She wouldn't want anyone else once she had a piece of me. She'd finally see what she'd been missing all these years. She could sell her house, maybe move in with me.*

"Looks like the water's too high to cross," he said, pointing ahead at the river.

Trish leaned across the car and grabbed Clark's crotch. "You like that?"

Clark nodded, at a loss for words. Of course, he did; what man wouldn't? He felt his head spinning. She didn't want to go, then she did, then she didn't, and now she wanted to risk their lives crossing a river they had no business crossing. "Damn, Trish, I don't know. Maybe we can hang out on the bank."

Trish released Clark's crotch and got out of the car. She moved to the front of the car—headlights illuminating her –

and unbuttoned her shirt. Her shirt draped lazily over her shoulders, exposing her breasts. She held up her index finger and motioned for Clark to follow. "Are you going to stay in the car all night?" she questioned.

Clark pushed open his door. "This can't be happening," he said under his breath.

Trish backed away, buttoning her shirt as she approached the bank leading down to the river and small canoe.

Clark, like a lonely, lost puppy, followed.

"I've long waited to have you to myself, Clark."

He glanced down at the canoe as the image of Trish's breasts raced across his mind's eye. *This is going to happen*, he concluded. *I'm getting my wish. Life has a way of working things out.*

"I'm always prepared," she said. "I hauled it down shortly after you left me today. Hope you don't mind?" She smiled at him and felt him wrapping around her little finger. *You're such an asshole, Clark.* She pointed at his pants. "Why don't you take those off," Trish ordered, trying hard to hang on to a fading smile. "We'll go across naked. It'll be fun."

Clark didn't have to be told twice. At first, he struggled with the zipper, his excitement an impediment to his end goal. Then the thought hit him—*what if he can't be ready? What if it doesn't work?* He shrugged off the worry, completely confident in himself. He stepped from the pants and then looked at the naked Trish. "No fucking way," he said. "This can't be happening."

"Yes fucking way," Trish replied. "And it is happening. Right here, right now." She placed her hands on her hips and then nodded at the canoe. "Get in." Her smile dropped, replaced by a frown.

There she goes again, Clark thought to himself. *Acting all weird. One minute hot, the next cold.* He stepped into the canoe and shivered when his testicles met the cold seat. "Whoa," he said. "Couldn't we get undressed on the other side?"

Trish rolled her eyes and stepped into the canoe. She sat opposite Clark and then handed him one of the paddles. "If you want a piece of this, you got to get us over there."

Clark jabbed his paddle into the water and paddled like an Olympic competitor. Even he was surprised at how fast they landed across the river, especially with Trish's paddle still desert-dry. Twenty years of waiting were about to come to an end. He jumped from the canoe and pulled it halfway onto the muddy embankment. He offered his hand to Trish —she took it gratefully—and helped her from the canoe. He quickly made his way to the oak, his mind squarely on Trish. He was finally going to do it, do her. He turned to face her, his smile as big and wide as the moon watching them from above.

But Clark's plan, just like twenty years ago, went sour. He made a move in her direction. "What the fuck are you doing?"

Trish stood about ten yards away, a gun in one hand, rope in the other. She tossed the rope at his feet. "We've both waited twenty years, Clark, just for something different."

As slow as Clark had been mentally in the past, his brain quickly put all the puzzle pieces together. Trish really was crazy. "You," he said.

"Yes, do you think you're the only murderer in town? Now get your ass up there."

Clark looked up at old Betsy. The twenty-four-inch limb they had swung from twenty years ago stretched directly out over his head. *The only murderer?* "You were there?"

"You mean when you decapitated the Sheriff?" Trish felt her index finger pushing against the gun's trigger. "I am happy the dog got away."

"Like you have room to talk," Clark said. "Offing your mother while she slept." Clark stopped only long enough to give Trish time to understand that people knew about her past. "That's right, I know what you did. The internet is one hell of a tool. Not sure I could do anything as messed up as you've done." He smirked. "What's it like to kill your mother?"

Trish's jaws clenched. She lowered the gun only slightly.

It took five seconds for Clark to understand what had just happened. He'd heard the gunshot, but the pain didn't occur right away. Maybe it was the adrenaline because he didn't realize he'd been shot until blood ran down his leg.

Trish's smile grew. "My dearest Clarky. It's my past that makes killing you that much easier."

Clark felt the blood running down between his toes. "There's something I don't understand. I researched you for hours. I couldn't find anything but that story. And I just stumbled on that." He took a calculated step forward—the pain in his left leg finally screaming out. He raised his arms to calm Trish. He could get out of this. He was sure of it. She had just answered many questions, like why she stayed here. Why she always acted funny around him? "You killed all those students, didn't you?"

"Yeah, old buddy, I did. Now stand on the chair."

"No way!"

Trish lowered the barrel to Clark's right leg. The gunshot was deafening as the sound echoed through the trees, drowning out Clark's squealing. She watched him languish on the ground. "Get your ass up, Clark. We're not done."

"You think anyone will believe I shot myself in each leg and then hung myself?"

"Doesn't matter," Trish said. "Nobody will miss you anyway. Besides, after this weekend, none of this will matter. Now climb up there and put the noose around your neck."

Clark paused momentarily but then realized Trish would shoot him again. Maybe the rope would break, or the tree limb would give way. Betsy had to be two hundred years old. He struggled up the tree, watching Trish disappear on the other side, reappearing with a chair. She was going to fucking kill him. As he tied the rope, he glanced down at Trish, who was watching the opposite bank. Clark followed her stare and thought he saw a man standing there, but then he blinked, and the man was gone. He gave the knot a little slack, ensuring it would come loose when it felt the full force of his weight. He let the noose end of the rope dangle above the chair and then crawled back down. The pain shooting through his legs reminded him of when the dentist had not given him enough Novocain and hit Clark's nerve. Clark shot from the chair and ran around the room screaming.

"Up on the chair," Trish ordered.

Clark struggled but managed. He stared up at the noose. "You can't do this."

"Step off, and you're dead," Trish replied.

Though he couldn't see her eyes in the darkness, Clark imagined them glowing red. She was enjoying this. "I'm dead either way," he replied, slipping the noose around his neck. "You know, I was tired of hiding anyway." Clark swallowed hard as the noose's fibers scratched his throat. "You're a slut, you know that. I never really liked you much anyway. I just wanted to fuck you, that was all. You're just a piece of shit, Trish."

Trish kicked the chair.

Clark dropped, swinging inches from the ground. He struggled initially, his hands clawing wildly at the rope—an animal caught in a snare. The quarter moon did just enough to brighten the terror on his face. His eyes rolled toward the sky and the knot he had tied. *It didn't break*, was his last thought.

Trish, naked and satisfied, turned to leave but then paused.

One down, four to go.

She faced the trees. It hadn't been her thought. Someone had put it in her head. "One down, four to go," she repeated.

10

Crystal Falls
Present Day

Laura turned onto Highway 55, the Escalade's leather seats keeping her as comfortable as the big recliner back home. The seats had been Richard's idea. "You'll love the comfort," he told her. The man made everything about her. Sometimes, she wished he didn't. Why couldn't he make things about him now and then? It would help with the guilt she felt about Hank McCoy. McCoy was a rain cloud that stayed over her head no matter how bright the day was.

Richard was already in the air on his way to Seattle for a carpentry conference. How much fun could that have been? Zero. The kids, also happy they were away, were already in the pool at the neighbor's house. Her secret impeded the family. They just didn't know it. They didn't know how often she teetered on the edge of an invisible chasm, ready to fall forward and end the guilt.

As Laura drove, she thought about the others in her senior class. Who would be the most changed, have the most kids, and be the most successful? She had been so career-driven through high school and college that everyone would be surprised to hear she settled for domestic life. Being a housewife and stay-at-home mom had its advantages. She loved to read and journal, activities a full-time job would not allow.

Jake seeped into her mind. That boy who had been her high school crush. Would she even recognize him? She still had the strawberry-blonde hair, freckles, and deep green eyes. She was only five pounds heavier than she was in high school. All the younger, dense babes at the gym watched her in awe. She wore her one-hundred-twenty-five pounds well on her five-seven frame. Every woman at the reunion would be hoping some other woman would show up fatter; every guy would hope some other guy would show up balder. *People are so vain*, she thought.

Her only not to do while in Crystal Falls—not go by the house she grew up in and stay away from the McCoy farm . . . if it still existed. She had not kept up with the town, especially after her parents were killed in a freak accident shortly after the three moved after high school graduation.

"You guys don't have to follow me to college," she said.

"We aren't, honey. We just wanted to experience something new, different. Your mom and I've lived in that town all our lives, and it was time that came to an end," Mr. Reeder replied.

Sitting in the backseat, next to her backpack, Laura noticed the manila envelope protruding from her backpack. *"And you gave me your will because?"*

Audra, Laura's mother, turned in her seat, her face serious. "We're getting older . . ."

"You're not that old," *Laura interrupted.*

"Laura, listen to me for a minute. With you being an only child, we wanted to ensure you were taken care of and that you would never have to return to that place. We want more for you."

When Highway 55 turned into Main Street, Laura felt her stomach sink. Everything was the same—still only four or five stoplights. The train tracks looked as unused as they had when she left. The stop sign at the corner of Main and Calvary was still bent from the tornado that came through during her first year in high school. She lowered her window and caught strangeness in the air—stale, unwavering, as if someone had placed a filter over the entire town, keeping it locked in a horrendous time capsule. No one sat in front of stores or walked the streets. The retirees always, at least before she left, sat out front, chattering, playing checkers, all those things you see in movies and dread would happen to you when you got older.

She pulled off Main and into Miller's Gas Station, except it was no longer Miller's; George's Service Station hung over the entrance to the cashier. There were two pumps to choose from—neither of which accepted credit cards; pay inside the sign read.

"Can I help you?"

Laura turned to find an old man approaching, one side of his overalls flapping as he walked. A red bandana hung from the center chest pocket. He chucked a ball of black spit onto the pavement, immediately reminding her of Hank McCoy. He wiped the excess drool from his chin with the red bandana. She grabbed the gas pump handle. "Wanting to fill up before I continue on my way," she said.

The man moved toward her and took the nozzle from her hand.

"Full-service," he said. He removed the gas cap and shoved the nozzle into her gas tank, making the whole thing seem sexual. He walked to the back of her car and glanced at her license plate. "Not from around here."

"Actually," she said, "I am. I grew up here. Laura Knox." She offered her hand. "Laura Reeder before I married."

The man's left eyebrow shot toward his receding hairline. "I'm sorry about your parents," he said. "I wish they'd never have left because they might still be alive."

Laura felt a pang of panic in her stomach. Why say something like that? "You knew my parents?" She managed, stunned by the man's comment.

"We went to the high school together. They were good folk. He studied her momentarily, his hand still holding the nozzle in the tank. "You staying or just passing through?"

"Here for the class reunion," Laura replied. She looked up and down the empty road. "Where is everyone?"

He released the handle and put the nozzle back in its cradle. He wiped his hands off on the dirty bandana. "People don't venture out much anymore. Especially here lately. The sheriff was killed earlier this week; the man who killed him committed suicide sometime after. Folks are a little scared."

Laura took a step back when the man approached her.

"I knew both your parents very well," he said in a lowered voice. I know you won't do it, but I will tell you anyway." He stuffed the bandana back into the chest pocket. He leaned against the Escalade. "You need to skip this reunion. Turn around and go back to what you were doing. You got family?"

Laura nodded.

"Then go on back to them. Nothing here for you but ten kinds of trouble, nine of those deadly." He shoved his hands in his pockets and stared at Laura. "Your parents would tell you the same thing."

Laura pulled three twenties from her purse and handed them to the man. "Thank you for the service," she said. She opened the door and slid into the driver's seat. "I'll be gone after the reunion."

The man moved closer. "It let you leave once; it won't let you leave again." He closed her door and moved back. "Please, just go on back home."

Head spinning, trying to process the man's warning, Laura pulled onto the empty road and headed toward the bed and breakfast. She knew the man was right. She should have stayed home and thrown away the invitation when it arrived. Instead, she let curiosity—Jake—get into her head. But then she also wanted answers. Why had her parents left? Why had they tried to keep her away from here? Did they somehow know about Hank McCoy? Maybe that was it. Was it a coincidence that they died the day after leaving Crystal Falls? No, of course not. The old man was right; the Falls had a grip on the people who grew up and stayed here.

She took a deep breath and tried to prepare herself for the evening, temporarily pushing the old man from her memory. She had a feeling that both he and his advice would rear its fangs again. She raised the window and concentrated on the road in front of her. But no matter how hard she tried, Jake Simon danced into her thoughts. Yeah, the evening was going to be epic one way or another.

The bed and breakfast stood outside town at the opposite end of Main Street. She could check in, drive around some more, and figure out where everyone had gone. Or, maybe she didn't want to know. Years of guilt were going to crash down and smother her.

A shiny, red Ford Mustang filled one of the parking spots. A rental car barcode marked the driver's side window. *Someone trying to show off for the reunion*, she thought. Inside, she checked in, gave the large lady behind the counter a credit card number, and headed to her room. As Laura walked down the hall, she heard a man's deep voice, talking intelligently on the phone, working out a business deal. *Didn't people ever leave work at work? And why would an outsider with any intelligence at all come here?*

In her room, Laura cringed at the quaintness of the bed and breakfast. Pistachio-colored wallpaper covered the bedroom and bathroom walls. Border with yellow roses encompassed the wall close to the ceiling. *A decorating disaster*, she considered. When she went into the bathroom, the decorating wreck continued. She suddenly realized the bathtub, no shower, looked like it had been painted white. The sink was chipped, but when she turned the water on, at least the water wasn't brown. She went back to the bedroom and lay on the bed . . . which was surprisingly comfortable. Maybe she could get some sleep, unlike last night when the thought of Crystal Falls filled her every thought. She had dreamed of Hank McCoy. She dreamed of his hand touching her face.

Jake placed his cell phone on the nightstand and plopped down on the bed, pleasantly surprised at the deal he had just closed and at the comfort of his bed for the night. The bed and breakfast met his basic needs: a place to crash, shower, and food. The Falls had one shabby motel—full for the night. The room could use a woman's touch, but not every place in the world could be as nice as his New York penthouse. His thoughts turned to Laura. He smiled while thinking about their first intimate night together, how Laura touched him, her soft lips, and remembered her body's warmth. The sex was uncomfortable, teenage sex at first.

The knock on Jake's door returned him to reality. "Yes, can I help you," Jake replied.

"Mr. Simon, I have the tea you requested," a deep female voice replied.

"Door's open." The woman creeped him out. She'd asked too many questions and had suggested the class reunion was not a good thing to attend. She wanted him to leave the past in the past, spit on its grave, and never return.

Laura jerked her hand back from her bedroom's doorknob. The lady had said Mr. Simon. Wanting to go find out where everyone had run off to, she was just about to leave. *Oh...my...god. He's staying down the hall! That's his Mustang in the parking lot.* She opened the bedroom door, watching the obese woman from the front desk waddling her way back down the hall. Laura thought she would have to wait until tomorrow night's reunion to see him, but now she could have him all to herself. *To herself?* What was she thinking of doing? She was married. All they would do is talk about what has kept them busy and apart for the past twenty years. But then, surely, they would have to talk about that night. Once the woman was out of sight, Laura opened the door and entered the hallway. The weight of the house suddenly fell upon her shoulders. Jake's bedroom door wasn't but about thirty feet away. Her feet moved forward, almost dragging. With each step, her confidence grew, and before she knew it, she was standing at his bedroom door. Closing her eyes like a schoolgirl waiting for a kiss, Laura raised her hand to knock.

"Can I help . . . ," Jake's trailing words opened Laura's eyes. "My God, Laura Reeder!"

"Jake," she managed to utter. She felt her knees weaken. *Hold it together. He's just a man. A very nice-looking man, no longer the boy who she had once loved. Loved?*

Jake couldn't find the proper words. "Um, come in," he said through smiling teeth. As Laura walked by, he breathed in her scent. Unbelievable. When he opened his eyes, Laura was smiling at him. "Sorry, it's been a long day," he said. Embarrassed at being caught *sniffing* her, Jake shut the door and took a deep breath. He couldn't believe Laura Reeder was in his bedroom, looking as hot as ever.

"What're the odds of us staying in the same place?" Too stunned for a coherent conversation, she didn't know what else to say. Jake looked even better than he did in high school. And he seemed to be doing very well financially, judging by the clothes he had been putting away before she tried knocking on his door.

"Pretty good since there's not another place to stay within an hour's drive. So how've you been, Laura?" Jake wanted to keep eye contact; maybe she still cared for him, but the shiny diamond on her left ring finger blazed like a noon-time sun. *Married. I should have figured as much.*

Noticing Jake's inquiring eyes, Laura subconsciously moved her left hand behind her back. "Yes," she admitted, "I'm married. Since my senior year at Harvard."

Disappointed, Jake changed the subject. "Tea?" As he poured, he tried to hide his regret. "Back in the Falls," he offered. "How's it feel?"

"Same old place, different decade," Laura said with a

chuckle. She remembered the empty streets and the old man at the gas station, especially his warning to leave. "You notice anything strange about the town when you drove through?"

Jake handed Laura the tea, holding the cup in her hand just long enough to feel the softness of her skin. "The empty streets, the gloom and doom in the air? Yeah, I noticed. It must be the latest hanging. I think people here are scared." In answer to Laura's puzzled look, "You don't know about the suicides?" Jake told her about the rash of suicides that had occurred over the years since graduation. "Early this week, it was Clark Hanson."

Laura stopped drinking her tea and almost dropped the cup.

"There's more," Jake said. He told her about the sheriff.

"And so the secret of Hank McCoy died with Clark?" She put the cup on the nightstand and sat on the edge of the bed.

Jake shook his head. "I'm afraid that secret will only die when the rest of us do. If Clark murdered the sheriff, which I think he did, others may also know."

"That makes me feel so much better," Laura replied sarcastically.

Jake shrugged.

"What about Clark's parents? How're they holding up?"

Jake stood at the window. "Clark's parents were killed in a freak accident the day they moved away to Florida. A sinkhole opened up and swallowed them whole, taking their entire house. Their bodies were recovered a couple of days later." Jake crossed his arms and studied the property across the road. He knew what question was coming next.

"Jake," Laura said. "How're your parents?"

He turned from the window. "They were killed in a car accident two days after graduation in Cincinnati." Jake noticed Laura's eyes beginning to water. "It's okay, it was a long time ago." He sat next to her. "The day we left seemed the happiest day of their lives, and then it was over. I stayed in Cincy, couldn't find it in me to return to this place."

Laura placed her hands on Jake's. "Mom and Dad were killed the day after we left town.

"I know," he said. "I spent quite a bit of time this past week searching the internet, researching the Falls. All I could find were stories about people dying after they left the Falls." He rubbed his tired face. "Nothing I read had anyone putting the facts together. You leave this place, you die."

"We didn't," Laura said. She moved from the bed and started pacing the room. "Why're we still alive?"

Jake stood and moved next to Laura, stopping her. "Something brought us back here."

Laura faced Jake, and the strain on her face made her entire body ache. A chill moved from her toes to the back of her neck. She told him what the gas station attendant had said. "There's something we need to do, something we need to finish in the Falls. Until we do, the oppression that hangs over the town will stay."

"We'll talk to the others," Jake said. "We'll figure out what to do."

"The old man said we will never be able to leave again," Laura replied. "My kids, my husband."

Jake considered Laura's words. He had no kids or wife, but he had money, a nice car, and a New York condo overlooking Manhattan. He would trade it all for her. "You know, I'm sorry for what happened that night."

"We all are. None of us had any intention of killing someone," Laura replied.

"That's not what I mean," Jake said. "I shouldn't have dropped you off that night without saying goodbye."

"Jake."

"Let me finish," he said. "Whether or not you accept my apology is up to you, but I need to say this. I was scared and didn't handle it the way I should have. I was so worried about how it would affect my future that I didn't think about anyone else. When I finally got my head out of my ass, I realized I had made a mistake. I let something that should have created a bond between us drive a wedge instead." Jake felt twenty years of heaviness slip from his shoulders. "So I'm very sorry for reacting the way I did."

Laura placed a hand on Jake's cheek and looked into his eyes. He met her stare. She moved to the tips of her toes and leaned in.

"Mr. Simon," a voice from the other side of the door called out.

Laura stepped away from Jake and brushed away the invisible wrinkles in her shirt. She needed to control her emotions. But how would that be possible with him sleeping under the same roof tonight?

"Yes, come in, Mrs. Crutchfield." Jake turned back to Laura, "It's the fat lady from the front desk," he whispered before she entered.

"Oh, I hope I wasn't intruding," Mrs. Crutchfield said when she spotted Laura. She pretended not to recognize Laura but knew who she was. She also knew about her and Jake.

"What can we do for you," Jake replied, still reeling from the interrupted, almost-kiss.

"Dinner will be served in thirty minutes. The other

guests should be arriving soon." Mrs. Crutchfield looked at Laura unpleasingly and then left.

When the door closed, Laura sat on the bed, her hands trembling. "Did you see the way she looked at me? What's wrong with the people in this town? I should have stayed home."

"I don't think you had a choice. I think whatever brought us back here would get you here one way or another," Jake said. He stood at the window again, knowing that if he sat next to her, he would want more from her than what was reasonable. "It's over there." He pointed out the window.

Laura moved next to him. She looked across the road at the farm and the large SOLD sign at the entrance. "What's over there?"

"Hank McCoy's farm."

Laura felt her insides catch fire. She leaned against Jake, not for intimacy, for protection. She understood now. Everything happening now had a reason. *It won't allow us to leave.*

"What the hell," Jake said, and the two of them watched the green SUV pull recklessly into the bed and breakfast, music blaring to a Jimi Hendrix tune. A rough character stepped from the vehicle. "I don't believe it. Landon Zeihm."

"That?"

Jake laughed. "Yes, that! Let's go!"

And they left the room, unaware of the eyes watching from the trees across the road. Satisfied, the thing slinked back into the woods and waited.

11

Crystal Falls
1891

Arthur Rhodes gave his horse a gentle nudge in the side. Although he had gone only three days, it felt like he had not seen his family in a month. He couldn't wait to have them jumping into his arms. The porcelain doll in his saddle bag would make Catherine a happy little girl; his way of saying sorry for being gone too long. And Isabella, he never forgot her. He ran his hand along the saddle bag hanging on his right—she would also be happy.

He enjoyed trying to live a normal life and especially enjoyed fitting in. But keeping Isabella on the straight and narrow had been a challenge like no other. She seemed to be a step from returning to the old ways. He wasn't sure how much longer she would last. They both knew what would happen if she reverted. Those who controlled "things" would come after them. He didn't want that for his family. But the evil buried inside Isabella was great, her desire to make Crystal Falls hers even greater. She had given him the daughter he never believed possible, having watched others over the past few thousand years raise a family without having one of their own.

He finally approached the small house, noticing a place on the roof needing repair. He would repair the roof tomorrow. The family would relax this evening, listening to Catherine's great tales of the fantastic, an imagination they struggled to control. As he rode up to the house, he thought it strange neither his wife nor Catherine was outside. And why was the front door standing open? He tied the stallion to the wooden trough by the porch—an empty trough. The trough was never empty. Something wasn't right. He started up the porch and stopped. Scratches and broken fingernails littered the wooden planks.

"Isabella! Catherine!" Arthur yelled, rushing inside. Empty. The hidden door in the floor stood open with dishes smashed around it. He checked the bedrooms. Nothing. They had been caught. He returned to the porch, closing his eyes to sniff the air. He smelled it. Something nearby had been burning.

He mounted his horse again and pressed the three-year-old stallion hard toward the town. The horse, fed and well cared for, didn't mind being pushed. These fools had no idea what they were dealing with. Killing Isabella would only be a temporary solution to their problem. Because when she came back, her wrath would be devastating for Crystal Falls. She would make them suffer a long, slow punishment. And there was no doubt she would play with them like a cat plays with a wounded mouse.

Arthur brought the horse to a slow gallop as he entered town. Those out walking the streets and doing their daily chores stopped only long enough to see the madness in Arthur's eyes. They cleared the streets one by one, retreating to porches or inside houses and stores. A young girl crossed in front of Arthur, his horse nearly trampling the girl to death. He stopped in the middle of town. "Where are they?" he yelled. "What've you done with my family?"

Cornelius Miles stepped from Perkins General Store and looked down the street at Arthur. He knew Arthur would be upset, but this was all for his own good. Having a wife who practiced the dark ways could only mean bad things for Arthur. Cornelius walked the porch that spanned several storefronts. Several other men appeared through Carver's Barbershop. Arthur stood nearly six feet seven inches tall, so it would take several men to subdue him if need be.

"Now Arthur, we had to do what was best for the town . . . and you." Miles swallowed hard. One of Arthur's hands was strong enough to strangle a man. Arthur didn't carry a firearm, which everyone thought strange, but he had once said he could care for himself and his family without a gun.

"Where are they, Cornelius?" Arthur demanded. He knew where they were. They were dead. But he wanted to hear it from Cornelius's lips before he snapped Cornelius's neck.

Miles stopped by the other men in front of the barbershop. "We had no other choice, Arthur. Isabella was involved in something very dark, ungodly."

"Where's my Catherine?" Arthur jumped from his horse, his large feet kicking up a small dust storm. Townspeople watched from windows to see what Arthur would do next. Arthur's horse whinnied and sent dust into the air when its left hoof scrapped the ground.

Two more men appeared to Arthur's right, then one to his back. They were surrounding him. The sun stood high above the town. Noon shadows hid among the trees. Arthur would not wait to be burned alive. He would rather die in the street, taking Miles with him. As he started toward Miles, every man on the street drew a pistol, steadying their guns in his direction. "This is just between you and me, Miles."

"I'm afraid it isn't, Arthur. It's between you and the entire town," Miles replied. He nodded at the men around him. They then formed a circle around Arthur.

"Strength in numbers is when cowards become brave," Arthur said. "I can't let you live after what you've done to my family. Where's Catherine?" Arthur stopped at the general store's planked porch. Nine men surrounded him, each with a gun. He'd be dead before he got his hands around Miles's throat. Arthur could return to the old ways, but if his family was dead and gone, he wanted to join them.

Miles raised his hands and then pushed down the guns of the two men next to him. "Arthur, go home. There's no reason for you to die as well. Come to the church in the morning and meet with the Council. We only did what was best for the town."

What's best for the town? I'll show you what's best for the town. Arthur turned away from Miles and the other men. The two behind him parted as he walked back to his horse.

"Don't go doing anything stupid now, you hear, Arthur." Miles's confidence grew with every step Arthur's horse took on the way out of town. "You hear me, Arthur?"

Arthur nudged his horse onto the road leading back to

his empty cabin. This was Miles's doings. The rest of the town was too afraid to do things like this. Miles had worked them up into a tizzy until they saw things his way. Arthur and his family had lived peacefully in Crystal Falls, not once causing any of their neighbors a problem. But that wasn't good enough for the likes of Miles.

Arthur rode to the cave where Isabella often stayed, practicing and performing for the ultimate master. He got off his horse at the cave's opening and stood there, the scent of blood empowering. Isabella had been doing what she loved. He entered the cave, glancing at the writing on the walls, turning his nose up at the blood to his left, and stopped at the opening at the back of the cave. It wasn't big enough for a man to walk through. Anyone had to get down on their hands and knees and crawl if they wanted to enter. This was how they got to the town. Unbeknownst to the people of Crystal Falls, the town had an underground that only the ungodly traveled. It allowed them to know what was going on in the town.

He sat at the entrance to the underworld and said, "Isabella? Catherine?" Neither answered. "I'm going to make this right, my loves."

Arthur got to his feet and dusted off his pants. Killing wouldn't bring enough suffering. Isabella had probably already cursed the town. There was nothing left for him to do. Or was there? He moved outside the cave and closed his eyes. Although she wasn't close, he could hear the woman humming. He raised his head to the clouds and breathed deeply, smiling as he opened his eyes. He climbed on his horse with an idea percolating in his mind. It would be the ultimate slap in Miles' face.

Nearly a mile outside town, Arthur caught a glimpse of the woman he'd sensed walking down by the river. He brought his horse to a slow walk and studied the woman. Arthur smiled the smile of a rich man. Miles's wife was reading a book as she walked along the river bank alone. He quietly dismounted his horse and tied the stallion to a tree. Arthur would have his revenge now—n*o need to wait until nightfall.* Arthur snaked toward his prey, sliding past trees and stepping over broken branches.

"Ma'am," Arthur said when he was close enough to grab her if she decided to run. He held a fake smile. "How're you this fine and glorious afternoon?"

Startled, Norah Miles dropped the book she was reading and watched it slide down the dirt and into the river. "I declare, Arthur Rhodes, you scared the living daylights out of me." Norah frowned. Arthur's wife had been burned alive just nights ago. "I really should be going. Cornelius will be looking for me."

As Norah started past him, Arthur grabbed her by the arms. "No need to rush away. I saw you down here and thought I would say hello before I headed home." It was not a complete lie. He *was* heading home.

Norah glanced down at her book. It floated down the river, open to the page she'd been reading.

Arthur stepped past her, glided down the embankment, and retrieved the water-logged book. "*Justine* by Marquis de Sade," he read. He smirked and then looked at Norah. "One of the most obscene books ever written." He handed her the book. "Does Miles know you read such heathenry?"

Norah turned away, watching the river as it lazily washed by. "It's a fine piece of literature," she offered. "I read lots of things." She glanced at the path that lay between her and Arthur. She had no doubts he would catch her. But maybe he hadn't been home yet. "I should be going."

Arthur grabbed her arm as she passed.

Norah looked up into his rage-filled eyes. "Let go of me, Arthur."

"You people killed my wife and child." He pulled her against his chest. "My only child."

Norah tried to fight back, tried to scream.

He dragged her to the ground and covered her mouth. "You scream again, and so help me. I will drown you in that river."

Norah nodded and thought better of fighting back. There was nothing she could do now but hope that he didn't kill her. Cornelius had done this, but she would be the one to pay the price. She closed her eyes.

Arthur removed his hand from her mouth. "Your family will be cursed for eternity. You hear me?" And then he moved his hand down Norah's body to lift her dress.

Arthur heard the horses as they approached his house. Miles, several other townspeople, and probably the entire council would surely be there. He had exacted his revenge on Miles. It was time to exact revenge on the rest of the town. Arthur got up from his rocker and fished one of the burning logs from the fireplace using his hand. He tossed the burning log into the center of the room. The rug quickly caught fire. When he was sure the entire house would burn to the ground, Arthur walked outside, where Miles and the other men watched in shock as the flames engulfed Arthur's house behind him.

"What did you do to my wife?" Cornelius removed his

gun from its holster. "She said you attacked her." One bullet to the left side of the chest was all it took to put Arthur on the ground. Miles had no intentions of killing the man right here. No, just like his wife, Rhodes needed to burn. Miles watched the other men push Arthur to the ground and shackle his hands and feet. "Time to burn in hell with your wife," Miles said, smashing his boot into Arthur's face.

Arthur blinked against the darkness of the trees, a blurry image of the moon slowly coming into focus. How long had he been out? Days, hours? And it wasn't the bustling of men around him that brought him from his stupor; it was the smell of kerosene. He drew in a long breath and then tried to move. Tied to a tree and unable to budge, he could only look at Miles and the other townspeople as they glared back at him. The entire council stood in front of Arthur. A short, rotund man, balding on the crown of his head with a beard over his belly, stepped forward and began reading from a book. Arthur recognized him as Robinson Crutchfield.

Crutchfield read the charges and spoke directly to Arthur. "How do you plead to these charges?"

Arthur pursed his lips and then spat into Crutchfield's face. "We did nothing to you people. We lived how we saw fit without bothering any of you. How do I plead? I plead the death penalty on this town."

Crutchfield stepped back, almost stumbling to the ground. He wiped the spit from his face and ran his hand along his trousers.

Miles, unafraid with Arthur tied to a tree, stepped forward. "You have disgraced my wife, and for that, you'll burn in hell with your wife. Give her my best." Miles raised his hand.

A tall, skinny man, face pallid and bony, moved forward

with a torch. "Herschel Ziehm," Arthur said. "Our dear Reverend." Arthur stared the man back to the crowd. "As sure as I burn here, each of your families will pay for what you've done to mine. May the town of Crystal Falls someday wither and die like a worm in the sun."

Miles stood on his toes and went nose to nose with Arthur. "You will never know, now will you." He paused and leaned toward Arthur's ear. "Something else you should know. Your daughter is still alive." Miles dropped the torch onto the kerosene-soaked logs at Arthur's feet and walked away.

"Miles," Arthur whispered beneath the sound of crackling wood. "Miles, come here. I have something to tell *you*." Arthur could feel his toes starting to burn, but he wanted to be the one to tell Miles.

Miles smiled and approached. "You sicken me, Arthur. You had so much, and you used it all for evil. You couldn't be like the rest of us, could you?"

"Your wife, Miles. She is with child."

Miles crooked his head. "What? What're you talking about?"

"I'm saying that your wife is pregnant . . . and you're not the father."

Raged, Miles grabbed the torch he had dropped and then shoved it into Arthur's face. Arthur's screams lasted only seconds before the flames engulfed his face. His body convulsed like a fish out of water, and then he fell limp. Dead.

Clouds rode the waves of a stiff breeze, blocking out the moon's glow. Trees around and above the burning body of Arthur Rhodes swished and scraped against one another, creating a burst of deafening laughter. The townspeople looked toward the swaying trees and then at Rhodes' body as it fell away from the tree. They mounted horses and wagons, hurrying away from the burning Rhodes and the trees that were snapping and falling around them, except for the tree that burned with Arthur and Isabella. Charred and black like the abyss they came from, it stood eloquently, a pillar to the revenge that had already begun.

12

Crystal Falls
Present Day

When Laura and Jake reached the bottom step, they saw Landon hugging the obese Mrs. Crutchfield. The two laughed and hugged some more. Laura and Jake glanced at each other and watched the happy reunion—though Laura couldn't help but steal glances at Jake from the corner of her eyes. He was as handsome as she had thought he would still be. Broad shoulders created a perfect V-shape down to a trim waist. She imagined firm and tight stomach muscles.

"Stop it," she said to herself.

"Stop what?" Jake said.

"Nothing, I was just talking to myself." *I've got to stop acting like a schoolgirl. If I keep this up, it's going to happen for sure.* She put on a fake smile as Landon approached.

"Pervert needs a haircut," Jake bellowed.

"Good golly, Miss Molly," Landon said, looking at Laura and Jake. "You two went and got married! How many kids do you have? Bet you left them back home."

Laura looked at Jake. That's pretty much the way it looked. "You need a haircut, and no, we aren't married," Laura replied.

Landon shrugged. "Been there a couple of times myself, just never worked out." He gave them each a hug and held Jake at arm's length.

Laura walked across the room to the front window, where a sofa and several chairs waited for visitors. She sat on the couch, hoping Jake would sit beside her. *I've got to get over whatever is going on inside me.* "I've been good, Landon. I'm married, two wonderful children." *And your husband; tell them about Richard.*

Landon rubbed his stubbled chin. "Yeah, sorry about the marriage thing earlier. I knew you two weren't married." Landon stared at his two old friends and realized there had not been a close friend since. They were much better off than him, which was okay, but he wished things could have turned out differently—like no Hank McCoy.

"Why were you hugging on the fat lady over there, Landon?" Jake crossed the room and sat next to Laura.

Landon squeezed between the two and put an arm around each. "Me and her?" he whispered. "Well, she's my Aunt, dumbass."

The three laughed.

"Can I get you all anything, Landon?"

"No thanks, Aunt Mary, we're good." Landon waited for his aunt to waddle into another room. The obvious question hung from his lips like a fish on a hook, "So, how've you been dealing with it?"

"I don't think it's ever left my mind," Jake said.

Laura pushed to her feet and crossed the room where she stared out the window, across the road to the farm that belonged to Hank McCoy. "I want to go over there," she said. "I want to make sure everything's okay." She turned around, still worrying about the old man at the gas station. "That's what brought us back here—killing Hank McCoy."

"I wouldn't do that if I were you," Raven said as she entered the room. "We need to let him stay dead."

"Wow," Landon said. "Twenty years, and you're still sporting the Goth look." He left the couch and circled Raven before hugging her. "You look hot." He looked at her suspiciously. "No kids, I bet. Working at a freaky bar. Doing things you shouldn't. Sporting a lip ring, probably have a tongue piercing."

Raven crossed her arms. "A son, married to a Reverend, and working as an accountant, doing all the right things." She stuck out her tongue and muttered, "No tongue piercing."

Disappointed, Landon walked away.

Laura was next in line for a hug. "You look good," Laura said. "How old's your son?"

"Fourteen going on thirty," Raven replied. She looked at the three of them and then down at her clothes. "Yeah, I'm as surprised as you are. This didn't happen until a few days ago. I got a call. The person said they were my 'old buddy,'" Raven said. "The call flipped out my brain, and the next day, I'm back to this: The Dark Mother."

"I got the same call," Laura replied.

"Shit, so did I," Landon said.

"I found the suicides on the Internet and then started researching some things." Raven sat on the sofa and opened the book she had brought. "What I found would explain the ghost town I just drove through."

Laura nodded, remembering the same thing. But she still wanted to go back to the farm. She didn't know why, but she had to. "After the reunion tonight."

"After the reunion, what?" Jake loved her eyes, the way they called his name. It would take every bit of willpower to keep his hands off her.

"We go to the farm, to the tree," Laura replied.

"You're not listening," Raven interrupted. "There's some bad karma over there. After I received the anonymous call we all got, I began looking into the town's history. Over a century ago, a woman was burned alive on that land before Hank owned it. And that tree trunk we stuffed Hank down . . . I think it's the tree used to burn the woman and her husband."

"Come on, you're telling me the place is haunted?" Landon sat back and looked across the road. "You saying the woman was a witch? Witch hunts, Salem, nothing but fairy tales. There's no such thing."

"I'm not finished," Raven whispered. "No, I don't think she was a witch, but the people of Crystal Falls thought she was something much worse."

"Why're you whispering?" Jake whispered.

"Three days after she was burned alive, the husband returns to town and discovers his family is dead. He rapes the wife of a council member who convicted his wife and daughter."

"Why should we care?" Laura thought she knew where the conversation was heading but needed to hear it from Raven.

Raven pulled a folded paper from the book and laid it on the table; a series of family trees was drawn on the paper.

Laura was the first to follow her lineage back to Arthur

Rhodes. "My great-great-grandfather was burned alive on that farm?"

"What's missing, Laura?" Raven asked.

Laura looked up at Raven, her eyes floating to Landon and Jake. "It doesn't say who his wife was for the second line he created."

Raven turned to Jake. "Arthur Rhodes was convicted of raping Norah Miles, Jake's great-great-grandmother." Jake is a descendant of Cornelius and Norah Miles. She turned to Laura. "You're a descendant of Arthur Rhodes and Norah Miles."

"You're saying that Arthur Rhodes and Norah Miles created the second line. . . and that leads to me?" Laura questioned. Her parents had never mentioned a word of any of this. She stood and walked to the mirror hanging over the room's fireplace. She looked the same as she did an hour ago, but now felt fake. Someone had peeled back a layer of her life she didn't know existed.

Jake stood and paced the room. "Laura and I are related?"

Laura whipped around, eyes wide as she watched Jake. *She'd had sex with him!*

"I'm not done," Raven continued.

"Yes, you are." Mrs. Crutchfield said. She sat a tray of cookies on the table. "I don't know why you four are so concerned about Hank McCoy's old place, but let me finish the story."

Mrs. Crutchfield explained how they were related to those involved. News of the trial never got very far, as most people thought it to be rumors. Besides, this was Crystal Falls, not Salem.

"I know what you kids did," Mrs. Crutchfield said. She made eye contact with each. "I saw you leaving Hank's property when I returned home late that night. Not sure what you did with his body, but I'm figuring you hid it pretty well." She gave them a minute to let it sink in. "And before you each have a heart attack, I understand what and why you did it." She retrieved a cookie from the plate and waited for a reply.

Landon felt as if he would lose his lunch. He stared in anger at his only living relative. "Why didn't you ever say anything?"

"I figured what was done was done. Besides, old Hank was doing something wrong on that farm. He was hiding something. I saw some things that made me question his sanity." She grabbed another cookie from the plate and nodded. "Have some."

"There's a sold sign at the main entrance," Laura said.

Mrs. Crutchfield finished her cookie and started reaching for another, thinking better of it. Her doctor had warned her about her blood sugar. "Financially, the Falls isn't doing too well. The town council found a company willing to build and hire locals. The town, or at least those who understand our dark past, know that if your roots are here, so are you. You can't leave for a job, so you must bring the jobs here." She crossed her arms and sat next to Landon. "Where did'ya stick Hank McCoy's body?"

"A tree trunk near the back of the farm," Landon said. "We'd thought about the river but figured he'd wash up somewhere. And us," he pointed at the others, "we didn't kill the old man. Clark did. He threatened to kill us if we didn't help him hide the body."

"Or if we told anyone," Raven said.

Jake stopped pacing. "Damn it, Landon, we agreed to keep this to ourselves."

Mrs. Crutchfield reached for another cookie. "I told

you, I already knew about it. And no need to use that language here." She stuffed the cookie in her mouth and leaned back on the sofa.

"We've got to move his body," Laura insisted. "Or bones, or whatever's left of him."

"When do we leave?" Mrs. Crutchfield asked.

"You can't go out there, Aunt Mary," Landon insisted. "Who knows what's out there?"

"Do you remember where it's at? I know most of that farmland. I even helped out the developers. Use to go visit Bertha all the time before she died."

"We should never have killed that old man in the first place," Raven said, closing her book. She couldn't believe they were going back out there. A week ago, she was as happy as ever. Or at least she thought she was.

Laura could feel the place calling her. She'd never forgotten what happened that night. At least once a week, she saw Hank in her dreams. Sometimes, she would even wake to his hand on her cheek. Other times, she was running through the woods in her pink bikini, listening to Hank slurping saliva back into his mouth as he chased her. A time or two, Hank caught her, and she didn't want to remember what happened when he did. Maybe this would end the dreams.

"Wait a second, what about Trish and Clark? Hell, Clark's the one who killed the old bastard anyway," Landon said.

Mrs. Crutchfield shuffled to the edge of the sofa. "Watch your mouth now, Landon. No need to curse. Besides, Clark Hanson killed himself."

Landon looked at the other three. "Clark wouldn't hang himself. He didn't have the balls to do something like that. He thought way too much of Clark Hanson."

"Who is that?" Laura said, pointing to a figure entering the tree line across the road.

The others moved to the window.

"I don't see anyone," Jake said.

Laura looked back out the window. "I swear, an old man was walking around."

Jake put his hand on Laura's shoulder. "It's stress," he said. "The reunion starts in a couple of hours. Lie down for a bit and get some rest. We'll talk about this later, after the reunion."

Laura turned to Jake and looked up at him. Jake slid his hand down her arm and briefly held her hand. "I should go upstairs," she said.

"Come on, child, let me get you checked in, and you can go up together," Mrs. Crutchfield told Raven.

Upstairs, Laura stopped Raven. "Damn, Jake looks good," Laura said.

"You better watch out, little Mrs. Married Thing. Keep your mind off him and on that farm. There's a reason we're all here, and it's not because of the reunion. The Falls wants to even a score."

"People are talking like the town has a mind of its own," Laura said.

Raven shook her head. "It does. The stuff I've read over the past three days was enough to give me nightmares. It's real. The town knows it and is scared as hell.

Jake and Landon continued to stare out the window. "I was a fool for dropping her off that night without saying a word. I've got more money than I know what to do with, a penthouse apartment, nice cars, but none of it compares to Laura."

Landon stepped away from the window. "She's married, so let her be. Don't confuse her any more than she's already confused." He started toward the stairs. "Besides, we need to concentrate on what's going on across the road." Landon stopped. "And that money you don't know what to do with, I can help you there." They continued up the stairs.

Mrs. Crutchfield moved across the living room and onto the front porch. Dusk was finishing up. She watched the old man reappear from the tree line, confused as ever but walking the same path he'd walked for at least the last thirty years. Until now, no one else had ever seen him. But now Laura had.

13

Crystal Falls
Present Day

Trish sat on a stool looking out the window while waiting for Fast Eddie to hand over her paycheck, scrutinizing the town she despised. She didn't know how much longer she could live in the armpit of America. The reunion was only a few hours away, and she still needed a shower and time to do something with her hair. She'd seen Laura Reeder entering Crutchfield's Bed and Breakfast on her way to Fast Eddie's. Then curiosity made her turn her car around. Hidden in the shadows, she waited to see if anyone would join Laura.

What Trish saw disgusted her—made her stomach act crazy, rollercoaster crazy—Laura and Jake almost kissing. They were close enough to show the flame still burned. Now, there was no doubt about it. Laura would have to die, and then Jake would be hers. If he refused, she would kill him as well. But she still needed to figure out a way to get Laura alone.

"Here ya go, Doll, don't be spendin' it all in one place!" Fast Eddie slithered the words through two gaping holes where his top front teeth used to be.

It would be time for Trish to move on when this was all over. She'd already had enough of Fast Eddie's grease pit, much less his innuendos and advances. How Fast Eddie thought any woman could be attracted to a no-count cook was beyond her. But all of Crystal Falls was beyond her. The town was just now putting in cable TV! "Thanks, Eddie, and you don't pay me enough to spend it in more than one place."

Eddie tossed a dish towel on the counter and waved at the last customer. "You going to the reunion tonight?" he asked.

"I'll make an appearance," she said. "Don't have a burning desire to see anyone in particular."

Trish made a move to leave.

Eddie rounded the counter and stood in front of her, removing his grease-smeared apron. "Too bad about your friend."

"Friend?"

"Clark Hanson—hung himself down by the river."

"I'm sure the world is much better without him."

Eddie leaned against the counter. "Thing is, I heard the two of you talking earlier that morning about going to the river." He slithered his tongue between the gape in his front teeth, a nasty habit he had when he thought he had the upper hand on someone. "I think maybe you had a hand in his death."

Trish slid off the stool, checking her butt for grease. She gave Fast Eddie a halfhearted wave and left the restaurant for the last time. Tonight, she would leave one shoe by old Betsy, the other next to the river, her purse caught in the trash that clung to the river bank. Suicide? Murder? It didn't matter. Crystal Falls would never see her again.

Eddie followed her through the front exit. "Don't forget, you got the early shift tomorrow."

Trish, already in her car, flashed Eddie the middle finger.

Trish meticulously brushed her wavy, brunette hair, standing naked in front of the mirror as she did after every shower. Tonight, however, she thought about Jake. His hands would be warm when they touched her. She cherished the thought of his lips on hers and their bodies pressed together. Maybe they could create a child this evening and be bound together forever. Jake Simon Junior—she liked that name. Being a stay-at-home mom sounded good to her. When Jake got home from work, dinner would be ready, and then after Jake Jr. went to bed, she would please him the way no other woman could.

She went to the closet in her bedroom and picked out a skimpy, black dress with matching black, high-heeled shoes. She shimmied into the dress and then checked herself in the mirror. *Beautiful*, she thought. Jake would never be able to resist.

"Hi Jake, it's been a long time," Trish mimed in the

mirror, turning her body one way, then the other. She pursed her lips and blew a kiss to herself. She imagined him approaching her from behind, his shirt off, his jeans unbuttoned.

And then her mother appeared in the mirror. She had appeared unexpectedly, not standing but lying in bed like all the other times. Trish watched a younger Trish in the mirror as the younger Trish entered her mother's bedroom. As best she could remember, it was midnight, maybe later. Her father was downstairs watching a John Wayne rerun, probably sleeping on the couch. He seldom made it through an entire John Wayne flick, but that was okay because if he could fall asleep imagining himself as the Duke, then life was good.

Trish was wearing her favorite Cinderella pajamas, the ones with the grape jelly stain over the left shoulder, where she had wiped her mouth late one night after sneaking downstairs to make a sandwich. Before entering her mother's bedroom, Trish snuck into her father's downstairs office, opened his bottom desk drawer, and removed the box holding her father's handgun. He had thought it wise to buy a box with a combination. Trish had been smarter. The combination was written on a slip of paper under the keyboard of her father's computer. Having just fallen asleep while reading a Dickens novel, her mother softly snored as Trish approached. Trish continued watching the scene unfold in the mirror. She knew what the twelve-year-old Trish was about to do. She'd watched the scene dozens of times since.

Twelve-year-old Trish looked down at her mother's chest as it gently bobbed up and down. She watched the slow beat of her mother's pulse as it strummed against the skin of her neck. Trish quietly removed the book from her mother's side and slid her mother's glasses to the nightstand. Her mother looked so peaceful. She would never know that her daughter had shot her while sleeping. Trish pulled the trigger. The recoil sent her stumbling backward. When she got to her feet, she watched a crimson halo form around her mother's head on the pillow.

Following much discussion on who was driving—who was getting plastered at the reunion—Laura was assigned the dubious distinction of designated driver. Her Escalade comfortably fit eight. She didn't mind since she had given up drinking after her first child was born. While she prepared herself for a night like no other—except for the one twenty years ago—her thoughts remained on Jake. What would she do if she and Jake were alone again? She thought about her husband Richard and how good he had always been to her. Surely Laura Reeder—Mrs. Congeniality—wasn't thinking about cheating on her husband.

"It works better if you put it in drive," Jake said. He sat in the front passenger seat, Raven and Landon in the back seat.

"You look like a penguin. You know that, right?" Landon said of the tuxedo Jake wore. Landon wore a black and white checkered sports coat, black slacks, and a black shirt that needed ironing—all last-minute purchases at a Walmart.

Laura looked into the rearview mirror as she pulled from the bed and breakfast, watching Hank McCoy's farm as it shrank in the distance. "Think Trish will go out with us tonight?"

Raven shuffled in her seat, her black mini-skirt riding up enough to grab a glimpse from Landon. Raven popped him in the back of the head. "The last I heard of Trish, she was still living here," Raven said. "I'm not sure what ever became of her father."

"You look like a freak," Landon joked. "Who wears black spider-web stockings to their class reunion? And what's up with the mesh top and jacket?"

"We know she won't get most changed." Jake turned to offer a white-fanged smile. "Man, this brings back memories, doesn't it? The four of us going out?"

Landon obnoxiously punched Jake in the arm, "Well, at least you all got laid in high school!"

Laura's hand shot to the rearview mirror, adjusting it so she could see Landon. "How did you know that?" She then stole an accusing glance at Jake, who was conveniently staring out his window.

Landon swallowed hard. "The whole school knew. What's the big deal?"

Laura turned her attention to Jake again. "You told the whole school?"

Jake turned to Landon. "No, I told him, and he told the rest of the school."

Laura re-adjusted her mirror. A car closed fast from behind. She thought it would run right up the back of her SUV, but at the last second, it swerved into the oncoming lane and passed too fast for them to see who was inside. *Idiot*, Laura thought to herself. Jake was right, just like old times. Except back then, he did the driving. Her parents were anti-teen driving. She had to wait until graduation to get her driver's license.

"So, what's it like being married to a preacher?" Landon asked.

"He's a Reverend."

"Yeah, that. What's that like?"

"Like I sold myself; forgot who I am."

Jake turned. "Giving up God?"

Raven shook her head. "Not at all. But I need to be me."

Jake nodded in agreement. "Look at Landon. He hasn't changed a bit."

"Screw you, Jake," Landon said. The two paused and then laughed.

Laura and Raven shared a quick glance and rolled their eyes.

When they pulled into the Crystal Falls High School parking lot, Laura saw the brown Chevrolet Camaro that had sped past them. The Camaro's door opened, and out stepped Trish Marcum.

"Trish! Trish Marcum," Laura yelled as she stepped down from the SUV.

Trish gave her and the others getting out of the SUV her undivided attention, making special note of how nice Jake looked as he got closer. He was dreamy, precisely what she thought of him in high school, exactly how she imagined he would look now.

"Wow, Trish, you look awesome," Landon said, tongue practically wagging like a dog's.

Unimpressed by Landon, Trish gathered every last ounce of goodness she could find within herself. "Nice car... I mean SUV, Laura. You must be doing well." Trish turned to Jake, waiting for a compliment.

The comment hit Laura like a splinter under a fingernail. Trish's body language was atrocious. Was Trish upset with her? For what? They hadn't seen each other in twenty years. "You look very nice, Trish," Laura replied—Miss Congeniality again.

Jake remained silent.

Landon left Raven's side and sidled up next to Trish, offering his elbow. "Shall we?"

"No, we shall not," Trish fired back.

Landon raised his palms. "Did I do something wrong?"

"Come on, guys, we haven't seen each other in years. No need to crawl under each other's skin." Jake paused to give everyone time to take a deep breath. "We noticed on the way over that Hank McCoy's place has been sold." Now Jake's eyes were steadily on Trish's.

Trish thought this moment would come much later in the evening, but since Jake was asking, she was telling. And obviously, he was out of compliments. "Rumor is that a strip mall is going up on the property, and the entire farm will be developed. The past is about to become the present, with brick and mortar." Well, okay, if they weren't going to offer. "I was thinking we could go out for one last hurrah."

The four looked at each other and then at Trish.

"We talked about going out there tonight after the reunion," Laura said. "We're all staying at the bed and breakfast across the street from the farm."

Trish wanted to smile. No, she wanted to jump up and down like a kid waiting for a ride at Disney. "I'm just going in to be seen for a bit and then head back home to change. Supposed to be storms tonight."

"It was a dark and stormy night," Raven said. "And then, who knows what happens next."

"If developers start clearing that place, we're in trouble. No matter how smart we thought we were, they'll find Hank McCoy's body." Jake felt as if he were trying to influence one of his clients. He stood next to Trish. "We're thinking of tossing what's left of Hank into the river."

"I was thinking the same thing," Trish lied. I'll meet you guys at the bed and breakfast around midnight." She motioned toward the school. "We should probably go make ourselves seen." Trish grabbed Landon by the arm and led them into the high school gym, where the festivities had already begun. She glanced at Landon and liked his rough look. Maybe she had been barking up the wrong tree. Nevertheless, she still had a score to settle.

They stopped at the reunion registration table and handed over their invitations. The woman at the table glanced at the invitations and then looked at them. "I don't know where you got these, but it seems someone made a mistake."

The five looked at each other.

"This is our twenty-year reunion," Jake said. "Why wouldn't we be invited?"

"Because the committee thought you would be a distraction," the woman replied.

Laura stepped forward, bent at the knees, and looked at the woman's name tag. "Okay, Karla, I'm not sure what distraction you're talking about, but we paid our registration fee, and we're all going in." Laura grabbed the marker from the table and wrote her name on one of the name tags. She attached the name tag to her shirt and walked past the table.

The others followed Laura's lead, except for Raven, who stayed at the table. "Karla Wheaton, right?" Raven asked.

Karla nodded.

"We had gym and science together, I think," Raven said. Raven took the marker from Karla's hand. She studied the woman, waiting to see why they weren't invited. Raven wrote her name on a blank tag and attached it to her shirt. She leaned in closer to the woman. The overpowering smell of breath mints made Raven's stomach convulse. She remembered that Karla had, on more than one occasion, said some pretty nasty things about Raven's lifestyle choice (Goth). Still getting nothing from the woman, Raven walked around the table and sat in the extra chair beside Karla.

"What're you doing?" Karla asked. "You can't sit here."

"I can't come to the reunion. I can't sit here." Raven's eyes grew wide. "What exactly can I do?"

Karla smiled a smile that began at one corner of her mouth and waved to the other corner. "You can leave."

"You little bitch . . ."

"Raven," Landon said. He hooked his hand under Raven's right arm and helped her up. "We were just waiting on you." He nodded at Karla. "Thank you, Miss."

"I was just about to slap her silly," Raven said, her face contorting with anger. "I can leave?" She struggled against Landon's grip. "Let me go." She looked back at Karla, who was now speaking to a needy-looking man and pointing at Raven. Raven thought she recognized the man but turned away when she and Landon found the others.

"So we weren't invited," Laura said.

Jake scanned the room, noticing the huddles of whispers and pointing fingers. "I think we need to make our stay short and sweet," he offered. "I'll get some drinks, and we'll hang out a bit." He grabbed Landon.

"Trish looks good, doesn't she?" Jake said at the bar.

"So what, you're going to make a move on her?" Landon asked. If Jake didn't make a move for Trish, he had every intention of doing so. He liked the mysterious thing she had going on. At least he would know her name the next morning when he nudged her in bed.

"No, of course not. But I can't help still being attracted to Laura." Jake turned back to where Laura was standing. Relatives? Really? It didn't matter, but what did was the ring on Laura's finger.

Laura smiled as Jake gave her a faint wave.

"Five beers," Landon said to the bartender. "Go for it, Jake, you two should have ended up together anyway."

Jake stood silent for several minutes. Maybe Landon, for all his immaturity, was right. They should have stayed together after graduation. But one thing stood in the way: the death of Hank McCoy. That night affected them all in different ways. When Jake dropped Laura off at her house the night of the murder, he was scared to death. Back then, he thought the easiest way to deal with it was by pretending it never happened and cutting off all ties with those who were there. Months later, in a drunken stupor, Landon contacted him and opened up old wounds. Jake then tried contacting Laura to say he was sorry, but she had already left for college—life's punch to the jaw, a resounding knockout.

Landon grabbed three of the beers the bartender sat on the bar, Jake two. As they walked back to the girls, Landon stopped. "You ever get a feeling in the pit of your stomach that something just isn't right?"

Jake frowned. "Now, what are you talking about?"

Landon sipped one of the beers. "Why do we need to go back out there tonight? Look at all the bad shit that's gone on in this town since we left. Ten suicides, Clark's suicide, maybe him murdering Sheriff Buford. It looks like he did anyway, according to my aunt. Trish even seems strange."

Jake hadn't given it a second thought...until now.

"And what's with all this ancient relative business Raven brought up? Maybe we should place going out to the farm on the back burner." Landon didn't care if Jake thought he was chicken-shit because this didn't feel right.

Jake shook his head in resignation and then started toward the girls. "Don't sweat it, Landon. We'll go out, find what we're looking for, and then get the hell out. Simple as that."

"Took you long enough," Raven said as she grabbed a beer from Landon.

"Landon's a little squeamish about tonight." Jake handed Laura one of the beers. "Let's just go now, get it over with."

"Not before a toast," Trish said. She raised her bottle. "To the Crystal Falls High School seniors." Trish looked around the small circle. "And to friendships that only last as long as they are allowed." She tapped each of their bottles, raised her bottle to her lips, and didn't stop swallowing until it was empty. "See you four in a bit," she said, leaving the reunion.

"She's just wrong," Landon said. "That's what I mean about something not being right."

"She must still be pissed," Raven joked as they walked through the small crowd toward the exit.

"About what?" Laura asked.

"You and Jake. She's always had a crush on Jake. Then you go off and screw his brains out."

Laura turned her bottle up and downed whatever was left—the whole bottle, forgetting her designated driver status. "This is going to be a lot of fun," she said, sitting her bottle on the sign-in table at the exit.

"Ladies and gentlemen; I use the term gentlemen loosely, of course."

"Of course," Landon offered as the four turned to find Mr. Saddlebrook staring at them. He offered his hand as a greeting and an apology for what he did in biology class over twenty years ago. "Mr. Saddlebrook, so nice to see you again."

"The feeling is not mutual, Mr. Ziehm."

Landon crossed his arms. "You're not still upset about me turning those frogs into finger puppets, right?" While Mr. Saddlebrook visited the staff lounge during class, Landon collected all ten frogs from each of the groups in the classroom. Already cut open, he slid a finger into each frog's throat and began his puppet show, the lead frog he appropriately named Kermit.

Jake stepped between the two. "It's good to see you again, Mr. Saddlebrook."

"Where're you kids off to so early? We still have awards and door prizes to give away." He studied each of them suspiciously, the way he studied every student who had ever gone through his teaching.

This time Laura butted in. "We thought we'd walk around the school, see if we could re-live some of the old memories."

Saddlebrook's eyes narrowed, his words brief but painful. "Then you and Jake need to stay out of the baseball dugout."

Laura eyed Jake.

"Yes, I saw what you two were doing in there after that football game," Saddlebrook chided. His mousey smile made them want to hurl.

Laura threw up her hands and walked out.

"Does everyone in this school know our business?" Jake asked.

The others followed Laura, but Saddlebrook grabbed Jake's arm as Jake tried to leave. "Yes, we know your business, and you should have stayed gone. Coming back here was the second biggest mistake of your lives." He looked around to see if anyone was watching or listening. "Don't bother doing whatever it is you five are planning. You're here now, and it ain't letting you leave."

Jake pulled his arm from Saddlebrook's grip. He stared into the man's eyes and saw that Saddlebrook was right. They were here for good.

14

Crystal Falls
Present Day

They stood outside the bed and breakfast, waiting on Mrs. Crutchfield and Trish. A cool breeze rushed in from Hank McCoy's farm. A full moon—the crater, Mount Olympus, looked down like a Cyclops watching over his dominion—cast a smear of silver over the trees and road. In the distance, unseen or heard, clouds and thunder worked in tandem. In fear, the cicadas had stopped their evening symphony.

Laura shivered when the wind brushed against her arms. "It's going to be cool and raining," she said. "I'm going to run inside and get a jacket."

Jake watched Laura ascend the porch steps. He wore blue jeans and a tight, white tee-shirt that showed every muscle—just for Laura. "That's probably a good idea." Jake followed Laura inside.

Landon leaned against Laura's SUV. "Those two should have stayed together after high school." He looked over at Raven. "And you should never have married a Reverend."

Raven adjusted her black leather shorts. "I was sorry to hear about your football accident. We were all looking forward to watching you on ESPN someday."

Landon nodded. He hated it when people brought that up. He'd tried hard to put that behind him, but others kept reminding him. "I try not to think about it anymore. It was my ticket to something better, fame, fortune, and now I have nothing." He reached into the SUV and opened the lid to the cooler they had filled on their way back. He grabbed another beer.

"Sorry for hitting on you. Totally inappropriate," Landon said.

Raven smiled, intrigued that Landon had been flirting. She hooked her arm in his and leaned her head against his shoulder. "I'm scared," she said.

"Me too," Landon replied and laid his head against hers.

"I feel like we've come back not just for our sins but also the sins of our forefathers." Raven toed a rock at her foot. "How can we make any of this right? We can't."

"If we go back, one if not all of us may not return." Landon held Raven tighter. "But, you know, I've lived with the guilt for so long that I'm prepared for whatever happens. That doesn't mean I'm not scared shitless. It means I know something wants to even the score."

Raven stepped away from Landon and paced in a small circle. "This is less about Hank and more about our families' past. Hank is nothing more than a conduit to that past."

The two turned to the farm and stared. It was undeniable what they saw. They held hands and waited for the others to come outside.

Jake knocked on Laura's door. "Can I come in?"

Laura turned from the closet. "Sure." Here they were again, alone. She stopped what she was doing and watched him. He reminded her of a Greek god she learned about in college. Apollo, she believed it was. His hair, although parted on the side, looked tussled. She could see the outline of his stomach muscles through the white tee. She would never have an affair, but seeing Jake like this made it difficult. When he began walking toward her, her heart sputtered. She wanted the same thing he did—live another night like they had in high school.

"I'll repeat it, Laura. I'm sorry I left you that night without saying goodbye. I was wrong and have always regretted leaving us that way." Jake raised his hand to Laura's cheek. "Honestly, I was scared to death."

Laura leaned into Jake, taking in his scent. Richard always smelled like a lumber yard. Jake smelled like a man should. "I never stopped loving you."

Jake held Laura's hand and then kissed her. The kiss was long and passionate. Seconds passed into minutes before Laura finally stepped away. "I can't do this, Jake."

Jake stepped away, disappointed but understanding. "Let's get back down with the others." That's not what he wanted to do. He wanted to stay here with her.

"Nice." Trish stood in Laura's doorway, the scowl on her face a mixture of rage and sadness. "Aren't you married, Laura?"

Laura crossed her arms over her chest. "Why is it any of your business, Trish?"

Trish raised an eyebrow and then walked away.

Laura followed Jake outside to join the others. This was getting stranger by the minute. Not only were they headed to the woods, but they were also going with a jealous psychopath. A blanket of tension met her and Jake. Landon and Raven stood silent, watching them. Trish stood at the edge of the road, arms crossed and face statue-hard. Mrs. Crutchfield gave Laura and Jake a sidelong glance and then returned to the map she had been studying on the hood of Laura's SUV.

"So what's the plan?" Jake asked. "I know someone had a plan."

Landon sighed. "You coming over, Trish?"

Trish turned. "I know where I'm going." She glared at Jake. "The plan is to walk across the street, down the path to the river, and see what we find."

Mrs. Crutchfield folded her map and grabbed the can of potato chips she had been devouring. "Well then, let's follow Miss Know-it-all."

"Anyone cares for a flashlight? Or we could feel our way through the woods." Landon handed each of them a flashlight. "I feel like a kid again," he said.

"When did you grow up?" Raven asked. No one laughed.

Jake wanted to put the fire out as fast as possible. "Look, Trish," he said while moving ahead of the others. "I had no idea you had a thing for me in high school."

Trish kept a straight face as she walked. "You pompous bastard. How do you know I had a crush on you? My life has been just fine without you."

"Trish, I didn't mean it that way." Jake moaned, exacerbated by Trish's stubbornness. What else could he say to her? He didn't remember one time when Trish so much as looked at him with a hint of flirtatiousness. Besides, he was dating Laura long before he knew Trish.

Laura flipped on her flashlight and beat it against her hand as it flickered. *Great, I'm going into the woods with a broken flashlight.* She dreaded what they would find. But what if they found nothing? There was a very good chance animals had carried off pieces of Hank. For all they knew, Hank's bones littered the farm. Laura kept her eyes on Jake and Trish. When Laura and Jake kissed back at the bed and breakfast, something lit a spark inside her, like her body was celebrating a coming-out party. Richard was a terrific husband and father. But Jake walked, talked, and looked like something immense. She admired his loose-fit jeans. Even his hiking boots were suave.

"You kids know there's a cemetery on the opposite end of the farm, back near that old oak tree?" Mrs. Crutchfield asked. "That's where Isabella is buried. Well, what was left of her. Arthur Rhodes is buried right next to her. Though she was never found, there's a third tombstone for Catherine. Rumor was that she probably died somewhere out west, wherever Thomas Templeton stole her off to."

"Succubus?" Raven's interest peaked.

Mrs. Crutchfiled stuffed four chips into her mouth and nodded. "Witch trials were long past. The people of Crystal Falls determined Isabella Rhodes came directly from hell. Crawled out of a cave on the property and into Crystal Falls."

"Right," Landon said.

"You kids don't get it." Mrs. Crutchfield closed her chips and rubbed her hands together.

"We're not kids," Trish said.

"You were when you murdered Hank."

Great, Laura thought. *This was just as spooky as the night they killed Hank McCoy.*

Trish left the group and started across the road.

Laura watched Trish go and dreaded being with her in the dark. The road to Hank's house looked like a meteor shower had hit. Laura felt her ankles give into the unforgiving ground on more than one occasion. Laura considered what she had learned about her past. First off, her great-great-grandfather had not only been an evil bastard, he'd also been a rapist. As if her anxiety and depression weren't bad enough, she was now attached to the most hated man to walk Crystal Falls. Yay her. She did find it interesting that there had been no mention of Arthur's daughter, who had escaped. Where could that bloodline have led?

When the group approached Hank's house, Trish moved forward. "I'll take over from here, Valedictorian," she said to Laura.

Laura grabbed Trish by the shoulder. No more knives in the back or smart-ass comments from the small-town girl who was never motivated to do more with her life. Besides, why should she have to pay for Trish's mistakes? Laura turned Trish on her heels. "So what, I screwed Jake. Nobody knew you had a crush on him."

Jake moved between them. Trish shoved him aside. "Stay out of this, Jake. So the little Princeton graduate wants to show herself."

Laura moved nose to nose with Trish. "Harvard, thank you very much." Laura had no qualms about a throw-down with Trish. She would probably get her ass kicked, but what did it matter. In less than twenty-four hours, she returned to Crystal Falls, kissed Jake—almost gone to bed with him—and now she was standing in the dark on a farm that scared the hell out of her. But before she got her butt kicked all over the place, she had a score to settle.

Trish's jaw moved like a horse eating grass. "I'll deal with you when the time is right." She walked away and made a bee-line toward the woods.

"I don't think so." Laura followed Trish into the woods. The others struggled to keep pace, including Mrs. Crutchfield, who could never do more than a slow walk. Laura quickened her pace, dodging trees and broken limbs on the ground. "Trish, stop. It's not safe out here. Please." Laura stopped her pursuit and then realized she was lost. "Jake! Landon!"

"Keep yelling," Jake hollered.

Laura did and, in a few minutes, was reunited with the others, minus Trish. "She disappeared. One minute, she was right in front of me. The next, nothing." Laura spun on her heels, confused.

Mrs. Crutchfield's breathing was heavy, like a perverted phone caller. "There's something you kids need to know about Trish." She sat on a nearby tree stump, chips snug under one arm, her flashlight under the other. She told them about her new internet service—how she learned about computers, setting up the bed and breakfast with wireless—that she had searched Trish's name—all their names, for that matter—just for kicks and giggles. The article she found about Trish had a headline that read, *Daughter Kills Sleeping Mother*. "The woman is an egg short of a carton if you ask me."

"She killed her mother?" Landon said, thinking he was no longer intrigued by the mystery surrounding Trish.

"I also think she killed your friend Clark." The four stopped talking and turned their attention to Mrs. Crutchfield. She shook her head. "I saw them drive by earlier, the same day Clark hung himself." She motioned them closer. "Coroner is a friend of mine." She smiled almost wide enough to show her back teeth. "He said Clark had a bullet wound in each leg. Also said he was as naked as the day he was born."

"Damn, she is nuts," Raven said. She started back the way they came.

"Where're you going," Laura asked. "We can't leave her out there."

"Are you serious," Landon said. "She's a fucking nut, not to mention she knows the farm better than us." He nodded toward Raven. "I agree, we need to go back. We can contact the authorities and let them find her."

Mrs. Crutchfield stood. "It's not gonna happen," she said. "The authorities have been in a shambles since the sheriff's murder."

"The State Police," Landon suggested.

"No way." Mrs. Crutchfield again.

"You're just full of good news, Aunt Mary." Landon waited for the others to pipe up. None did. Landon shrugged. "So now what?"

"We go after her," Aunt Mary replied. She closed the can of chips and wiped away the crumbs that had gathered on her shirt.

"Wait," Laura said. She pointed at Aunt Mary. "You're not telling us something."

Aunt Mary opened the chips and removed a handful.

"I'm right, aren't I," Laura continued. "You've been hiding something since we walked in your door."

"Calm down, Laura, don't talk to her like that."

Jake moved toward them and pushed Landon against a tree.

"Stop it," Aunt Mary yelled. "You're exactly doing what this town wants you to do."

"Which is?" Raven asked. Things were going to shit faster than she expected.

"Fighting amongst yourself, pulling your friendship apart." Aunt Mary moved to where she could look directly at them. This day would come. She knew that. And damn, how she hated it. "Laura's right. There's more. When they killed Isabella, they only made her stronger. All the deaths in Crystal Falls—Isabella."

"She's dead," Landon said.

"No," Aunt Mary replied, "she's alive and well. We don't see her, but I'm sure you've felt her presence. She's got a hand in all this. And now you kids are back, and she's ready to finish off Crystal Falls."

"This is bullshit," Raven said. She glanced down at her fishnet stockings. What had happened to her? When had she started to lose her mind? The night they stuffed Hank inside a tree, or years after that?

"But we were able to leave," Jake said.

"That's because she can only kill one generation at a time." Aunt Mary looked at them and then stared at the ground.

"What, Aunt Mary?" Landon asked.

"You were safe until you came back. Now she won't let *you* leave. Each of your parents was a buffer. That buffer died when they died."

"Our kids . . .," Raven said

Aunt Mary looked up. "You're their buffer now."

"Can you get us to the old oak tree? I think we can find the tree stump from there," Laura said. "Trish may be there waiting for us."

Mrs. Crutchfield pulled the area map from her back pocket and shined a flashlight on it. In minutes, they were traveling a path she had highlighted on the map earlier in the day.

Laura felt another breeze raise the hair on her arms. She also felt that maybe they weren't coming back from the woods.

15

Crystal Falls
1892

Cornelius Miles sat on his front porch, twirling his hunting knife, his insides burning like a lake of hellfire. Norah's screams were deafening, keeping the entire town awake and on edge. Couldn't they pull the Godforsaken thing out of her? He didn't care if they both died. He hated what was inside her, hated what it would become. So he would do the proper thing: kill the child, the monster created by a demon.

Word had spread quickly after Arthur Rhodes attacked and raped Norah. Everyone knew the child about to slip from Norah's womb did not belong to Cornelius. Just like he could never forgive Rhodes, Cornelius would never accept the bastard child who was causing his wife so much agony—causing his family so much pain. He and Norah had argued repeatedly over the past nine months—Cornelius wanted the baby slaughtered as soon as it poked its head out. Norah vehemently fought the notion that anything should happen to the child. It was still a part of her, so she would treat the child as her own. Yes, she hated Rhodes as much as Cornelius, but this was a human life they were talking about.

Doc Carrigan had promised to bring the child right out so Miles could take it off into the woods, slice its neck, and give it an improper burial right next to Rhodes and his wife. Carrigan had argued the point until Miles suggested that maybe Carrigan's wife had been too close a friend with Isabella.

In a private gathering, the Council expressed concern that a baby born from such evil became the same evil, a point proven during the old Salem witch trials—when Miles's great-great-grandfather assisted in sentencing supposed witches. The opinions were unanimous: kill the child upon birth. Other council members volunteered, but Cornelius disparaged the idea. Problems don't disappear just because you let someone else deal with them. No, this issue was his.

Miles brushed a speck of dirt from his boot and touched his holster. Norah would have to understand. They had four other perfectly normal kids who needed their love and affection. And imagine the ridicule their other children would receive at school and in the town; they would have to move to another state to hide this abomination.

"Miles," George Babcock said as he approached. Babcock winced at the scream that followed from inside the house. He shook his head. "There's word Catherine is traveling through Arkansas with a family. They're heading to California." Norah screamed again, a drawn-out, eardrum-busting sound bordering on inhumanity.

Miles sheathed the knife and stood, doing his best to ignore the bloody screams. "Finally, some good news," he said. "Take three men with you. Bring her back here."

Babcock nodded.

"And, Babcock, I want her alive. Don't fall for any of her tricks."

"Yes, Sir."

Miles looked up the road and saw Thomas Templeton walking with an armload of wood. "Thomas," he called out. "I need a word with you." He considered Templeton one of the less intelligent townspeople, a man who needed his mind set straight by a doctor. But Miles also remembered when another man called Templeton dumb to Templeton's face. Templeton smiled only briefly before driving the other man into the ground like a fence post.

Thomas continued to his own house and dropped the wood on the front porch, the same chore he performed every day at the same time. He brushed his hands off on his pants and headed toward Miles. Every time he saw Miles, he saw what was wrong with the world. He hated the man—what he stood for. "What can I help you with, Miles?"

Norah screamed again. This time, it sounded more like a scream of relief. Miles listened for the sound of a baby crying, but none came.

"You hear that?" Miles said. "When we find Catherine Rhodes, I will make sure she screams just as loud." Miles took a step back, noticing how close Thomas had moved. "And when, not if, I find out you helped her escape, you and your family will be punished."

Thomas, at least four inches taller than Miles—a solid fifty pounds heavier—closed the gap between the two men. He noticed Miles's face run pale. Miles was weak when he was alone. "You get anywhere near me or my family, and you'll swing from that oak down at the river you like so much."

Miles straightened his jacket. Words hung on the tip of his tongue. But what he saw in Thomas's eyes made him think better of saying them. "We'll see," he finally said.

"I believe we will," Thomas replied and walked away.

He watched Thomas go, and the anger building inside nearly caused him to shoot Thomas in the back. He removed his hand from his gun and returned to the porch, acutely aware that Norah had not screamed in several minutes. Half relieved, half worried, he knocked on the door.

"Doc, everything okay?" He wanted this to be over with. The weight of the town was heavy on his shoulders.

Nothing.

Miles squeezed the door handle and nudged the door open; the hinges purred, and he smiled. Miles considered himself the supreme craftsman since he built the house with his own hands. "Doc, I'm coming in."

The first thing Cornelius noticed was that Doc Carrigan's coat and hat were no longer hanging on the rack next to the door. In only four or five strides, Cornelius went to the bedroom where Norah lay motionless in their bed, her stomach much smaller than it had been yesterday —Doc Carrigan nowhere to be seen. "Where is it?" he said.

Norah struggled to sit up in bed. "I'm sorry," she said. "I couldn't let you kill him." She reached out, wanting his assurance.

Him, Cornelius thought. They had tried to have a boy for years but ended up with four girls, and now she had delivered a boy. "Where'd you send the child?" he asked. "So help me, Norah, if you've set that child free."

"What?" she screamed. "You'll kill me like you want to kill him?"

"Where?" he yelled and grabbed her by the shoulders.

"No, Cornelius. You're not killing anyone else."

Miles grabbed her by the neck, squeezing until she began to turn blue. He let go, allowing her to fall back onto the bed, a fit of coughing and gagging taking over. "I'll find him myself."

Norah reached for him again, but he angrily stepped away.

Miles moved to the window and touched a small blood spot on the window stool.

"Cornelius, don't," Norah pleaded.

He pointed at his wife. "You tell anyone that little monster was born, and I'll see to it that you hang." He started out of the room and then stopped. Rage made him turn back to her. "And I'll bury you right next to that bastard and his whore of a wife."

Miles hurried to the front door. Carrigan had taken the child. He rushed around the side of the house and followed the tracks—two sets of footprints—into the woods. *Who was helping Carrigan?* He pressed his hands against his temples and then made a sound that echoed through the valley. Letting that monster child away would be worse than allowing Catherine to escape, and he wouldn't let that happen. He returned to the front of the house and mounted his horse, leading the brown stallion back around the house and into the woods. Norah yelled for him through the open window as he disappeared.

The tracks stayed fresh for the first few miles, leading across neighboring properties. It wasn't until the last property that Miles stopped his horse and dismounted. Rhodes had paid a good bit of money to have a rock wall built around his property—and no one was ever real sure where he got that much money.

"Stay here, big boy," he said to the horse and tied the reins to a nearby oak. He climbed the wall and headed toward the burned-out cabin, following the tracks of, based on the boot sizes, two men. Surely Templeton wouldn't be dumb enough to cross him a second time?

Miles approached the cabin and saw nothing but charred remains. The stone fireplace was an ornament to the evil living there. The tracks led to the right of the house and straight into the woods—toward where he'd burned both Isabella and Arthur. *This was good*, he thought to himself. *He could burn the little creature right where he burned the little bastard's father*.

As the woods and brush began to thin, Arthur recognized Doc Carrigan and Thomas Templeton. He stepped into the small clearing and removed his gun from its holster. "Gentlemen," he said. He motioned toward the baby. "You got something I want."

Thomas handed the baby to Carrigan and then turned to Miles. "We can't let you take the child," he said. "The child didn't ask for any of this." He put a few steps between him and the baby.

"You took the other child," Miles said accusingly. He took a step forward. "I want both of them."

Carrigan laid the sleeping baby next to the blackened tree. He moved next to Templeton, blocking Miles's view of the baby.

"Too late," Thomas said. "She's already out west somewhere."

"Then I'll just take the newborn, and we'll call it even." Miles started forward but stopped when he felt cool steel press against his temple.

"Put the gun down, Cornelius. This is over. You can't have the baby, you can't have Catherine, and you can't keep doing this," Norah said. "Let them finish what they're doing."

Miles dropped his gun and shook his head at his wife, who turned on him. "Why're you doing this? All of you? Why?"

Norah backed away and grabbed her stomach, the pain dropping her to her knees. Through blurring vision, she reached out for the child. "Simon."

Miles looked from Norah to the baby. She had named the abomination? He reached for his gun but felt the air leave his body when Templeton bowled him over. Miles managed to roll to his left, away from Templeton's surging hands. He lunged for the gun again but felt his teeth give when Carrigan connected with a booted foot. Miles rolled to his back and looked up into a starless sky. Blood flowed from the corner of his mouth. His head lobbed to the left. He could see that the two men were trying to help Norah, the baby unguarded. Miles scrambled on hands and knees toward the sleeping baby as rocks and limbs cut through his clothes, burrowing into his skin.

Miles stopped. The pain seemed to begin before the sound. He dropped to his side.

Norah fired a gun at an actual person for the first time and did not miss the intended target. Miles's right knee exploded in a mass of blood and bone. He fell over, hands grasping at the knee that was no more.

"Get the baby," Carrigan yelled, still holding Norah in his arms. "It's going to be okay," he told her. But it wasn't. Norah glanced over at Cornelius one last time and then closed her eyes.

Thomas grabbed the screaming baby and held him

against his chest. He looked down at Miles, who was scooting his way to a sitting position against the charred tree. Thomas moved away, joining Doc Carrigan and Norah's lifeless body. He rewrapped the baby in the bloodied blanket the child had been placed in. "We need to get him someplace warm, or he's going to die out here," Thomas said. "We can take him back to my place until the morning, then he'll have to leave the Falls." He placed a hand against Norah's pale face and looked at Carrigan.

Carrigan shook his head no. "She's gone." Carrigan glanced at Miles and the knee that needed his help. "Happy?" He asked. "We'll take Norah back to the house; tell everyone she died giving birth and that the child died during delivery," Carrigan told Thomas. "Everyone wanted the child dead anyway."

"And what about him?" Thomas nodded toward Miles. "He won't stop until him," he held out the baby who was sleeping again, "and Catherine are both dead."

Carrigan lifted Norah's body from the ground. "With that knee, he's not going anywhere. The wound's too large to heal. An infection will set in soon, and his leg will swell. Add in all the blood he's lost, and he's a dead man." He laid Norah over his horse's saddle. He took the baby from Thomas and then gave the baby back when Thomas settled atop his horse.

"Wait," Miles said, his breathing heavy with pain. "My daughters."

"We'll make sure everyone is well cared for," Thomas said. "You should've just left the kids alone. That's all you had to do. You thought this town was here for you instead of you being here for the town. It's not going to work that way anymore." Thomas tightened his grip on the baby and then nudged his horse.

Miles took a deep breath and winced in pain. Norah had shot him—his own wife. This was Rhodes's fault. All of it. He took another deep breath and felt the pain travel into his groin. It was getting worse. No worries, death would be here soon. He closed his eyes and tried to relax.

"Death."

Cornelius opened his eyes.

"You don't deserve to die."

Cornelius squinted into the darkness. "Rhodes?"

"I won't let you die, Miles. That would be too easy on you."

Cornelius looked up. Arthur Rhodes sat on the burned tree six feet above him. "You just won't die, will you . . . just like your kids," Cornelius said.

Rhodes jumped from the tree, the sound of his feet hitting the ground as soft as a cool breeze. He moved to one knee in front of Cornelius. "As long as rock walls surround my land, you'll be imprisoned on my land. You'll never forget what you've done to my family and me and what *you* did to your wife and kids. Until the day that you die, your lineage will pay for what you've done."

16

Crystal Falls
Present Day

Aunt Mary turned the map clockwise, studying her archaic drawing beneath the beam of a flashlight. A drizzle continued working in from the west. A rumble of thunder reminded them that time was short. "I'm not exactly sure where we're at," she said. She pointed at the map. "Things don't look the same, like the trail just up and changed itself."

With hands on hips, Laura stared toward the dark woods before her. "This way," she said. She stepped around a group of thickets and began dodging around the trees.

Jake quickly moved forward, trying to slow Laura. "How do you know where you're going?"

"I don't know," she replied. "But I think we head this direction. Trish is heading for the tree trunk. We all know that." She stopped only briefly. "We're supposed to find the tree. That's why the Falls brought us back.

Jake grabbed Laura's arm. "Wait for the others. We're not running into the woods halfcocked."

Landon, Raven, and Aunt Mary stood watching them. A raven landed in the trees above, drawing their attention.

Raven, who was standing next to Landon, watched the black bird. "That can't be a good sign."

Something jostled in the darkness ahead. Landon moved toward the noise. A part of him expected Hank McCoy to come walking out of the night. If that happened, he would call it quits, sacrifice himself if only to be done with this nightmare. His flashlight danced between trees, eventually finding a foraging opossum. "If I'm being honest here, I gotta say, I'm scared enough that my heart might beat right out of my chest."

Jake left Laura's side and stepped to Landon's side. "Don't go chicken-shit on me again," Jake said.

Landon shined the light on Jake's face. "I'm not chicken. None of this makes a lick of sense. Suicides, murders, Trish acting bat-shit crazy, not to mention the five of us walking around in the woods . . ."

"Lost," Raven added. She grabbed the back of Landon's shirt. "Don't leave me."

Landon reached back and took Raven's hand. "Not a chance." He started forward, but his mind went in another direction.

Landon glanced at the scoreboard as he ran to the huddle from the sideline with a play that would send him over the defensive line and in for a touchdown. They were down five to Michigan, the team every Ohio resident vehemently hated. He passed the play onto the quarterback, who then repeated the play to the others circling him. The players in the huddle clapped and moved into position. The quarterback moved under center. Landon lined up behind and to the right of the quarterback. This touchdown would secure his place in OSU football history. Everyone across the nation would know the name Landon Ziehm. His only regret was that his parents were not here to see him become famous. He breathed steadily, calming his nerves, his eyes on the white line he only needed to touch. At ten years old, he began dreaming of this moment: being hoisted up on shoulders, cheering with the crowd, pumping his fist into the air, and slamming the ball to the ground in victory.

Forty-six, he heard the quarterback yell. The play would begin on eighty-nine. Landon leaned slightly forward, ready to push off the balls of his feet. He could hear the fans screaming his name. Sixty-four. His eyes focused on the quarterback. Eighty-nine . . .

Landon sprang forward, opening his arms as the quarterback turned with the football. Landon felt the ball hit his stomach, his arms squeezing the pigskin as if he were a hero carrying away a bomb that would surely end the world. He heard shoulder pads and helmets clashing and young men groaning in pain. He heard his coach yelling for him to jump. He heard the fans shouting his name. To the left, he saw a lineman break through the offensive line. In a millisecond, Landon changed the play. The defense had managed to stand up the offensive line, making it impossible for him to go over the top. He cut to the right, where another lineman had broken through. Through the player's mask, he saw the nightmare from the summer—the face of Hank McCoy. Landon *spun from the lineman and saw an opening in the end zone. The lineman who had originally broken free to Landon's left closed in. Landon looked at the lineman, his face that of Hank McCoy. And as Landon sprang for the small opening to the end zone, both Hanks went for his knees. He felt the ligament tear one way and then another. As he went to the ground, Landon reached forward, the ball hitting the ground a foot short of the white line.*

When Landon finally came around, a nurse and doctor stood at the end of his bed, reading from a clipboard. Other than the doctor and nurse, the room stood empty—no parents, girlfriend, or friends. Both knees felt sore. He pulled back the sheets covering his legs and, taking one look at his knee, Landon left consciousness.

Landon fell to his knees, Raven falling over him, landing with a thud against a fallen tree. Landon shook the cobwebs from his head and stared at the others. "He was there," Landon said. "It was him."

Jake helped Raven to her feet. "Who was where?" He asked. "And you about broke her neck."

"Hank McCoy was at the Michigan game when I shredded my knee." Landon sat up and winced in pain. "On the other team."

The others shared a worried glance. Jake offered his hand. "Hank McCoy was dead long before you played that game. You're just spooked." He turned to the others. "I don't want to leave Trish out here alone any more than the rest of you, but we need to think about our safety as well." He helped Landon to his feet. A purplish streak of lightning raced across the treetops close enough that they could feel its emanating energy. "We'll go back to Aunt Mary's, wait the storm out, and come back in the morning when we're not falling over each other." He looked at Landon. "Sound good?"

Landon pulled leaves from his hair and shirt. "Perfect." He headed back the way they had come, a noticeable limp, a new addition to his repertoire. Raven caught up with him and laid his arm across her shoulders, supporting him.

Aunt Mary followed but kept stealing a glance at the woods behind. She felt Trish's presence and guessed the woman was watching them from the shadows, not lost at all.

Jake sidled next to Laura, who seemed to be in another world. "If we're going to make this work, figuring out why the hell we're here, you need to be a team player." Laura, obviously hurt, looked at him. "I'm serious," Jake said. "You can't go off running into the woods without us. The only way we get through this is by sticking together. Trish'll be fine."

Laura watched the ground as she moved along the trail they had followed. "It's not Trish," she said. "It's something else. There's more here than Trish." She noticed Jake's hand dangling close to hers. She slipped her fingers between his. Not an intimate gesture, but one of comfort, of protection. She considered getting into her Escalade and leaving when they returned to Aunt Mary's, but she believed the old man at the gas station. The Falls would not let her go until it had dealt with her. "We'll have to let this play out," she said.

In the shadows, not thirty yards away, Trish walked parallel to the friends she now considered enemies. Laura was right. There was something in the Falls keeping them here. And when she noticed Laura take Jake's hand, that something bore its way deeper into Trish's soul. She watched Jake with severe intensity.

Trish watched the others cross the road from the tree

line and return to the bed and breakfast. The night had not been a total loss. Landon's limp meant that he would not be able to run, making it easier on her when the time came.

17

San Francisco
April 17, 1906

Twenty-five-year-old Catherine Rhodes gazed at herself in the mirror and tried remembering her parents. She looked nothing like either: blonde hair, freckles that bunched at her nose and then scattered along her cheeks, maybe her father's height at almost five feet ten inches tall.

Although only fifteen years had passed, the memories were beginning to blur, like a photograph left in the sun too long. But one of the strongest memories of her mother was also Catherine's guiding light—the special powers. Stories of witches, witchcraft, and demons dominated her classroom studies. She learned of exorcisms, the Salem witch trials, the devil, and, most importantly, how to spot a practitioner like herself. The key to staying safe and avoiding the religious folk and "ghost hunters" was creating a normal life.

So she became part of the family that had whisked her away from Kentucky, studied like a regular schoolgirl, said all the right things, and did all the right things—attending church service an absolute must. Fit in or get out was her mantra.

But then she also set aside time for herself and adventures in the California woods. She loved the woods and felt at home with the trees, animals, and all of nature. Here, she learned her craft, a natural talent that only needed to be stoked, tested, and put into practice. She did not consider herself a witch—the word represented the old world, not the one she lived in now. The world had changed for the better—no more burning people at the stake or hangings. Now they stuck people like her in big buildings called asylums—the reason she learned to be "normal."

Her mother never called people like them witches or warlocks. Those were names made up by outsiders who didn't understand how to become one with the natural world. She was proud of herself and her parents.

Tonight, a quarter moon rested between two swelling gray clouds; a hint of rainfall swept in from the Pacific. Catherine tied her hair back into a ponytail, laughing as it flopped side to side each time she soared over a downed tree. She loved taking deep breaths in the forest and filling her lungs with virgin air. The good found in nature was limitless to that found in the city where crime, rape, and murder were household words.

Nearly two miles into the redwoods, Catherine leaned against a tree as wide as she was tall. She sat at the tree's base in the lotus position and unpacked her bag. She gazed at the giant trees, much larger than she remembered trees to be back in Kentucky. These were ancient and had seen strange things for over a thousand years. Best of all, when she spoke to these wooden centurions . . . they talked back.

She broke the bread she had carried in the bag and shoved a piece into her mouth. She chased the sourdough with a swallow of water. The burp that followed echoed through the trees; the trees seemed to giggle amongst themselves.

"Time," she said. She retrieved a ball of rope from her pack—her adopted father would surely miss it but would never think to ask her, his little princess—and strung the rope around a circle of trees, creating a thirty-foot perimeter. She collected an armload of sticks within the circle and made a stick body along the ground. She then gathered the smattering of moss in the ring and positioned the moss around the top of the stick head. Catherine closed her eyes, concentrated on the image in her mind's eye of a girl her age, and then opened her eyes.

Catherine moved to the center of the circle and kneeled in front of the young woman lying on the ground, her eyes closed, her body not moving. She parted the woman's lips, lowered her mouth, and breathed life into the lifeless.

The young woman sat up and took a deep, violent breath, choking momentarily. A meandering string of spit flew from her mouth and landed on Catherine's shoes. Catherine laughed and helped the young girl to her feet. "Remember the rules," Catherine said. "Stay inside the string." The first three or four times Catherine tried this very trick, the woman darted into the woods and, thirty feet in, fell to the ground in a heap of sticks.

"Samantha," the young woman said and pointed at herself. She then pointed at Catherine. "Catherine."

Catherine smiled, impressed with herself and her gift. She skipped around the circle, and Samantha followed, skipping along with her. "Good girl," Catherine said. "Now this." Catherine spun in place, stretching her arms and looking up at the few stars between humongous branches.

Catherine looked down to see Samantha spinning in place, her pigtails floating in the air. Catherine laughed and reached for Samantha's hand, which dissolved into a branch and dropped to the ground. Catherine stopped and, in shock, looked down at the pile of wood and patches of moss.

"My apologies for such an abrupt entrance."

Catherine turned on her heels and held her palms out, ready to strike. Only once had she used her gift to harm a person. A man, drunk and falling over himself, attacked her in an alleyway in San Francisco. She should never have been alone in the city. The drunkard ripped at her clothes, telling her she didn't need to be a virgin anymore. It took one twist of her wrist, and the man's bones disintegrated, leaving behind a pile of skin and organs. She ran home and never mentioned the scene to anyone.

The man slipped his knife back into its sheath and dropped the cut rope, breaking the circle.

"Who're you?" Catherine asked, still holding up her hands, ready to strike. Before she killed him, she wanted to know why he had entered the circle and what he had seen. No one, including her new parents, had a hint of her gift.

"Names Babcock," he replied. He stepped forward and nudged the pile of branches and moss with the toe of his boot. "Nice trick. Miles wasn't kidding when he said to be careful."

Catherine studied Babcock, trying to remember if they had ever met. The name Miles was familiar. Her eyes grew wide. Cornelius Miles, the man who had killed her parents. "He sent you after me?"

"He did, sort of."

Babcock noticed Catherine's eyes narrowing. A stiff

wind rushed through the trees. He raised his hands. "Don't," he said. "I'm just here to see what all the fuss was about, not to take you back to Miles." He waited for Catherine to lower her hands. When she did, he eased his way to a tree stump and sat.

"You owe me a rope," Catherine said. She gathered the pile of branches and placed them next to the tree where her pack sat closed. She sat opposite Babcock. "You've seen what you needed to see. Now it's time for you to go."

Babcock chuckled. "I can't just up and leave, not after coming this far and losing four good men. Besides," he dug a piece of jerky from his pocket and placed it between his cheek and gum, "I want to make you an offer."

"An offer," Catherine retorted.

Babcock stood.

Catherine raised her hands. A stiff wind followed.

"Just calm down, little lady. I told you I'm not here to cause you no harm. I only want to talk, offer you something." Babcock stood and pulled a sheet of paper from his back pocket. "Miles is long gone, killed by his wife. But even with Miles gone, the town seems to think there's some curse on it." He looked at Catherine sharply. "They say your mother put the first curse before she died. Then your father added to it before he died. It has been fifteen years."

"They didn't die," Catherine said. Babcock looked confused. "They were murdered."

"Fair enough," Babcock said. "The town would like you to return and lift both curses."

"They murdered my parents," Catherine said, appalled that anyone would think this request would be okay. Why not ask her to make it rain when the crops were dry or warm the day when it was below freezing? But appease those who had set her parents on fire? "No."

Babcock walked around the circle, thinking. He turned to Catherine. "Do you remember the name Thomas Templeton?" He asked. "The man who saved your life?"

It was Catherine's turn to stop and sit.

She put her arms around the man and looked back at her mother, who stood on the porch, waving goodbye. He ran through the woods, telling her to hold tight and that everything would be okay. She was safe now. She wanted to ask about her mommy and why she wasn't coming with them. But she was old enough to process what was happening. Her mother was staying so Catherine could get away. The mean men were coming back, and the only way for Catherine to stay safe was to leave. And this man, his name Thomas, was going to make sure she got away safely.

Thomas ran with her in his arms until they reached the river, where a small boat waited. In the boat were a black woman, a small black child, and a white man who looked very nervous.

"Hurry it up, Thomas. We need to get going before dawn breaks."

Thomas dropped her to her feet and kneeled in front of her. "You have to go with these people," he said. "You'll be safe with them."

Catherine looked back at the three people in the boat. "Okay," she said.

Thomas brushed back a stray strand of hair from Catherine's face. "But there's something you have to promise me, okay?" Catherine nodded. Thomas smiled the best he could. "You can never come back to Crystal Falls. Okay?" He paused and took a deep breath, trying to slow the adrenaline. "Do you promise me that?"

Catherine promised.

Thomas lifted her into the boat. Catherine sat beside the other little girl and watched sadly as the boat pushed away from the bank. Thomas waved, and she waved back.

The small boat emptied into the Ohio River hours later, and the four occupants began heading west. They stopped along several towns, taking handouts from strangers, though the man in the boat seemed to know about everyone and everything. She was well taken care of—given a doll by a well-to-do woman in Evansville—so Thomas's promise had been true.

It was not until two months later that they stopped for good. They paddled into a small town called Memphis (though Catherine called it Memis). Here, she was introduced to a family willing to take her in as their own.

Thomas had saved her life.

"I will never forget Mr. Templeton and what he did for me," Catherine said.

"Good," Babcock replied. He didn't mean it to be a wry smile, but that's how it came out. "Thomas is very sick. About four days ago, the last word I got was that he was nearing death. If we leave now, in time to catch the train, we could be in Crystal Falls in less than ten days."

"You should be a snake oil salesman," Catherine said. "And you should've told me about Thomas in the beginning. I would've agreed without your games."

"I see," he said, but he didn't. He was a man of many means and would always do what was necessary, even if it involved a game of cat and mouse.

Catherine retrieved her pack and slung it over her

shoulder. "Since you followed me out here, I assume you also know where I live."

Babcock nodded.

"I need clothes and supplies," she said. "Be waiting at five tomorrow morning." She turned to leave and then stopped. "I'll need a horse," she added, disappearing into the woods.

Pleased with himself, Babcock whistled for his horse and made camp in the broken circle. This was the part Babcock cherished—the deceit. The part he didn't like was the fitting in. He listened to Catherine's footfalls until they were no more. He smiled and closed his eyes.

Catherine stood at the corner of Fourth and Mission, looking up and down the street for Babcock, who was five minutes late. *A liar*, she thought to herself. *And she had fallen for it.* The city began to wake, and dawn broke the eastern sky. In another hour, her new parents would awaken and find her gone.

"I'm sorry," Babcock muttered as he approached. "The horses seemed spooked about something and were giving me trouble."

Catherine mounted the spare horse. She also considered apologizing for thinking Babcock was a liar but then thought better of it. She still didn't trust him and never would. "Follow me," she said.

They headed down Mission Street just as the ground began to rumble. Catherine's horse was the first to rear up on its back legs. Catherine leaned forward and grabbed the horse's mane, steadying herself. Babcock wasn't as lucky. Though he leaned forward when his horse raised, the ground beneath the horse opened in a loud rumble, swallowing both the horse and Babcock.

Catherine, still trying to control her horse, screamed and kicked the horse in the side, urging it to move. The horse bucked again, and instinct told the animal to run from the widening chasm. Catherine grabbed around the horse's neck as it charged down the road. The buildings in front of them were beginning to crumble. Catherine felt a sharp pain in her shoulder and a warm stream race down her back. The brick that had hit her danced off the horse's hind quarters and bounced into the gutter.

When she managed to grab the reins, she maneuvered the horse down the next street. The horse hurdled a new vein opening in the road, almost throwing Catherine to the ground when it landed awkwardly. She needed to move away from the taller buildings. She jerked the reins to the right, heading toward an older part of town, where the houses and buildings were single-story. Clearing the tallest part of town, Catherine looked back.

The earthquake had only taken a few minutes to flatten the town. Catherine looked toward Third Street, where her family lived. Though she couldn't see for sure, the absence of buildings suggested that her family had been crushed to death while they slept. She looked toward the train station and felt her heart sink. Flames higher than some of the buildings waved in the western sky. For the second time, she had lost a family. She and the horse were on their own.

She encouraged the horse southward toward Los Angeles. The Santa Fe railroad stretched from Los Angeles to Chicago. However, she knew she would never make it back to Crystal Falls to save Thomas Templeton. Like her two families, he was also dead.

On the southern outskirts of San Francisco, Catherine stopped to rest and eat what little food she had gathered from strangers. She retreated to the woods, where she felt safest.

She slept all day and well into the evening. She woke to find her horse gone. She tried to look up and see the stars, but the sky was a slate of blackness. She glanced around at the trees and listened for small animals. Nothingness. Everything was gone. Lonely darkness crept over her . . . and she liked the way it felt.

18

Crystal Falls
Present Day

The smell of bacon and eggs made Jake open his eyes. Sunlight gleamed through his windows and heated his bare chest. He stared at the small water stain on the ceiling and wondered if last night had been a nightmare or if Crystal Falls was truly the rectum of Kentucky. He closed his eyes and thought about waking up in New York City . . . until something moved next to him. It wasn't so much a scream as a murmur of terror that he made.

He bolted from his bed and stood terrified next to the bathroom door. The covers unfurled, and Laura looked at him blurry-eyed. "What's wrong?" she asked.

Jake rubbed his face and stared. "What the hell are you doing in my bed?"

Laura pushed back the covers, fully dressed, and left the room. The look on her face was both hurt and anger.

Jake followed, still in his red boxer briefs. He entered Laura's room, where she sat on the bed crying. "I'm sorry," he said. "I was just a little shocked to see you in my bed."

Laura shook her head as if he never got anything right. "You asked if I would feel better staying with you last night," she said. "So I did."

"Did we . . ."

"No, we didn't," Laura said. "Why do you think I still have my clothes on?" She looked up at him, still angry. "Go eat, Jake. I'll be down in a bit."

Jake stood in the middle of the room, half-naked, unsure what to say.

"Go," Laura said.

"Okay. I'm sorry." He stopped at the door and looked back. "I wish that we had stayed together." He closed the door, continued to his bedroom, dressed, and met the others in the dining room.

Landon smiled and bobbed his head, waiting for a report on how the night went with Laura.

"Don't," Jake said and sat down. The headache working behind his eyes was enough to put him in an instant bad mood. Hell, Crystal Falls would put anyone in a bad mood. "Nothing happened, and nothing will." As much as he still loved Laura, he wouldn't allow anything to happen between them.

Aunt Mary entered the room with a bowl of gravy and a tray of biscuits. She placed the food on the table and cleared her throat. "Well, what's on the agenda for today? Hunt for vampires; try to find the Leprechaun's pot of gold?"

Raven sighed and grabbed a biscuit. After speaking to her husband, Daniel, on the phone last night, she was ready to throw in the towel and call it quits. To hell with Hank McCoy, Trish, and the rest of Crystal Falls. She wanted to return home, quit her accounting job, and get a job at Barnes and Noble. One Goth chick already worked there. Would another hurt? Goth chick? Thirty-eight and a chick? She highly doubted that. Daniel had told her to come home and insisted that she do so. The reunion and her brief interlude into the Goth world were over. What kind of message was that sending their son? Being abnormal was no way to mold a young boy into the man he needed to be. Shortly after two o'clock, she fell asleep with the phone in her hand, Daniel still barking orders. His message at the crack of dawn this morning: "When you're ready to grow up, you can come home."

Laura entered the dining room and sat beside Raven, adding more silence to an already silent room. She could feel Jake staring at her and could see Landon watching her. She put her elbows on the table—she never allowed her kids to place their elbows on the table—and looked up. "I'm leaving," she said. "I have a family at home that needs me. I'm supposed to be chasing my kids around the house, not chasing a grown woman through the woods." She felt it coming and could do nothing to stop it. "And you!" She pointed at Jake.

"What?"

Laura stood. Her face turned hard, unwavering. "You couldn't even say goodbye. You left me at my doorstep and drove off into your life." She slammed her fist against the table. Raven backed away. Aunt Mary grabbed a biscuit. "All you had to do was get out of the car and walk me to the front door . . . you know, like you did on prom night or any other night we had sex." She rounded the table, making a bee-line toward Jake. "Scared?" She screamed. "You were the toughest kid in the school, and you were too fucking scared to get out of the car and put your arm around me?

Tell me everything would be okay and that you would protect me."

Jake stood, not knowing what else to do. None of his clients ever acted like *this*. "I'm . . ."

"Don't say it!" Laura screamed. "Don't you dare say you're sorry to me again. Sorry isn't going to fix any of this. Sorry isn't going to free me from this God-forsaken town." She burst into tears and leaned into Jake's arms.

Raven finished her biscuit and sipped her black coffee. "The Falls won't let us leave," she said softly. She wanted to cry as well, scream like Laura. But the Falls would do what the Falls wanted to do.

Laura wiped her face on Jake's shirt and looked up at him. "You deserve that."

"You're right," Landon said, "he does. But that doesn't change the fact that we need to come up with a plan to get the hell out of this shithole." He pushed from his chair. His khaki shorts let them see the twelve-inch scar along his knee. He glanced down. "A permanent reminder," he said. He pointed toward the farm. "There's something over there that wants us. The Falls has a score to settle, and it ain't letting us go until the house is square."

"So we need to go back," Raven said. She left her chair and started toward the stairs leading to the rooms.

"Where're you going?" Landon asked.

"To get ready."

Aunt Mary spooned gravy onto her biscuit. "She came back last night. Drove off quietly so no one would know until the morning." She forked a bite of biscuit into her mouth. A drop of gravy splattered her blouse. "She's involved with all this. I just haven't figured it out yet."

"We all are," Laura said. "She was with us that night."

"Uh-huh," Aunt Mary said. "There's more to this than

sticking some old coot into the center of a dead tree." She finished off the biscuits and pointed at them with her fork. "I think the Falls wants Laura. But I think it wants you," she pointed at Landon, "Jake and Raven dead."

"What about Trish?" Laura asked. She moved away from Jake and the heat of his body and the smell of his skin. "What makes her so special?"

Aunt Mary put her fork down and wiped her mouth. "I haven't figured that out yet. But I will." She started collecting dishes from the table. "Trish isn't from the Falls, remember? So maybe the Falls has no connection to her. Maybe she's a conduit to get you kids here."

When Aunt Mary carried the dishes into the kitchen, Landon pulled the others into the living room. "Go get your keys," he said to Laura. She hesitated. "Go."

Laura disappeared up the stairs.

"We're all in this," he whispered to Raven and Jake. "I can't let Aunt Mary go into those woods again."

"Agreed," Jake replied.

Laura returned with her keys.

"The county line is right down the road," Landon said. "We need to see if we're really stuck here, and if we are, we make this stop today."

They followed Laura to the Escalade, leaving Aunt Mary to the dishes in the kitchen. Raven sat in the front with Laura. Jake and Landon climbed into the back. Laura adjusted the rearview mirror and found Jake staring at her. She turned the mirror away. She pulled onto the road and headed west toward the county line.

"Slow down," Landon said as they approached the county line sign.

But Laura didn't have to slow down. The Escalade sputtered and coughed like a sailor with a sore throat. They rolled to the road's shoulder and stared at the sign.

"Only one way to find out for sure," Jake said, climbing out. "Wait here."

Jake stood beside the Escalade and waved at an older couple who drove past him, entering Crystal Falls. *That's a good sign. Now, I only need to walk the twenty steps to the line.* He wanted to look back and get reassurance from the others but thought better of it, not wanting to appear weak. He felt a trickle of sweat slide down his temple. He wiped it away and deposited it on his jeans.

His first step, accompanied by a cool breeze that brought the smell of firs, was the easiest, but the next nineteen, not so much. What could happen? What could happen if a business deal went bad? Lose a little bit of money, make it back on the next deal. He wondered if this went bad if there would be another deal.

"Today, Junior," Landon yelled from the SUV.

Jake raised his middle finger. "Ten more," he whispered to himself.

It occurred to Jake that Landon should be making this walk. What did Landon have to lose? Raven and Laura had kids. Jake had a multi-million dollar job.

To the left, on the opposite side of the road, a rabbit nibbled a daisy. "Not a good place to eat a meal," Jake said. He shooed the rabbit out of the road, and the fur ball scurried back into the brush.

At the sign, Jake watched leaves blow across the road a few feet before him. Another car passed by—he had saved the rabbit from a crushing death. Who would save him? He extended his right hand past the sign. Nothing. That's a good sign. He felt his throat relax and let out the breath he had been holding, apparently for no reason. To be safe, he reached out his left hand before stepping forward. Nothing. A better sign. He turned and looked at the SUV. "I think it's going to be okay," he yelled, taking another step.

Jake climbed out of the SUV. "Wait here," he said. He moved in front of the Escalade, shooed the rabbit, waved at the old couple driving by, moved forward, and watched another car go by. He stood at the sign again and reached out. Nothing. He stepped forward and stared back at the Escalade once again.

"Well, if you're not going to do it, then I will," Landon said. He looked back at the road and then stepped from the SUV.

Jake watched with intense curiosity, though he knew exactly what would happen. Landon walked toward the sign, not hesitating. As soon as he passed the sign, he was back sitting in the SUV.

Landon looked over at Jake. "Well, if you're not going to do it, then I will," Landon said. He opened the car door; Jake grabbed his arm. Laura and Raven turned in their seats.

"Wait," Jake said. "You've already done it." He motioned toward the sign. "I've been twice."

"Bullshit," Raven said. "You never left the Escalade."

Jake nodded. "I did. And I walked past the sign only to end up back in this seat." He shook his head and glanced out his window. "The Falls won't allow us to leave."

"Raven's right. This is bullshit." Laura jumped out of the SUV and ran for the sign, reappearing in her seat when she crossed the county line.

"Shit," Landon said.

Laura looked at him questioningly.

"We're stuck here," Landon said.

"No, we're not!" Laura reached for the door handle. Jake grabbed her arm.

Jake pulled his wallet from his back pocket and handed it to Laura. "Before you pass the sign, lay my wallet on this side of the county line."

Laura approached the sign and did as Jake asked. She passed the sign and reappeared in the SUV.

Jake explained what he had done moments ago. They all agreed that he never left the SUV and his wallet should not be lying on the road by the sign. The four exited the vehicle. And although, from this distance, they saw a brown object by the sign, none were sure what it was. They approached together.

"My wallet," Jake said. He opened it and showed them his driver's license. Jake headed back to the SUV. "Laura, get in and put it in neutral. We need to get it turned in the opposite direction. Landon and I'll push."

They pushed the Escalade across the road, doing a U-turn where the rabbit had been feeding minutes ago. "Start it up," Jake said. The SUV purred to life.

"I'll be damned," Landon said.

"I think we already are," Raven replied.

They returned to their seats and drove back to the bed and breakfast, where Aunt Mary sat on the porch waiting for them.

"Falls ain't going to let you leave," she said. "There's work to be done." She descended the porch steps and told them to follow her across the road. She leaned against the fence separating the sold land from the road. "There are some other things you need to know. Things your parents knew but never told you." She retrieved a Twinkie from her apron pocket. "It's time you knew. Before you kids went your separate ways, and right before Hank McCoy's death, your parents met at the old church building at the center of town. I know because I was there with them."

They had once considered burning the church to the ground. Not that they weren't considering it again. But the building was too close to the daycare on the right and McNamara Dentistry on the left. Everyone in Crystal Falls—present company excluded—was too afraid to level the place. It was, after all, a church.

The pews had been removed in the mid-seventies— replaced with nothing. The vestibule—made of oak so heavy that none dare tried to move it—still stood empty in front of an even emptier baptismal. In the eighties—when Reagan was telling Gorbachev to tear down the walls—the town boarded the windows to keep the local teens from playing target practice with their favorite rocks. Every ten years or so, the town selected four strong men to paint the outside and refinish the wooden floors. Since no one in their right mind wanted to spend too much time in the place, the job generally took no more than three days—four if the weather turned bad.

The night I was present, everyone in attendance managed to remember their own chairs, except for me. Joe and Emma Ziehm, accompanied by Joe's adopted sister, Mary, sat beneath the vestibule. Carter and Sally Simon sat together but were partially separated by the basket of food Sally thought everyone might enjoy. William and Debi Templeton—the parents of the only Goth child in the Falls— sat on the opposite side of the Ziehm's. Closing out the circle and the last to arrive were Samuel and Vanessa Reeder, the parents who owned the smartest kid in the Falls.

I was an outsider, brought in to take notes, keep everyone on task, and make sure things happen in their proper order.

And because I could not have children, I would be the only one in the group to die a natural death. I didn't know that tidbit until later on. I suppose I could have left the Falls and been happy doing so at any time.

No one wanted to be the first to say it, admit to the truth they all knew for some time.

Carter Simon cleared his throat in a gesture to break the silence. And although he was afraid of the truth, he chose to speak up and get it over with. "We have a choice," *he said.* "We can either stay here and make sure our kids never have a life to live, or we leave and give them a chance at things we never had."

Joe crossed his arms and nudged his glasses up the bridge of his nose. He squirmed in his chair, afraid to be the one who came across as selfish. "We leave, we die. It's that simple. Where does that leave them, then?"

"We make sure they don't ever come back once we take them away," *Debi Templeton said. She glanced at her husband.* "It breaks the cycle . . . as long as they never come back."

William Templeton nodded, though I could tell he was suspicious of the plan. He didn't think it would work. Like their kids, they had nothing to do with what happened in Crystal Falls well before they were born. But, like their kids, they had been a Falls victim. "They'll have to be told why." *He looked at the others sincerely.* "We'll tell Raven once we reach our destination. We plan to leave the week after graduation. It won't be easy and will take some time, but we'll tell her."

Carter reached into the box sitting next to him. "I've written a short history of the Falls, explaining to our kids what they're up against." *He motioned for me.* "Mary will go *back through the books and ensure I've left nothing out. She'll return the books to you once she's done."*

I smiled, took a cookie from the small package beside me, and wrote more notes. I can't say I believed much of what they said, but I did what they asked. Later on, I realized it was all true.

Joe began to speak but was distracted by a noise outside the church. He turned from the group and headed to the front door. When he opened the door—the others gathered behind him. Outside, he found a crowd of townspeople approaching. He looked back at the others, puzzled.

"We need to talk to you folks." Mr. Saddlebrook moved to the first step. "We think it's best if your group leaves the Falls. Maybe things will be normal around here."

William Templeton stepped around Joe. "We'll decide when we leave," he said. He looked at every member of the crowd. "Your kin were just as big a part of the Falls' history as ours were."

Saddlebrook glanced back at the crowd. "That's not true, Bill, and you know it."

Carter thought the situation resembled the old Frankenstein movie—those in the church were the obvious choice for Frankenstein's monster. He descended two steps—a step higher than Saddlebrook. "Where're your torches and pitchforks?" He asked. Several in the crowd mumbled, pointing at them.

"We've said our peace," Saddlebrook said. He noticed Sheriff Buford's cruiser pulling into the small church parking lot and rubbed his chin. The sheriff left his cruiser and shook his head as he approached. No law enforcement officer could ever be prepared for what Buford would experience in the Falls.

"Church meeting?" Buford said.

Saddlebrook glanced up at the group standing above him. "Just a friendly conversation, Buford."

Buford looked at each group. He knew what the meeting was about and why it had to happen. It was about the town's history, the suicides, and the strange shit that he never experienced in a larger city. He also understood that he was in a bad situation, standing between the two groups. "Are they bothering you, Joe?" He asked Joe Ziehm.

Joe made eye contact with the couples behind him. They nodded, and he turned back to the sheriff. "We were just getting ready to tell Saddlebrook and the others that we'll leave the Falls after our kids' graduation." He watched the small crowd smile, whisper, and pump their fists in victory. "Having said that," Joe began. He didn't bother to look back at the others. "If you think we're the Falls' only problem, you're all in for a great surprise." He acknowledged the sheriff and returned to the church with the others.

"Go on home now," Buford told the small gathering. He was as pissed off as ever since arriving in the Falls. One set of townspeople had no business running off another set. He understood the history but also believed people should stick together. At some point, they'd all need each other. He climbed the church steps and entered with the others.

Buford waited for everyone to take their seats. He liked everyone in the room. If he had to pick who was the sanest in this messed up town, he would have pointed at those in the room because they were the ones trying to get out. "I'm sorry about that," he said. He was sorry. "There's no need for you to leave town." He knew that wasn't true, but Buford always tried to be diplomatic.

"You know the history," Emma Ziehm said. "They'll always blame us for the town's problems. They always have."

"We need to go, Sheriff," Sally Simon added. She looked

at the others. "We don't want our children stuck here the way we've been stuck here. It's not fair, and it's certainly not healthy."

Buford nodded, not in agreement but in understanding. "I hate it for you, I do. You know my stance. I DO NOT believe in witches, witchcraft, or anything else." He didn't believe any of it. He did believe the town was about as fucked up as any he had ever visited—and pardon his French. He wanted more than anything to provide a safe place for EVERYONE to live.

Carter stood and shook Buford's hand. "We appreciate that, Buford."

The others followed Carter's lead and thanked the sheriff.

While shaking the sheriff's hand, Joe placed his other hand on the sheriff's shoulder. "We'll instruct our kids never to come back to this place. But I can't say that they'll listen." Joe waited for acknowledgment from the others. They motioned for him to continue. "If something happens to us," he held out his hands toward the others, "we ask that, if they do come back, you make sure they're safe."

Buford removed his hat. "I give you my word."

"Witches," Jake said. "I'll give you the fact that the town is strange and always has been. But witches? Come on." He crossed his arms and sat on the bottom porch step. He should have stayed in New York, where things were always weird—you expected that. But small-town America? Not to mention that Laura was totally off limits now . . . or was she?

Sitting on the swing hanging from the porch ceiling, Raven spoke to Aunt Mary. "Our parents left because they thought it would break a cycle." She considered what Aunt Mary had said. "Now we're back."

Aunt Mary shook her head.

"The cycle started again when we came back," Laura interjected.

Aunt Mary nodded and ate another chip, satisfied it was all beginning to sink in.

19

Little Rock, Arkansas
1925

She studied the six-foot snake as it slithered across her ankles. The snake, indifferent to Catherine's presence, continued its way. The silvery scales shimmered in the early morning sunlight. The last cicadas were droning on, ready to bury themselves for a long sleep. She enjoyed their music the most, probably the sound of crickets a close second. This was the nature she wanted to experience

Catherine retrieved a healthy red apple from her bag and used a single fingernail to slice the apple in half. She offered half the apple to her horse, who happily accepted, chewed twice, and then swallowed. They were both hungry and in dire need of food and water. She took a deep breath and glanced up at the trees.

The Ozarks paled compared to the majestic California redwoods, but for now, the Ozarks were all she had. Truthfully, Catherine loved the Californian forests and preferred to have stayed there. However, Kentucky called. Crystal Falls called. Sure that Thomas Templeton—her childhood hero—was long dead, there was another reason to return to the place of her birth—learn about her gift.

She gathered the clothes strewn across the ground, barely recalling the previous evening: a fire, some dancing with Samantha (creating life from twigs and branches had become her favorite "trick"). Since her departure from California, her gift and understanding of the gift had grown. The final question . . . where had the gift come from? From her parents? Was that why they were brutally murdered by Crystal Falls? And there was her reason for returning.

Catherine pulled on her raggedy clothes. Her left breast peeked from a tear that had occurred during an attack upon her arrival in Arkansas. She considered her attacker momentarily, mulling over her actions, her mind finally giving way to the flock of vultures that ate well shortly after she left the man in a bloody heap.

She mounted her horse and patted the well-behaved mare on the neck. In the grand scheme of life, animals could be trusted far more than any human Catherine had come to know. The horse headed northeast along the path they had been following the past two weeks. Less than a mile into the morning's journey, a girl's scream caused them to stop. Catherine slid from the horse's back, tied the horse to a branch, and then slipped into the thick brush lining each side of the trail.

She moved slowly toward the sound of voices, dodging around trees, watching her step. Of course, she had no idea what she was walking into, but the girl's scream gave her a pretty good idea. Humans were being humans again.

"Please," a young girl pleaded.

"Hold her legs, Frank," a man ordered, cackling as the girl screamed again.

Catherine stepped into the clearing.

Two men held down a young girl. Catherine guessed the girl was fifteen or sixteen. The men were old enough to be the girl's grandfathers.

The men saw Catherine, and both grinned. Not so much in surprise—beautiful women were always stalking the forest—but in anticipation of each having their own. "Pretty lady," the man holding the girl's arms said. "I'm guessing you'll be next." He released the girl's arms, and her fingernails instinctively went to her attacker's eyes. The man screamed and rolled to his side in pain.

The second man stood and pulled up his pants. He approached Catherine with an arrogance that would soon deflate like an untied balloon. He stopped less than a foot in front of her. He tipped his hat back and hooked his thumbs into his side belt loops. Turning his head to the left, he chucked a chewing tobacco ball onto the ground. "Me and you gonna dance," he declared.

"That's a nasty habit you have," Catherine said. She looked around the man and at the other filthy man balled up in pain. The girl was quickly recovering.

"Frank, you okay?" The man said to his horrid friend on the ground. He squinted at Catherine and then raised his left arm.

It always started in the pit of her stomach. Deep, sometimes as if her insides were as vast and dark as the universe above. Sometimes, it felt like the onslaught of a powerful orgasm. Other times, it was but a small spark. It never mattered how it started because the results were always the same: a power so destructive that nothing around her stood a chance when it escaped. She raised her hand to the man's face and tapped him on his snout.

"That supposed to scare me?" He asked.

Catherine grinned. "Did it?"

The girl on the ground retrieved her panties and scampered between two large oaks. The oaks were less impressive than a redwood, Catherine noted. The girl's eyes thanked Catherine.

"Hey, you listening to me?" The man interrupted. "I said . . ."

"I heard what you said," Catherine replied. "And here's my answer." She raised her right index finger and placed her fingernail at the top of his forehead. Cross-eyed, the man looked up at her finger. She drew her finger down the middle of his face, chest, stomach, and legs. He smirked and looked back at his partner. "Goodbye," Catherine replied.

The nameless man—they had all been nameless—frowned and then looked upward. His left side was the first to fall away, his right side falling next, creating a large X on the ground. Catherine recognized the sound as a towel full of water being wrung dry.

"You little whore," the second man yelled. He went for his holstered gun.

Catherine wagged her finger at him. His hand relaxed. "Come here," Catherine said to the girl hiding behind a tree. The girl obeyed. "This man was bothering you?" Catherine asked. The girl nodded. "Does he deserve to be punished?" The girl nodded again.

Catherine motioned for the man and then pointed at the ground in front of her. "Now," she commanded.

"You the devil," he replied, then complied with Catherine's order.

Catherine looked at the girl who stood at her height. "What's your name?"

"Agatha," she replied.

"Well, Agatha, I'm Catherine, and this man will die. The question is, how will he die?" Catherine placed her hand on Agatha's shoulder. The two looked at each other and then back at the trembling man.

"They were going to rape and kill me," Agatha said.

"We weren't," the man pleaded. "I promise." He put his hands together and began to pray. "Please, Lord Almighty. Please save me from these wretches."

Catherine breathed deeply. She hated when they did something bad and then pleaded forgiveness when caught. They would never have talked to this Lord Almighty person if they'd gotten away with whatever deviant act they were doing. Begging and pleading after the fact was cowardly. She stared at the man a moment longer and made the decision.

Agatha held her hands around Catherine's waist tightly as the horse carried them along the trail. She glanced back only once to see her second attacker strung up in a tree by his ankles, his head dangling less than a foot from the ground. Catherine suggested that if the man had the wherewithal to escape, he deserved to live. If not, many forest animals would partake in the free hanging meal. Catherine's redolence calmed Agatha's trepidation in joining Catherine on her journey. Catherine had assured Agatha of her protection and guidance and that she would never leave her by herself again, unlike Agatha's parents.

Catherine also explained that they were heading for St. Louis via a stop in Memphis where they would procure transportation other than a horse—though their need for finances may require an extended stay in Memphis. During the three-week journey, Catherine confided in Agatha her brief history, leaving out much talk of Catherine's gift, though Agatha had seen its brutality firsthand. Agatha shared her story, including the point at which her parents had abandoned her. She gave Catherine no justifiable reason that her parents would do so, and Catherine took Agatha at her word. Agatha was not shy with her inquiries into Catherine's gift. But Catherine politely refused, expunging further details.

Upon their arrival in Memphis, Catherine immediately searched for a job working in the house of a well-to-do family, which she found on a plantation north of the city. Agatha was hired as kitchen staff, Catherine a sitter for the family's two children: a boy of twelve and a young girl who had recently enjoyed her eighth birthday. And what Catherine found most promising was the thick forest that lined the eastern edge of the Chesterfield property. Their new employer, Alan Chesterfield, gave them a grand tour, including a stint in the forest nestled to the mighty Mississippi. Although he carried on about the Mississippi and its long history with the moving of goods, Catherine was well aware that the Mississippi—and its connection to the Ohio River—had played an integral part in saving her life.

On their return to the Chesterfield mansion, Mr. Chesterfield stopped at a modest two-story house nearly a hundred yards from the primary residence. "Though small," he said, "there are two bedrooms upstairs, a meek kitchen and dining area on the first floor." Almost as an afterthought, he added, "There is plumbing throughout the house, although the bathtub drain can be pesky at times."

"We are very grateful, Mr. Chesterfield," Catherine said and placed her arm around Agatha's shoulders (Agatha was none too pleased that she would be working in a kitchen). When Chesterfield turned to leave, Catherine said, "We've not seen Mrs. Chesterfield."

He stopped and looked solemnly at the two women. "Patricia is very ill and rarely ventures from her bedroom. She was struck with an unknown sickness several months ago." He rubbed his chin and seemed to consider further conversation. He moved closer to Catherine and Agatha. "I do not expect her to last much longer." With that said, Chesterfield left them standing in the small living room of their new house.

"Well," Agatha said. "Better than living in the woods."

Catherine studied the room and then plopped in the middle of a sofa sitting against the wall. "I wouldn't exactly say that," she replied. Through the window in front of them, she watched Chesterfield enter the rear of the mansion and disappear. At ten years her senior, she found him handsome and intelligent. He cared for his dying wife, so Catherine would not pursue her intent until Mrs. Chesterfield passed.

"Do you have any idea how to raise kids?" Agatha asked. "What if they behave like adolescent baboons?" She noticed Catherine staring out the window. "We're not leaving anytime soon . . . are we?"

Catherine shook her head. "I'm going to send a letter to St. Louis." She grabbed her bag and retreated to her room upstairs.

20

Crystal Falls
Present Day

Laura ended the call and collapsed on the bed. The kids were safe—for now. Witches? Really? Nothing but fairytales by people who had nothing better to do than conjure the make-believe and scare others. Staring at the ceiling, she wondered what her parents had been thinking. Why had they never said anything before? Maybe her mom had. Laura was never allowed to be a witch on Halloween. She was never told why.

The whole situation with witches, curses, and other bullshit was all so stupid that she filed it in a drawer in her mind. She marked the drawer "ridiculous theories."

And the book Aunt Mary spoke of . . . Laura had never bothered to open the book and may have even thrown it away after her parents died. The stories were crazy. Trish—

crazy. The town—crazy. The existence of witches—crazier. Clark was dead, and that was half the problem.

She walked to the bathroom and stared at herself in the mirror. She pushed at the bags under her eyes and examined the young wrinkles at the corners. The Falls had aged her ten years in the two days she had been here. She closed her eyes and rubbed the back of her neck. Seeing the darkness of her eyelids, she considered the wild fairy tales of the Brothers Grimm, a favorite book her father had given on her tenth birthday. She loved stories of the macabre. Her father loved the stories as well. How many times had she watched him disappear into the woods for a long walk to gather his thoughts?

"Now you're just searching for reasons to think you were born of something so ridiculous," she said to herself.

"It's not so ridiculous."

Laura opened her eyes and slammed her hand against her mouth, covering a scream that demanded an escape. She jerked around, knocking her hip against the sink, and faced her father.

"When you were a child, you had the imagination of a writer," her father said. "You believed that anything was possible. You believed in monsters and fairies and everything in between. To you, nothing was impossible. And then, like most adults, you stopped believing and lost your imagination."

Laura walked toward her father. He backed away as she approached, leading her into the adjoining room. "I need sleep," she said. "This town . . ."

"Is not what it seems," he finished for her.

Laura sat on the edge of the bed, staring at her father.

He sat in the chair next to the window. He stared across the road at Hank McCoy's property.

"I've completely lost it," she said.

"We tried to keep you kids away from here. That's why we moved in the first place."

"You knew you would die?"

He nodded, put his hands together, and placed them on his knee. "It was either us or you all."

"And now that we're back, it's us or our kids." Laura felt tears building in the corners of her eyes. "Mom?"

Sam moved to his feet and sat next to his daughter, wanting nothing more at that moment than to hold her in his arms. He missed those times when she could crawl up next to him in a recliner, sit on his shoulders, and share an ice cream. "Your mother's in a good place. She's doing well. She's watching us now."

Laura glanced around the room, seeing nothing but the dreaded wallpaper. "What's going to happen now? I mean, what are we supposed to do?"

He put his arm around her, though neither could feel the touch. "You're going to have to fight this thing and not let it win." He pushed from the bed and paced the room. "You know where we came from," he said. "We have a dark side that I was always careful not to explore, especially careful not to let you experience."

"The walks in the woods," Laura said. He nodded. "So you're saying all this nonsense about witches is true?"

"It's more than that," he replied. "It's not about witches. It's about the power that people have inside." He tapped his chest. "I have it. You have it." He sat in the chair again. "Some don't use it, some use it for good, and, unfortunately, some use it for their own gain."

Laura felt her temples beginning to throb. "Arthur Rhodes used it for evil," she flatly said as if he were the reason the Falls was such a terrible place to be.

"No," he said. "He was provoked. Once the darkness took hold, there was no turning back. And that's what you have to be careful to avoid."

"Wait, you're telling me I have these 'powers'?"

"Yes," he replied. He stared at her, remembering the child she once was. "I have to go, Laura." He stepped forward and placed his arms around her. Although neither could feel his touch, they knew he was there and always would be, watching over her, doing his best to guide her.

"Do people outside the Falls know about us and its history?"

Sam shook his head. "No, because we were never allowed to leave. When we did, we died." He lowered his head. "All the parents should have explained what happened back then better. Humanity is all about paying for the sins of their forefathers."

"Where did you go in the woods, Dad?"

Sam watched the farm through the window. "There's a cave on Hank McCoy's property. It's where this entity comes from. It could never get me to enter the cave, but I stood and listened. I fought what it wanted me to do." He held his daughter's hand. "There is a place after this life." He tried to wipe her tears. "We'll have an eternity together."

Laura watched her father fade into nothing. There was no denying who and what she was. Who or what any of them were.

"Who were you talking to?" Jake asked, standing in the doorway.

Laura frowned. "Don't you knock?" She returned to the bathroom and began filling the tub with warm water. She hoped he would leave but knew he wouldn't. But then maybe she didn't want him to leave. Maybe she wanted him there with her. Not in the bathtub but in the room to keep her safe or at least make her feel safer.

"My father," Laura finally said. She poured a small container of bubble bath into the water. "He was here, in the room."

"Okay," he said slowly.

"Don't patronize me," Laura said. "He was standing in the very spot you're standing in now. He told me I had the power to change what was happening." She closed the bathroom door, leaving a small crack so Jake could hear her. "I think we still need to explore Hank McCoy's farm. Whatever's running this town into the ground is over there waiting for us."

Laura slipped from her clothes and laid them across the sink. She stepped into the bathtub and sank to her shoulders, the warm water and tiny exploding bubbles relaxing every muscle. Jake tapped on the door. She smiled. "You may enter, but you have to keep your eyes closed."

Jake pushed open the door, his eyes closed.

"I was kidding."

Jake opened his eyes. The fading sunlight entering between two barely closed curtains bounced off the bubbles and gave Laura's face a miraculous glow. She was as beautiful now as she had ever been. "Relatives," he said, reminding them they were related.

"Sponge, please," Laura replied, pointing at the sponge beside her clothes. She watched Jake cross the short distance to the sink and felt her heartbeat skip. For all the obstacles: marriage, being related, kids, distance, she still loved him and, she supposed, she always would. He handed her the sponge. "Thank you." She dipped the sponge in the warm water and brought it across her shoulders. "There's at least four generations since my relative raped your relative," she said.

"We sound like the Hatfields and McCoys," Jake said. "Though I'm not sure Hank McCoy would find any of this funny." He sat on the floor next to the tub, gently leaning his head against the warm porcelain. He pulled his knees up and rested his arms on his knees. Bubbles popping echoed in his ears. As Laura raised the sponge from the tub, the trickle of water made him want to turn.

"Jake," Laura said, "you can look at me." She looked into his eyes and saw the boy who treated her so well during high school and the young man who had made love to her dozens of times. And then Hank McCoy walked into their lives and messed it all up. Her husband Richard was a good man but wasn't Jake and could never be Jake, no matter how hard he tried. Could she give up everything she worked so hard to create for an opportunity to be with the only man she ever truly loved? The answer was simple . . . no. She laid her hand along his cheek. "I'm sorry it can't be different," she said.

Jake started to reply but stopped when someone knocked on Laura's door.

Laura lowered herself chin-deep into the water. "Who is it?" she yelled.

"Raven."

"Great," Laura whispered to Jake.

"Come on in," Jake yelled.

"What're you doing!"

"And Landon," Landon said when they walked into the bathroom. "Oops, sorry," he added without turning away. He winked at Jake and then leaned against the door jamb. Raven took a seat on the closed toilet. "Well, here we are."

Laura sighed and smiled. Things could always be worse

—Jake could have been in the tub with her. But they were still friends and had certainly experienced life together at its least desirable time. "What now?" she asked.

Landon slipped a pack from his back. "Flashlights, a few flares, a map, some Snickers bars. Treasure hunt, anyone?"

Raven glanced at Jake and then at Laura. She then caught a glimpse of Landon from the corner of her eye. The more she spoke to Landon, the more time they spent alone, the more she wished he had been after her that night at the oak tree instead of Trish. But every guy was freaked out by Raven. Giving up the Goth lifestyle was not in the cards back then—or now.

Before coming to Laura's room, the two shared a seat on the porch swing, talking about everything but Hank McCoy. Mostly, she listened to Landon's nocturnal relationships with women he couldn't remember. While they spoke, her husband called and demanded that she return home or there would be consequences. The more she thought about her marriage, the more she realized she had been the Reverend's wife, not her person. She did what he asked regardless of the request—because she figured it would put distance between the lifestyle that she longed to live and the one people told her she should live. Those days were over. And, of course, there was her son. The young man that she loved more than anything. She thought he would understand—he had even asked her once upon a time why she didn't look the same way she had in her yearbook pictures. She explained to him that people had to grow up. He asked why. She replied that it was just the way life worked. But now she knew that not to be true. Life only worked that way when you allowed it to.

So, she made the decision. When she returned home,

the ultimatum would be laid out on the table for Daniel. Accept her as she is, or he could leave. He would most likely pack his bags and leave, never accepting her for the Raven she truly was. He would attend church the following Sunday—without her—and once again preach about how God loves everyone, every sinner. Yet he, a simple preacher, couldn't do the same.

"Raven. Raven?"

Raven looked up and saw her three friends staring. "Sorry, zoned out there for a minute. What were we saying?"

"Come along," Landon said and hooked his arm around hers as if he were leading her to prom. "Laura needs to find a toga." He looked back and smiled, winked at Jake again.

"Get out," Jake said jokingly. Jake turned to Laura, who sat chin-deep in the bathtub when they were gone. "Knock on my door when you're ready to go." He left the beautiful and naked Laura Reeder to herself, not noticing that the scenes in all the pictures hanging on the walls in the hall had changed. Instead of a quiet, serene Crystal Falls, the images portrayed a violent, murderous Falls.

21

Memphis, Tennessee
1936

Catherine stood in the ballroom with Alan Chesterfield as the Memphis elite poured into celebrate Chester and Catherine's tenth anniversary. Visitors commented on her youthful looks, many willing to sell their souls to age like the beautiful Catherine, some suggesting she'd found the fountain of youth somewhere in a hidden corner of Memphis. Catherine assured them that she was as old as dirt... because she was.

Agatha, however, had undoubtedly aged over the past ten years and looked at least ten years Catherine's senior. She didn't rightly mind, though, as she had taken full advantage of Catherine's ten-year rise to a Memphis elite. She figured Chesterfield either hadn't noticed the non-change in Catherine or was so enamored with her beauty that he had not kept up with the years.

Once the ballroom filled, drinks in hands, hors d'oeuvres making the rounds, Chesterfield thanked his guests and praised his wife Catherine and her work on the mansion—none of which required her to step foot into the fields, barns, or gardens. He mentioned her work at the orphanage and her visits to Stone Asylum to help the mentally deficient. In unison, the crowd raised their glasses to the Chesterfields and wished them many more years to come. On the rags to riches scale, Catherine had scored an astounding ten-plus. Every need, want, and desire had been and would continue to be filled. No more dancing in the woods with stick people, foraging for food like an animal. And the gift? There was no need to worry about that when she was treated like a queen without it.

Chesterfield hooked his arm around Catherine's as the guests returned to their conversations. "I believe we have a grand celebration upstairs this evening," he said, patting her hand. "But for now," he added, "there are business deals to make." He kissed her on the cheek and headed for a group of men at the far end of the ballroom.

Catherine watched her husband and admired his ability to converse and mix with anyone regardless of their Memphis rank. With the thoughts of returning to Kentucky firmly behind her, she had worked tirelessly to become the Mrs. Chesterfield that the previous Mrs. Chesterfield had not. She scanned the room and sighed with angelical gracefulness. She worked the room and the crowd, noting those who had attended and those who hadn't. Those who hadn't would find out tomorrow what they had missed.

She finished crowd perusing and landed next to Agatha, who remained at the bar, drink in hand, eyes scanning the room for *that* one bachelor. "Why so glum?" Catherine inquired. "A crowd of people, a glass of wine . . ."

Crystal Falls: A Witch's Revenge

"Twenty-six and not yet married," Agatha replied. She glanced around the room and motioned toward the group. "The good ones are either married or tend toward the feminine side." She took the last sip of her wine. "I'm interested in neither." She watched Catherine gaze around the room, obviously pleased with the attendance. "You've had a good ten years," she said.

Catherine lifted a glass of wine from the bar. "And here's to another ten good ones." She raised her glass in celebration, clinking it against Agatha's. "Alan was telling me about a banker friend of his. The friend is well-off, has never been married, and lives in Memphis's better area."

Agatha motioned to the bartender. He poured her another glass of wine and placed it on the bar. Agatha gulped half the glass and looked across the room. "I've had my eyes on that gentleman over there," she said. "He appears to be single."

At first glance, the man's face didn't register in Catherine's mind. He was not one of Memphis's well-to-dos, and she had never seen him at another event. When he turned to face her, Catherine felt every muscle tighten. It had been a long time since she watched in horror as the man was sucked into the depths of a San Francisco street, his horse tumbling in. He raised his glass into the air, toasting their reunion. Catherine placed her empty glass on the bar. "I'll be right back," she said.

Agatha tried to protest but knew that when Catherine had her mind set on something, nothing would turn her back, so she turned to the bartender and smiled.

Catherine gingerly walked across the room, politely declining invitation to chat. She hooked her arm around the man's and led him to the patio for a clandestine meeting. Outside, she let go of his arm. "You're dead!"

George Babcock held his arms out from his sides and looked down at his own body. "I'm very much alive," he said. "And you are looking quite ravishing . . . and young, I might add."

And then Catherine understood. Babcock had not aged a day since the last time she had seen *him*. "You're like me," she said.

"Guilty," he replied and bowed slightly. "And I'm afraid you're going to have to leave for St. Louis . . . tonight," Babcock replied. "There are people in St. Louis who are eagerly awaiting your presence. Be there, or those in St. Louis will come looking for you."

Catherine's face turned to horror. "I can't leave here," she demanded. "I'm normal. I don't need the gift."

Babcock grabbed her by the arm. "It's not a gift, Catherine, and when you get to St. Louis, don't call it as such. What you have is a curse from the devil himself. Don't act otherwise." He stared through the glass patio doors. "You've had your fun with these people . . . it's time to leave." He noticed Agatha slathering all over the young bartender. "And make sure she comes with you." Babcock turned and made his way down the patio steps. He looked back. "The people in St. Louis should not be played with," he said and disappeared around the corner of the mansion.

Catherine felt as if one of her favorite redwoods had fallen and squished the life out of her. Leave? Was he serious? She looked toward the stables, the manicured property, and the large fountain adorning the patio. Give it up? She walked around the fountain and stood at the rail overlooking the tree line. Along the east side of the property, shadows moved from the forest that lined the Mississippi—dozens of shadows.

"Who're they?" Agatha asked, stepping next to Catherine. Catherine jumped. "What's wrong with you . . . and why are they out there?"

Catherine placed her hands on the rail, her stomach a thunderstorm of rage. "We have to leave tonight," she said. There was a stench on the wind coming from the shadows or the river or both.

"That's not funny." Agatha ignored the shadows. "We can do anything we want."

Catherine turned on her heels, anger lacing her face. "It wasn't meant to be." She glanced back across the gardens. The shadows were gone. "We'll leave after midnight. Meet me at the bottom of the porch steps." She moved to the patio doors and took a deep breath.

"At least tell me where we're going?"

"St. Louis, of course." Catherine opened the doors and returned to the party.

Catherine lay in her bed watching Alan as he stood by the open window, his silhouette powerful against the billions of stars looking in on them. She had given herself over entirely to him and, like the passionate man he was, pleased her in ways she never could have imagined. She didn't know how she could leave such a man. He had made no qualms about caring for her, giving her everything she had ever dreamed of. There were knights in shining armor, and Alan Chesterfield was one of those knights unequivocally. But then this was just another one of those things life had given her and then ripped away.

"Children," he said from where he stood by the

window. "At least two, though three or four would be fine." He moved back to the bed and gently climbed on top of her. "We have all these things but no children."

Catherine stared into her husband's eyes and nodded, the pain of leaving him and the life she had rebuilt almost making her renege on her promise to Babcock. She looked deep into his eyes, finding his gentle soul. She couldn't tell him. She knew that fleeing in the middle of the night was the only way. She decided to leave a ripped sweater and a lone shoe along the bank of the Mississippi. It would have to look like a terrible accident—a slip, a fall, a splash into the black waters of the Mississippi River. He needed to think she was gone forever.

Catherine kissed him again and then wrapped her arms around him. He told her he loved her and then moved to her side, where he quickly faded into sleep. She watched him with a mixture of regret and sadness. She whispered his name when his breathing relaxed, and his sleep deepened. With no reply, she kissed his forehead and caressed his cheek with the back of her hand. Two families and a husband—lost. Never again. She slinked out of bed, changed, and retrieved the already-packed bag from beneath the bed. She looked down at him, fighting the sobs that threatened to thwart her plan.

The servants had retired for the evening, so she was able to traverse the halls and down the stairs undetected. Once outside, Catherine glanced back at the mansion and the life she was abandoning. She didn't know those in St. Louis but did know it was unfair of her to bring them here. Alan would assure her safety, but his protection was impossible against these people.

Agatha met her near the bottom of the porch, and the two moved through the shadows toward the Mississippi, each carrying a single bag. Recent rain made the footing difficult, filling their shoes with thick Mississippi mud. Short on time and short on notice, the river idea was the best she could come up with. Outright leaving would never be an option as Alan would come searching and never stop. Once he found her stuff along the river bank, he'd have every worker scouring the river down to the Gulf. He would eventually write her off as dead, a drowning victim, and hopefully continue with his life. There was also the issue with kids. Though Catherine wasn't positive, she didn't think she could have kids. She claimed she was on birth control for ten very long years, if only to appease Alan, putting off the inevitable.

At the banks of the Mississippi, Catherine retrieved a pair of shoes and a sweater from her bag. She tossed the sweater down the bank, snagging it on a tree that had recently fallen over, its roots still digging into the Tennessee soil, the branches licking at the muddy water. She then used a long stick to shove one of her shoes into the mud about two feet from the water. She tossed the other shoe as far as she could into the swift current of blackness. The two stared at each other and then turned their attention to the small boat heading toward them from the far side of the river.

"Move back into the trees," Catherine said. She waited until Agatha was out of sight and skirted the bank northward. She'd told no one except Agatha. She looked back toward the trees and noticed Agatha following along, keeping in the shadows. A beam of light landed on her eyes, causing her to turn away.

"Catherine Rhodes?" The man in the boat called. "I'm here for you and your friend."

Catherine raised an open hand toward the man and then squeezed her hand as if squeezing a sponge. She heard the flashlight crack and then adjusted her vision to the darkness.

"There was no need for that," the man said. He navigated the boat to the bank. He looked around Catherine, trying to get a better view of Agatha. "Tell your little friend to come on out of there. Times wastin'."

"Come on out," Catherine said. Agatha moved from the trees. Catherine positioned herself in front of Agatha. "Are you one of them?"

"James O'Malley," he said. "And no, I'm not one of them." Catherine could hear his mind swirling. "I know what you can do to me," O'Malley said. "I'm only the messenger, and you know what they say about not shooting the messenger."

Catherine grabbed hold of a tree root jutting out toward the river and carefully descended the slope to the boat. She stepped into the boat and turned to Agatha, who was unsure about their next adventure. "It's okay," Catherine offered. She reached out to Agatha and helped her down the slope and into the boat, where the two sat side by side, looking at the rugged old man powering the boat.

They headed north along the western bank of the Mississippi—not at any great speed, as one never knew what would be floating toward them in the dead of night. Their guide only said that a car awaited them two miles north and that he was paid to pick them up and drop them off without question. Catherine and Agatha didn't bother to speak to one another, though both often glanced back south at the life they were leaving.

Almost an hour after the boat left northern Memphis, it pulled alongside the western bank of the Mississippi and stopped. Here, the slope was less steep, and they were greeted by both wooden steps and a man who appeared to be in his early twenties. The young man helped them up the steps and then waved to O'Malley (Catherine sensed relief on O'Malley's face that he had done his job, made a few dollars, and stayed alive).

Their new guide shuffled them to an awaiting car. He stowed their two bags in the back and opened the passenger door. Catherine looked at the young man and caught his soul in her eyes. He was not one of them, but she felt he was just as dangerous. She and Agatha crawled into the back and glanced at each other. Catherine considered killing the man, taking his car, and heading back west. That would work for a few weeks, maybe a month, but if Babcock had found her in San Francisco, there was no hiding from these people. She put her hand on Agatha's and gave her an affirming squeeze. Things were about to change back to the way they used to be. She felt powerless to do anything about a storm coming her way.

They entered the St. Louis city limits that evening under a dark, cloudy sky. As they pulled to the front of a gated building, Catherine accepted that life would never be as it had been.

22

Crystal Falls
Present Day

They had waited all day for Aunt Mary to leave the house, but that didn't happen until after dinner when she was heading to the Crystal Falls public library to meet with her book club. Before she left, she made the four promise not to go tromping over to Hank McCoy's old property until after breakfast the following morning. They promised her—they lied.

Jake led the way across the pavement and down the dirt road to the tree line. Laura hugged his side, keeping in perfect step with him.

Raven repeatedly checked her flashlight to ensure it would properly work when they got lost. Getting lost was the only way this was going to turn out. She could only hope that lost and dead were not on the menu for the evening.

Landon looked back over his shoulder as the sun dipped behind the bed and breakfast, shooting sunlight through the house, making fiery eyes of the front windows. He felt bad about lying to his Aunt—his last living relative—but, especially at her size, she didn't need to be hiking through the woods. And then there were her stories that seemed to scare everyone. All the talk of hocus-pocus and ancient, evil entities. He didn't believe in such things.

They picked up the trailhead and entered the woods; Jake and Laura side-by-side, Landon and Raven joined at the hip. Five minutes into the journey, the four flicked on their flashlights.

"Got dark awful quick," Landon said. He shined his light to either side where the trees pushed against the trail, crowding them. "It's not the same."

Jake stopped and turned. He stepped between Landon and Raven. "The trail," he said, "It's gone." The others sidled next to him. The four stood at a line of trees where the trail behind them abruptly ended. "Shit," Jake said. "Trees are on the trail."

"The town got us here, and now it's going to try and keep us," Raven said matter-of-factly. She had already accepted that they would never leave the Falls, so this new surprise was no surprise at all.

"The town is changing, redefining itself to meet its needs," Laura said.

"And we're right in its belly," Landon added. He checked his pockets. "Forgot the map."

Jake turned and faced the trail that was still leading into the woods. "Don't need it. The Falls is leading us where it wants us to go."

Laura moved toward Jake. She slipped her thumb

through one of Jake's empty belt loops. "Don't leave me again," she said. He nodded. She looked back at Landon and Raven. "Holy..."

Raven felt a chill sweep across her chest. She looked down to see what Laura was so worried about. Landon stopped and stepped away from her. She ran her fingers across the black bikini strings of the top she had not entered the woods wearing. "What the hell is going on?" She looked up at Laura. "Laura..."

Laura glanced down at her body, the bikini top and short shorts she had not worn since high school. She suddenly remembered that the last time she wore this outfit was the night they encountered Hank McCoy. She turned her attention to the others and realized that they were all wearing the same clothes they wore the night McCoy was murdered. "It's recreating the night at the tree," she said.

"And nothing we can do to stop it." Landon ran his hands over his bare chest and stomach. He raised his light to Laura's face and then to Jake's. "We're all younger."

Raven turned toward the trees behind her and took a step forward. Her leg, up to mid-thigh, disappeared, and she stopped. She reached forward. Her arm up to her elbow vanished. She pulled her arm away from the darkness before her, and it reappeared.

"Step back," Laura said. Raven and Landon complied. Laura stood two feet behind the spot Raven had occupied. She reached out, and her arm disappeared. She pulled her arm back from the darkness and scooted the others backward another three feet from where she had just stood. She reached out again. Her arm disappeared again. "It's following us, closing in."

Still standing on the path, Jake reached out to the trees

on each side. Both his hands vanished. He took a deep breath. "Let's go."

As they slowly moved along the path, they could see both the forest and the path recreating itself as it guided them deeper into the woods and their destination. Occasionally, Landon would reach out to his side and swipe his hand into the darkness, watching it weave in and out. And although none of them mentioned it, they were aware of no sound, smell, or touch of a breeze. Jake intentionally stepped on a branch to see if the crunch would make a sound. It did not.

The path took a sharp right turn, and they stood at old Betsy and Crystal River. A fire blazed from the same pit they had used twenty years ago. A tattered rope hung from the old oak tree, waiting for its next victim.

"Why?" Laura asked. "Why bring us to this spot?" She walked to the murky water's edge and glanced upriver, knowing that the evening fog would have the area covered very soon. That night, they managed to avoid the fog and the danger it presented.

"Laura," Jake said.

Laura turned and felt her skin turn inside out. Hank McCoy stood opposite the others. She stepped back and felt the cool water wrap around her ankles. She stepped back onto dry ground and looked down at the black sludge covering her feet. She stepped forward and watched the inky water edge its way from the river, following her. "Jake," she called. "Jake, the water." She walked backward from the water, shrieking when Jake touched her shoulder. She felt Jake's hand pulling her back, glanced at her feet, and screamed at the burning flesh.

"What!" Jake shook Laura and looked at the ground and

the dry cracks in the soil. "Laura!" Laura turned her head. Her face dripped sweat and tears. "There's nothing there. Look." He pointed at her feet.

Laura looked at her feet again, her pedicure shiny and untouched. "I felt . . ."

"The Falls," Raven said. "It's messing with our heads."

Laura turned around. Hank McCoy was gone, as was the fire. She looked back at the river and the oak—gone. "I can't do this," she said.

"You don't have a choice," Jake replied. He cast his light where the trail should have been behind them—gone. He then moved the light across the clearing, where the trail continued into the woods. "The Falls won't let us go anywhere but forward." He motioned to the trail with his light. "We should keep moving."

Jake started along the path, and the others followed, Raven and Laura between Jake and Landon, bringing up the rear. None spoke, eyes constantly darting left and right as they scanned the trees. A breeze wafted toward them from up ahead, the trail behind them disappearing with every step forward. Landon found himself lagging, his curiosity toward what was happening behind him now much greater than what was ahead. He slowed to a standstill, allowing the others to move several yards ahead. He could feel the darkness behind him tickle the nape of his neck, and then he felt it whisper into his ear. He stopped and turned. The beam of his light stopped shining inches away from the flashlight. He slapped the flashlight against the palm of his hand, but nothing changed. Thinking better of the situation, he turned back to the others—gone.

Landon yelled, but his words dropped with a thud against the ground. He turned in a circle, repeating the move until dizziness brought his spinning to a halt. The Falls had boxed him in. He reached out in every direction. His hand disappeared in every direction. He tried yelling again, but although he felt the sound vibrations in his throat, he heard nothing. Then he felt the darkness pressing at his shoulders, crowding him. His mind began flipping like a Rolodex through almost thirty-five years of memory until it found what it sought.

At eight years old, Landon was swimming in Crystal River with family and friends. It was shortly after lunch. As a kid, he thought you should wait thirty minutes after eating before entering the water. He hadn't. The pain in his calves felt like large needles. He began to sink despite his struggles to stay above the water. He opened his eyes to floating moss and muck, heading straight to the riverbed. He swallowed river water and snorted the nasty muck up his nose. Then, a hand was around his wrist, pulling him toward the sunshine.

Landon opened his eyes and gulped a large breath of stale air. The box was sucking the air out of his lungs. He yelled again—nothing. He looked up. Blackness pushed toward him. *I have to run*, his mind screamed. *I have to step into the darkness.* He took another deep breath, closed his eyes, and surged forward.

Raven screamed, dropped her flashlight, and covered her mouth.

Laura and Jake turned, their lights dancing on Raven's back and the inky darkness gliding toward her. It didn't register at first. But then they both realized that their group of four was now a group of three.

Jake moved to Raven's side and then felt his heart skip a beat. A wall of darkness stood less than an inch from the tip of Raven's nose and toes, toying with her. The wall reached for her and then contracted. "He was right behind me," Raven said. "And then he was gone."

"Take my hand," Jake said. "Laura, take my other." He gently tugged on Raven's hand, trying to pull her away from the darkness.

"It's going to take us," Raven said. "No matter what we do, we belong to the Falls." She let herself be pulled away, retrieving her flashlight as they moved. "Don't let go, Jake."

Jake nodded and glanced behind Raven. Although he and Landon had not spoken as much as they should have over the years, Jake still felt a connection to Landon. Landon had been that friend Jake could always talk to, tell stories to, bitch and moan to. And Jake's ears were always open for Landon as well. Jake wanted nothing more than to step into the abyss following them and see if he could find his childhood friend, but Jake also needed to take care of Raven and Laura. He hoped that Landon, wherever he was now, understood that and would have done the same.

Laura led the way, her right hand reaching back and holding Jake's left hand. If the Falls tried to take one, it would have to take all three. She enjoyed—as much as anyone could while scared to death—the feel of Jake's warm hand in hers. Warm hands, cold heart, the saying went. But she doubted very seriously that Jake's heart was cold. No, far from it, she realized. He had never been married, and now she wondered if he had been waiting on her.

Nearly thirty minutes after Landon disappeared, they stepped into another clearing, a scene none had forgotten.

Laura released Jake's hand. "It hasn't changed a bit," she said. She circled the tree like a shark circling its prey. "All these years, and it looks the same." She moved closer to the tree trunk and studied the carved initials.

Raven released Jake's other hand and stood before her twenty-year nemesis. She was not filled with the same awe that seemed to envelop Laura. This thing, this dead monument, still ate away at her soul. She hated it, the farm, and now, for the first time in twenty years, she hated everyone who had talked her into joining them that night. She stared at Jake, who studied the tree as if trying to figure out a way to look inside. She watched Laura, who had no fear on her face. She watched Jake stop next to Laura. The two stood there, staring, *worshipping*, she thought. And now they were laughing and giggling like a couple of high-schoolers. Friends had died or disappeared, and here they were, yacking it up.

She stepped to the left and noticed something shiny at the tree's base—the knife they had used to carve their initials into the tree trunk. Why had neither of the other two seen the sparkling blade? She approached the tree and felt like she might spew her dinner on the charred bark. Was this the direction Hank McCoy faced when they lowered him to his death? She moved to one knee as Jake and Laura carried on obnoxiously. The knife felt cool against her clammy skin and fit snuggly into her hand. Raven stood and carefully slid the blade between her back and shorts. She pretended to examine the tree, the slick bark that looked neither weather-worn nor old. They were ignoring her again. Always, always ignoring her, like last year in science class when she presented her project on photosynthesis. The two sat in the back of the room whispering. She adjusted her bikini top and made a mental note to inform her parents she needed a larger top. Always ignoring her is what these two were famous for. A few weeks ago, dateless for the prom, she sat at their table. They ignored her. And now she was stuck in the middle of nowhere with all of them, Clark trying to get into her shorts. She then noticed Jake moving away from his little whore girlfriend. Raven advanced. She curled her hand around the knife and charged.

Laura saw the gleaming blade coming at her and dodged to the left an instant too late as the knife caught her cheek under her right eye. She fell to the ground and wiped at the blood, shocked. She looked up at the charging Raven and rolled from the oncoming blade. The blade stuck firmly into the ground.

"Raven," Jake yelled. He grabbed Raven from behind and rolled her away from the knife, landing on top of her. He pressed his knees against her arms. He looked down at her sweaty, terrified face and waited for her to stop struggling. "Stop! Raven, stop."

Laura scooted across the ground and back to the knife. Using both hands, she jerked the knife from the tree root it had impaled. The root bled darkly crimson. She then crawled toward Raven and Jake, knife in hand.

Jake reached out to Laura a second too late. The knife dug into the ground less than an inch from Raven's ear. "Shit, what're you doing?" he said to Laura.

"She tried to fucking kill me, Jake," Laura screamed. "Let her go!"

Jake looked down at the sobbing Raven and eased off her arms, eventually sliding off her stomach. He sat on the ground between the two girls and leaned against the tree trunk. "It's beginning to rain," he said, another drop splashing in his eye.

Laura held out her hand, feeling nothing. "It's not," she said and reached for her flashlight. "You're bleeding." She moved closer to Jake.

Jake felt another heavy drop land on top of his head. He swiped at it with his hand. He moved his fingers closer to his face and scrambled from the tree. He grabbed his flashlight and illuminated the top of the tree trunk, where blood was beginning to pour over the jagged opening. When the mangled, blood-stained hand appeared over the lip of the tree, all three pushed to their feet to run.

23

St. Louis, Missouri
1936

Catherine and Agatha followed the driver up cracked and dirty stone steps. The metal doors in front of them squealed as the driver entered the building. He turned and waved them forward.

"Wait here, and someone else will be right with you," he said and returned to his car, leaving the two women alone in the foyer.

"Keep quiet, and let me speak for both of us," Catherine said.

Agatha saluted half-heartedly and slid into a nearby chair. "This place is creepy. We should be back in Memphis and all the comforts we deserve."

The black and white checkered floor fanned out toward three different hallways. Before entering, Catherine noticed the building had east and west wings. Broken signs and equipment suggested a hospital long past its use.

"It's not as bad as it appears."

Agatha leaped from the chair and took her place next to Catherine. Catherine nudged Agatha back and stepped in front of her. "Catherine Chesterfield," Catherine said, offering her hand to the approaching gentleman.

"Adrian Carmichael, Miss Rhodes," the man replied. "If you follow me this way, several people are waiting for you." He looked around Catherine. "You too, Miss."

Catherine followed hesitantly. No one had used the name Rhodes since the night Thomas Templeton saved her from the town of Crystal Falls. Agatha crinkled her nose and pointed at the man leading them down the middle hallway. Catherine nodded, surmising that Agatha was ridiculing the man for how he dressed, a fashion she had not seen since she left the Falls over forty years ago. She also noted that the inside of the building was as unkempt as the outside: thick cobwebs in the corners, art covered in dust, peeling paint, and wallpaper. The small lights overhead flickered and threatened to either fade or explode.

They stopped at a set of shiny wooden doors, the scent of turpentine so strong that Catherine felt slightly dizzy.

"Wait right here, and I'll make sure they're ready," the man said. He opened one side of the doors and slid in, blocking their view of those inside.

Catherine only knew that "they" existed, a fact shared with her by the man who had navigated the boat on the night Thomas Templeton helped her escape. He also provided her with an address and the assurance that if she ever found herself in a bad situation, those in St. Louis could help. At the time, Catherine felt a sense of loyalty to these people she had never met because they were looking

Crystal Falls: A Witch's Revenge

out for her. When she mailed her letter to this address ten years ago, she had only addressed the letter to the address and no specific individual. In that letter, Catherine stated that she had found a more suitable life. She had everything she could dream of and didn't need her "gift" to get her through life any longer. She thanked those concerned about her and sent her best regards. And now, although she had left Memphis behind, she still had no intention of returning to her life before Memphis.

"Please come in."

Catherine and Agatha followed the man into the next room, where seven people sat around a fireplace, each in their own leather chair—three women, four men, varying ages. Catherine didn't bother shielding Agatha from the group. They were here, and their opportunity to forget this whole charade evaporated when they entered the building.

"Catherine Rhodes," one of the men said.

"Catherine Chesterfield," Catherine replied.

"I'm afraid not," the man said and stood. "Our kind can only be married by our kind. Anything else is unacceptable. So, in those terms, you are Catherine Rhodes." He walked between two others and approached Catherine. "Ellis Perry," he said. He held out his hand, but Catherine declined. He retracted his hand and then said, "Please have a seat. We have things to discuss." He led Catherine and Agatha to two empty leather chairs.

"You're all like me," Catherine said flatly. "I had been told there were others, even told where you were."

"Yes," Ellis said. "And we've all read your letter from ten years ago." He glanced at the others around the room. They were all dressed in Victorian garbs. "We had hoped this wouldn't be necessary, bring you here to clean up a problem created by your selfish parents." He looked to take pleasure in the apparent condemnation of the Rhodes'.

Catherine bit her bottom lip. She was not easily scared and never found a place or person creepy. However, as she glanced around the room at the dust on the furniture and the footprints left behind on the floor, it was apparent that these people rarely inhabited this place. So then, where did they come from?

"She's angry," one of the women said. The woman's smile reminded Catherine of a Jack-o-lantern she'd carved as a child, the smile huge but menacing. Although her skin was young and smooth, Catherine surmised that the woman was much older than Catherine. The woman's eyes, although gleaming blue, suggested a wicked soul somewhere behind.

"What situation?" Catherine asked curtly.

"Your parents left Crystal Falls in dismay, threatening our way of life."

"You mean murder, destruction, despair. Those kinds of things?" Catherine said.

Ellis stood, obviously the man in charge. "Call it what you want, Miss Rhodes, but the fact remains that your parents created a problem that you have to fix. We expect that you go fix that problem . . . now."

"And if I refuse?"

"Bring the girl here," Ellis said.

Two of the other men stood and dragged Agatha from the chair. Catherine shifted in her seat to get up but found herself cornered by two women. The two men held Agatha in front of Ellis.

Catherine trembled, her rage growing. The fourth man watched with only a hint of interest, his eyes shifting back and forth between Catherine and Agatha. And then

Catherine realized that it was not Ellis who was in charge. "You," Catherine said to the man still seated. "I'm not interested in being one of your monsters. My parents weren't monsters, and Crystal Falls brought their troubles upon themselves. My parents never bothered anyone in that town."

Semia, still seated, nodded to the other three men. "Take the young lady away. Miss Rhodes and I have a lot to discuss." He turned to the three women. "You may leave as well." He waited for the door to close and then gave his full attention to Catherine. "It's not often I let a subordinate speak to me the way you have. Let me suggest that you not let it happen again."

"Who are you people?" Catherine asked.

"We're called the Dispatch." He stood, placed his hands behind his back, and began walking around the room as he spoke. His early Victorian clothes hung limply from his gangly body. Catherine noticed a six-inch scar along the side of his neck. "We keep rogues like your parents in check, preventing them from drawing attention to our cause."

"Your cause," Catherine said. When he passed behind her, Catherine caught the rancid smell of the man's clothes and wondered how long it had been since his last bath. "Mr. Babcock said that I should never refer to myself as a witch, but isn't that what I am," she held her arms out. "What all of you are?"

Semia laughed and returned to his seat. He looked at Catherine thoughtfully. Although it would take time, he had little doubt that Catherine could be coerced into returning to the old ways. She needed a little prodding. "We *are* man's free will and have been since man's beginning," he said.

"Adam and Eve?" Catherine shook her head in disgust. "I don't believe in fairy tales."

"Yet you believe in witches," Semia said.

"Only because that's what I have been referred to as." Catherine frowned. Needing no further explanation, Catherine pushed from the chair and headed for the door.

"Don't bother," Semia said.

Catherine looked down at the doorknob as the lock clicked. She grabbed the handle anyway and pulled. Locked, she turned to Semia. "People know where I'm at. They'll come looking for me."

Semia pointed at the empty chair. This time, Catherine obeyed his directive. "You were found hours ago, sneaking along the banks of the Mississippi. No one has any idea where you are, and it would be much easier on everyone if you would accept our offer to set Crystal Falls back to the way it was before your parents made their mistakes. Every town and village from here to China has representatives controlling man's environment. When that balance is thrown out of whack, bad things happen."

"Isn't that what you want, chaos?" Catherine tried to raise her level of rage but felt something pushing it back. It was him controlling her emotions. "My parents were good people who kept their wickedness at bay, not once harming another soul. And yet, those people had to interfere. They got what they deserve." She shook her head. "You're obviously on the side of those murderers."

Semia sat in the seat directly across from Catherine, lit a pipe, and took a long drag. A ball of smoke floated from his mouth and dissipated above his head. A vanilla smell filled the room. "We do our best to stay in the middle, with the occasional step to either side."

Catherine released a heavy sigh. "I don't get it," she

said. "What did they do that was so wrong?" Then she looked him squarely in the eyes. "You're afraid of something . . . what is it."

Semia returned the look of reproach. "When things or situations get too far out of whack, other issues begin; bad ones, to say the least." He stood again and began pacing. "You've heard of the kudzu plant?" Catherine nodded. "Plant a single kudzu near a tree, and within a year, it has encompassed the tree. What happens to the kudzu if it's allowed to thrive? It will take over an entire forest. We, Miss Rhodes, are the gardeners, ensuring the plant does not thrive." He stopped at the drink cabinet again. "If you don't return to the Falls and undo what your parents have done, the evil they've created will continue to fester, spreading itself."

Catherine swallowed a blistering laugh. In her mind's eye, she saw her loving mother and father, who always brought her things when he returned from his travels. She would not go against her parents' wishes. An epiphany raced through her head. "You could've stopped their deaths," she said.

Semia's jaws tightened. He swallowed a glassful of liquor and placed the glass on the cabinet. "They died because they made a poor decision."

"They died because you wouldn't help." Catherine jolted to her feet. She raised her hand toward Semia, tried to exert her powers, and failed as if her gift had never existed. She started toward Semia, wanting to kill the man with her hands, not the gift that had suddenly disappeared.

Semia rushed forward, meeting Catherine in the middle of the room. His hand went to her throat, raising her two feet off the ground. Like a dog flinging a stick, Semia tossed Catherine across the room.

Catherine rolled onto her back, bracing her fall. She turned back to the approaching Semia. This time, she jerked to the right, his fingertips catching the hairs on the back of her neck. She flew toward the door but a step too late. With Semia's hand firmly snarled in her hair, Catherine spun and drove the palm of her hand against his nostrils.

Semia fell backward, grabbing his nose before landing in one of the leather chairs. He sat there not in disbelief but in amusement. Like her mother, Catherine was a fighter. He righted himself. "Truth be told," he said, still smiling, "your father was sticking his nose where it didn't belong, so he had to be exterminated, which he was. Unfortunately, I was naïve to think his kindness had no end."

"You were there," Catherine said. "In the church when we were on trial. I saw you talking to Miles as we were being taken out."

"And I was there to see both of them burn," Semia retorted. "And I will be there to see you burn as well." He turned to the door. "Ellis, get in here." Ellis and the two other men entered the room. "Take her to Waverly and make sure she's secure." He moved toward Catherine as the other men surrounded her. "Eternity in a room of mirrors will suit you well."

The train ride to Louisville, Kentucky, bordered on insanity for Catherine. The mirrors covering the inside of the box had kept her from thinking evil thoughts or screaming for help. She had known about the mirrors but surmised that the mirrors caused one to view oneself in a particular way. Not settling on a specific theory, Catherine settled in for a worse stay than dying by flame.

She thought of Agatha, who would still be safe in Memphis if Catherine had not insisted on her joining Catherine. She thought of those men taking her away and tried to push out the thought of what they might do to Agatha.

She heard the same men entering the freight car and felt them lift the box, her body swaying as they carried her down an incline. She heard them discuss back roads and watching for potential trouble. The truck ride—she assumed it was a truck based on the engine's roar—was bumpy, giving her the hope that the glass inside the box might shatter. It did not. She then felt them lift her from the truck, place her on something with wheels, and then felt the slow decline as they pushed her toward her destination. They lifted her again and then put her on the floor. She took a deep breath and waited for them to let her out.

They did not.

24

Crystal Falls
Present Day

Landon lolled his head to the left and then back to the right, where a woman sat on the ground, watching him. Once again, he had awakened next to a woman. Except this time, he knew her name. He moved to his elbows. "Trish," he said.

Trish stood and then offered Landon her hand, which he took, and then helped him to his feet. "I see you've experienced the Falls firsthand." She crossed her arms and looked at him, waiting for the questions. When none came, she said, "You aren't the least bit curious about what's been going on here while you and the others have been out living life?"

"I hate to sound like Captain Obvious, but things are pretty fucked up. One minute, I'm thirty-nine years old. The next, I look and have the body of my nineteen-year-old self. How any of this is possible, I have no clue." He looked around, realizing he was still in the woods on McCoy's property. Then he noticed the two gravestones behind Trish. "Isabella Rhodes," he said. "Arthur Rhodes."

Trish didn't bother to turn. "Yeah, and the reason things are so fucked up, as you so eloquently said."

Landon turned, trying to find a way out. Darkness pushed uncomfortably close.

"It'll let you go when it decides to let you go," Trish said.

"I was afraid you'd say that." He studied the younger Trish, rekindling an old flame. "You know," he said, "when we figure all this out and get the hell out of here . . ."

"I'm not interested," Trish replied harshly. "Why do you keep trying?"

"Why do you keep acting like you want everyone at arms-length? Like you can't stand any of us? Well, except for Jake." Landon regretted the words as soon as they left his lips. He glanced around at the darkness and then at Trish. "Wait, what're you doing out here?"

Trish meandered around the inky darkness. "The Falls has made me do things," she said. "Things that I'm not proud of."

Landon regarded Trish's younger body and then forced himself to push his perverted ways aside. With the thoughts of Trish's body formerly out of his mind, Landon realized that, even when they were young, he actually loved her for her and not just her body—he cared. "Why didn't you just leave like the rest of us?"

"I tried," she said. "But it wouldn't let me go. It used me against me." Seeing Landon's confusion, she went on. "Somehow, the Falls knew about my mother. It knew what I had done, so it clung to my despair, using it to make me do things."

"You killed all those people," Landon said.

Trish nodded and refused to look at Landon. "Then it used my jealousy toward Laura." She raised her head. "The Falls wants me to kill the four of you, Landon." Tears formed at the corners of her eyes. "I can't. I can't do it." She moved into Landon's arms and let him hold her. "The Falls thought you would come back someday, and that's when I would do it."

"You sent the reunion invitations," Landon replied. He held her at arm's length. "To get us here."

Trish let her eyes meet his. "No," she replied.

"Then who sent the fucking invitations, if not you or the class committee?" Landon said.

"There's something I need to show you," Trish said. She raised her hand and pressed against the darkness; as she did so, the darkness moved away. She took a step forward, following a path previously hidden.

"I don't get it," Landon said. "Why does it let you move around like you can?"

Trish continued moving forward. "The Falls has trust in me." Using both hands, Trish parted the wall of darkness in front of her, and the two found themselves where Crystal River turned into Crystal Falls, the water lazily pouring over the fifteen-foot drop to make its way down the Ohio to meet up with the Mississippi. Trish led Landon to the base of the falls, where she then led him into the water. They swam to the middle of the falls, Landon still able to bounce on the tips of his toes against the limestone rock below. Trish pushed the foaming, white water away as she dog paddled toward the falling water. The full moon behind them created a billion sparkling chandeliers against the wall of water in front of them. Trish went below the water and then beneath the falls, reappearing on the other side of the thunderous splash of water. For a moment, she thought Landon had changed his mind but then felt a pang of relief when he emerged next to her. And although he tried speaking to her, Trish could only hear the roar of Crystal Falls. She pointed behind him at the opening in the rocks. She crawled up the bumpy façade and slipped through the slim opening. Landon followed.

They walked several yards along the oval-shaped tunnel before Trish finally halted and turned to Landon. Cold and drenched, Trish shivered violently. "It never gets above sixty degrees in here," she said, teeth chattering.

As cold and miserable, Landon pulled Trish into his arms, pressing his body firmly against hers. Trish raised her head and let her eyes meet his. "We'll freeze to death if we don't do something," he said.

Trish moved her hand into his, and she stepped back. "I come down here to escape the Falls," she said. "For some reason, it can't control me here." She touched the smooth walls surrounding them. "It's almost as if I'm inside the thing doing all this. Like it can control the environment without but not within." She pointed further along the tunnel. "I have wood and matches for a fire. Maybe some clothes that you can wear."

Still holding Landon's hand, Trish continued into the cavern before stopping in a small domed area where a lantern glowed just enough to show a bed, supplies, a stack of wood, and a box of Twinkies.

Landon motioned toward the tunnel that led past the domed room. "Where does it lead?"

"To the abandoned church in the middle of town," Trish replied and began undressing.

They stood against the wall of darkness and watched the tree give birth to a mangled human form. It would only make sense that Hank McCoy would reappear from his monolithic grave someday, but as the form rose over the edge of the hollowed tree trunk, Laura, Jake, and Raven guessed that this man could not be Hank McCoy.

The slender body lurched down the tree head first, its protracted fingernails chipping away bark as it secured its decent. At the base of the tree, the man stood erect, though unsteady, as if he'd been a lifelong alcoholic. He stepped toward them, and his right knee buckled, the horizontal wound beside his kneecap opening up and puking a wad of white, wiggling bodies. The man read them toe-to-head, his attention focusing squarely on Laura. He stepped forward again, the wound closing and hiding the wiggling forms beneath his dirty skin. He raised his left hand and pointed at Laura, and as he did so, a small patch of slimy skin dropped to the ground. Taking his eyes off Laura, he reached down and retrieved the swatch of skin and shoved it into his mouth. He returned his attention to Laura. "You," he moaned and pointed at Laura. "You caused all of this."

Laura's mouth dropped open.

Jake stepped in front of both Laura and Raven. "What're you?" he said.

"Cornelius Miles," Raven interjected.

Miles turned his head to Raven. "Templeton," he said. "Thomas Templeton." Miles reached for Raven, but Jake intercepted him, pushing him back. Miles's arms flailed as he stumbled back against the tree trunk. He studied Jake.

"Great-great-grandson," Jake said, feeling as if a large circle was beginning to close. The man in front of him was the beginning, Jake possibly the end.

"Release me," Miles said to Laura. "Please, I beg you, release me from this place." Miles slumped against the tree trunk, resting his elbow on his knees. His knee opened again, allowing a gush of small, white, squirming bodies. He plucked one from the open sore and tossed it into his mouth.

"You can't still be alive," Laura said. She stepped away from Raven and Jake, approaching Miles.

"Laura," Jake said. "Don't"

But Laura ignored Jake's plea. She moved to her knees and rested her butt on her heels. "You're Cornelius Miles," she said. Miles nodded. Laura glanced back at Raven and Jake. "Why is this happening?" she asked Miles.

Miles lowered his head and took a deep, wheezing breath. "A man came to me several months before your parents' death. He told me that Isabella was a witch." Miles coughed, and the wound next to his knee split apart. "He said it was a matter of time before she released her demons upon Crystal Falls. I didn't believe him at first. He was a stranger passing through town. He told me he would have another man stay with us to ensure Isabella was dealt with." Miles raised his head. "He told me that Arthur knew nothing of his wife's power, that she had made him blind to her real self. So I believed him and convinced the town to believe him. He left after the trial, leaving behind the man to ensure our safety." Miles coughed and swiped at the line of mucus pouring from his nose. "The man that stayed behind left after Isabella was declared dead." Miles began to sob. "I sent him away to find Catherine, Arthur and

Isabella's daughter, who escaped the night before Isabella died."

"Arthur Rhodes took revenge on you and then the town," Laura said.

Miles nodded. "And only Catherine can end it."

"How?" Laura asked, not sure she wanted to hear the answer.

Miles turned his head to Jake and Raven. "Kill the descendants."

Laura pointed at Jake and said to Miles, "That's your great-great-grandson, Jake Simon."

Miles shook his head and dropped his hands into his lap. "Doesn't matter. He needs to die like everyone else."

"This is bullshit," Jake said.

Laura stood. "Give me the knife, Jake."

"It's not happening," Jake said.

"Jake, give me the knife," Laura said slowly. Jake looked at Raven.

"Don't do it," Raven said. "We can figure this out."

"No, we can't," Jake said. "We already know we're stuck here."

"The knife," Laura insisted. "Now."

"Jake," Raven pleaded. She grabbed his arm, but, as Laura wished, so Jake offered

Laura grabbed the knife from Jake's hand and stared at both he and Raven. And then, with what could only be described as a ninja movie scene, Laura, facing away from Miles, dropped to a knee and swung the knife backward, hitting Miles directly in the Adam's apple. The blade passed through Miles's throat, slicing through the back of his neck and lodging deep into the tree. The speed with which she moved surprised them all. She released the handle and stepped away from Miles.

Jake took a knee in front of Miles and studied the man's face, recognizing his facial features in Miles's. "You just killed my only relative," he said to Laura.

"Tough-titty-said-the-kitty," Laura replied. "He's one of the reasons we're here, why we'll always be here."

And just as fast as Laura stabbed Miles in the neck, Jake swung his hand and landed a punch against Laura's chin. Laura fell back on her ass and stared up at Jake. Jake then tried to dislodge the knife from the tree. "You're dead," he said to Laura.

Raven took a quick step toward Jake and veered to the right as his hand approached her head. Jake's momentum sent him across Miles's body and rolling across the ground. Laura moved quickly, sitting on Jake's chest. Raven grabbed his arms, and the two struggled to keep him at bay, screaming for him to come to his senses. Jake thrust his hips upward. Laura bounced skyward but locked her legs around Jake's side.

"Jake, stop!" Laura pressed her full weight toward the ground, not easing up when Jake's body seemed to relax. "Stop," she said softly.

"What the hell is going on?" Jake questioned. Raven released his arms, and Laura slid from his chest. He scooted along the ground away from them. "I'm sorry," he said.

"We've got to keep it together," Raven said. "The Falls wants us at each other's throats.

All three took a deep breath and stared at Miles. They looked at the top of the tree trunk.

Jake moved to his feet. He then stepped opposite Miles's body to the side of the tree trunk. He shimmied to the top and asked Laura for a flashlight and a small rock. The light illuminated a solid surface far below the tree's base. He dropped the rock and raised his eyebrows when the rock pinged against rock. "That's our way out."

"You've got to be kidding me," Raven said. "I'm not going down there."

Jake jumped from the tree. "Look around you, Raven. What do you see? A way out of this mess? A dead man pinned to a tree? We're out of options." He pointed at Raven and Laura. "I'm not waiting to be offed by our ancient relatives." Jake shimmed back up the tree trunk, pausing momentarily to look at the initials they had carved twenty years ago. He offered his hand to the approaching Laura. Raven followed, and the three hugged the tree like a family of monkeys.

"I'll go first," Jake said. He moved to a sitting position atop the rim of the tree trunk and grabbed hold of the opposite edge. He scooted forward and clung to the rim with his hands. He thought the drop to be no more than seven or eight feet, and if he landed just right, he could avoid breaking a bone. He dropped and landed with a thud but stayed on his feet. A tunnel led to his left and right, a decision one of them would have to make.

Laura tightened her lips and stared at Raven. "You next," she said.

Raven grabbed the opposite rim and glared at Laura before dropping into Jake's waiting arms. She moved away from Jake and turned on her heels to see the tunnels leading in opposite directions. "Which way?"

Jake pointed at the tunnel leading toward town. He ran purely on adrenaline, his mind working hard to forget Miles. When it was over, they could all mourn the loss of the dead. "The other way should lead back to the river," he said. "Even though the Rhodes died here, I think the real problems lie at the heart of Crystal Falls . . . in the middle of town." He moved beneath the tree again. "Ready," he yelled to Laura.

"Ready as I will ever be." She prepared to jump.

"There's something that's been bothering me," he said, waiting for Laura to drop down. "We know where everyone is, all the descendants, except for Catherine's. Where's her offspring?"

"Maybe she was caught, killed like her parents."

"I don't think so. If someone went through all the trouble to help her escape, they would ensure she was safe." He squinted toward the opening above him. "Laura?"

"I'm coming down," Laura yelled.

But as Laura maneuvered over the entrance, the tree folded in upon itself, closing the opening.

25

Crystal Falls
Present Day

For once in his life, Landon felt like there would be no more waking up next to a strange woman in his bed. Trish really was the *one*. He had always known that but had long ago given up hope that they would meet again. Yes, his best friend and two other friends were missing, but any silver lining was worth grasping at. As he approached the tunnel leading to the town center, he grabbed Trish's hand, determined not to lose her again. "How far?" He asked.

Trish momentarily considered the question and said, "It's about two miles, though the tunnel meanders most of the way, so probably thirty minutes." She looked down at their connected hands. If they made it out of this mess, they could leave the Falls and never look back. She let a smile slip across her lips.

"What?" Landon questioned.

"Nothing," Trish replied. She nodded toward the tunnel. "We need to get moving."

Landon grabbed a flashlight from a box of supplies that Trish had brought into the tunnel several weeks ago as she prepared to murder her high school friends. He clicked the light on, and the two began the trek through the tunnel, heading toward town and whatever new surprises the Falls had waiting. Nearly a hundred yards into their journey, Landon stopped. "Crystal Falls no longer controls you," he said.

Trish shrugged. "Something has changed," she said. "I used to feel the Falls inside me, squeezing my soul."

"Then you can leave." He looked down at the slick, rocky ground. "You don't have to do this. We're the ones who can't leave and who need to fix this."

Trish pulled away. "I'm not leaving. This place has ruined my last twenty years of life, and now I have an opportunity for payback." She also didn't want to leave Landon. "I want to help even the score," she added.

Landon shook his head as if Trish were nuts. "Come on," he finally said.

"Wait," Trish replied. "There's something else."

"Great."

It was Trish's turn to study the ground. "There're miles of tunnels beneath Crystal Falls," she said. "And there're at least a dozen entrances to the system."

"Okay," Landon said slowly. "What am I missing?"

"There's an entrance directly under the tree trunk that we placed Hank McCoy in," she replied sheepishly. She waited for Landon to show he understood. When he didn't, Trish continued, "Hank is still alive . . . down here . . . in these tunnels."

Landon crossed his arms and stared at Trish. "You're

shitting me," he said. "I thought you buried him?" He shook his head. "Another lie."

"I'm sorry," she said. "I told you, the Falls made me do things. To say things that weren't true." She lowered her head. "But not anymore."

"This is unreal," Landon said. "Come on then, we need to keep moving."

They followed the snake-like tunnel for another twenty minutes, the smooth, cold walls sending chills up Landon's arms each time he pressed a hand against the rocky surface. Yes, he was scared to death at what he might find around the next corner or the corner after that, but he had also found a new purpose in his life—Trish. She would push away the twenty-year blown-out-knee-pity party. Yeah, they had to figure out how to get out of the Falls, and once they did, it would all be downhill after that. He felt a tug on his arm and then remembered where they were.

"There's a light up ahead," Trish said.

Landon noticed a shadow bouncing along the walls. "McCoy," he whispered to Trish. He eased toward the shadow, his mind working through his first move with McCoy. He turned the flashlight off and felt in the darkness for Trish's hand, finding it and squeezing it tightly. They moved to the opposite wall, pressing their backs against the cool rock and continuing slowly forward. Landon glanced down at the heavy-duty flashlight in his hand. The junction up ahead would bring the two tunnels together before continuing northward to the middle of town. He and Trish arrived at the intersection first, still plastered against the wall. Landon raised the flashlight over his head and waited.

"Last week," Raven said as she followed behind Jake.

Jake listened to only half of what Raven had to say, his thoughts still on Laura and the fact she was either dead or walking around the Falls alone. He had let her down again, leaving her alone to deal with what began twenty years ago. But he also understood the fallacy in that way of thinking. What plagued the Falls began at least a century ago. They were just lucky enough to be part of the present problem.

"We're going to need help," Raven said. She nearly knocked Jake over when he suddenly stopped. "What?"

"There's no help," Jake replied, still angry about leaving Laura behind. "It's us or no one."

Raven massaged her temples, fighting back a migraine. She needed sleep as badly as she needed to get out of Crystal Falls. Dealing with Jake was like dealing with her teenage son. Talk slowly, let things soak in, and then scold him for being a jerk. "I found something else online while searching our past," she said slowly. "It's about Catherine, the Rhodes's daughter."

Jake crossed his arms and listened.

Raven steadied her eyes on Jake's. "I think she's still alive."

Jake's shoulders slumped. "You've got to be kidding."

She placed her hands on her hips and sighed. "I don't like being made fun of," Raven said. Jake held up his hands in surrender. "Thank you. There's an urban legend about a witch buried near Waverly Hills in Louisville." Jake started to say something, but Raven raised her eyebrows, a mother's scolding. "The legend also stated that she was brought there from St. Louis."

Jake rubbed the back of his neck and tilted his head side-to-side. "You're not making any sense."

"A young woman, Catherine Chesterfield, disappeared from her Memphis mansion in 1939. It was assumed she drowned in the Mississippi."

"Okay."

"St. Louis sits on the Mississippi, Jake. Louisville sits on the Ohio River, which empties into the Mississippi." Raven held out her hands in a don't-you-get-it motion. "Crystal Falls River empties into the Ohio!"

Jake surrendered. "Okay, let's say what you're saying is true. Then what next? We can't leave town."

Raven smiled victoriously. "We can't, but Trish can."

Jake considered this for a few minutes and looked up and down the tunnel. Trish was nowhere in sight. Raven had a point. Trish had nothing holding her here. She was an outsider as far as the people of Crystal Falls had always been concerned. Yes, they had all accepted her, but the townspeople would have had no trouble shoving her right out the door if push came to shove. "So you want to send Trish to an insane asylum . . ."

"An abandoned tuberculosis hospital . . ."

"Okay, an abandoned tuberculosis hospital to find a witch who we think lives there, based on an urban legend you found on the internet." Jake paused and said, "Because we all know everything you read on the internet has to be true."

"Screw you, Jake. Just forget it." Raven padded past Jake and into the darkness of the tunnel.

"Well," Jake said, "hold on a second." He lit the way with his flashlight before Raven tripped and broke her neck.

He hurried to get in front of her and then looked up as something shiny came down from the tunnel's roof and smashed into his head.

Laura didn't bother to scream, yell, or panic. She stared at the ground, not in shock but in weird fascination—the Falls certainly had many tricks. They had all underestimated the power of the past and whatever was creating the chaos in the present. She noticed the darkness pushing against them had disappeared, allowing a full view of the woods and the trail from where they came. There was only one way to go—take the trail. One thing to do—tell Aunt Mary.

The trail seemed to meander less than it had when she was with the others, her path back to the road taking half the time. She crossed the road and ascended the steps leading to the front door, expecting Aunt Mary to come running out with a bag of chips and a look of terror on her face. Laura opened the front door and slowly stepped inside. She yelled for Aunt Mary, but her call was met with a resounding silence. She walked through the kitchen and looked out the window for Aunt Mary's car—gone. She glanced around the kitchen and noticed nothing had changed since the previous night. Aunt Mary was known for her early morning bread baking, pie making, and canning operation. She placed her hand on the oven—cold.

She climbed the stairs leading to her room, stopping to study the pictures hanging on the wall leading up the stairs. In some form or fashion, each image depicted a part of Crystal Falls's history, from the first settlers to the new service station near the middle of town. At least a dozen family photos graced the wallpapered wall. She paid particular attention to one of the black and white photos she guessed was set in the mid-1800s: parents and a daughter who appeared to be ten or eleven. Laura lifted the frame from the wall and turned it over. She removed the back and read the notation: Arthur, Isabella, Catherine. Laura removed the picture from the frame and stared at the three faces. She continued up the stairs, taking the picture with her, not noticing the eyes in the other images following her. At the top of the steps, Laura pushed open her bedroom door, oblivious to the vanishing stairs behind her.

In the bathroom, Laura gazed into the mirror, studying her face and then glancing at the picture. She looked so much like Arthur Rhodes that there was no doubt where she had come from. She placed the picture on the back of the toilet and then closed her eyes, resting her hands on the edge of the bathroom sink. Her father had told her to stay strong—that's what she intended to do. But what was her next move? Eyes still closed, she thought about the Falls, the evil, the town, and places in the town. The church, she decided. Relieved that she had some sort of plan, Laura opened her eyes to see, in the mirror, Hank McCoy standing behind her.

At first, Laura thought Hank was only an apparition or her mind playing tricks, but then he grabbed her shoulder, and all thoughts of him not being real faded. She turned and lashed out, striking him in the face, coming away with a stinging, dirty hand. Hank cackled in amusement and swiftly—as swift as an old, rotted man could move—tore away her bikini top.

"I remember those," McCoy said. He laughed and

lunged forward, missing Laura as she dodged to the right, nearly falling into the bathtub she had enjoyed yesterday.

Laura looked back at McCoy as she darted from the bathroom. Nothing about McCoy was different from that night. Like them, he had somehow reverted to the McCoy of twenty years ago. She went for the door handle, but instead of her grabbing the handle, the handle grabbed her. She screamed and pulled away, backing toward the bedroom window.

"Where are you going, Sweetheart?" McCoy said. "We got some things to do. Some people to see. Though I think those people can wait just a tad bit longer." He slowly worked his way around the bed that stood between them. One side of his overalls flapped as he approached.

Laura turned to open the window, but as she did, a black, inky film descended from the top, throwing the room into darkness. She slid across the bed, nearly reaching the other side before feeling a gritty hand around her ankle. She screamed again, but her screams bounced from wall to wall, never escaping the room. She managed to flop onto her back, pulling her free leg toward her chest and then ramming her heel into McCoy's nose. She felt a crunch along the bottom of her foot. McCoy's grasp faltered. Laura, her other foot now free, sent both heels flying toward McCoy's face. One foot found solid purchase, the other a glancing blow. She heard him call out in pain before falling into the nightstand. The light from the bathroom showed a bloody and slumped Hank McCoy. She raced to the bathroom and grabbed the picture. Catherine and Arthur were unchanged. However, Isabella's slack face had been replaced with a menacing smile.

"Not done," McCoy said. He stood in the bathroom doorway, his large arms crossed over an even larger chest.

As fast as Laura turned, McCoy disappeared quickly, replaced by another man staring at her in disbelief.

"Richard?" Laura said. Her first instinct should have been to run into his arms and thank God he was there. But this was the Falls and those instincts no longer existed. "What the hell are you doing here?" She looked around him. "Where are the girls?"

"In the car," he replied.

Laura rushed past Richard, out of the bedroom, and down to the SUV, where her two girls watched a Disney video. She opened the door, and both girls looked at her in horror. They moved away, pressing against the opposite door. Laura's eyes widened and slowly lowered to her young, bare breasts. She was still the eighteen-year-old Laura. She backed away and then screamed when her back slammed into Richard, who was holding a tee-shirt.

"What're you doing here, Richard?" She grabbed the tee shirt and pulled it on. "You're supposed to be at a conference." She glanced in the SUV. "And they're supposed to be at the neighbors."

"And you're supposed to be thirty-eight years old," Richard retorted, confused.

"You have to leave, now? Take the girls and go."

Richard shook his head. "I'm not leaving without you, and certainly not until you tell me what the hell's going on." He stepped toward his wife, who took a step back. "What the hell, Laura?"

Laura placed her hands on her head and took a deep breath. "Why're you here?" she asked calmly."

"Okay," Richard replied. "I received a call on my cell that you were sick and wanted me to bring the girls to see you. So I took the first plane home, picked up the girls, and here we are." He looked at her suspiciously. "Okay?"

"Okay, what?"

"Tell me what the hell is going on."

Laura paced in small circles, her throat clenching in panic. They wouldn't be able to leave. None of them. "How'd you know I was here?"

"I didn't," Richard replied. "I was headed to the church downtown and turned wrong, wound up out here. Saw your car and stopped."

"The church," Laura whispered as she stared at the ground. She jerked her head up at Richard. "Listen to me," she said and paced faster. "You have to take the girls and leave." He shook his head. "Please, you have to do this for me. I'll explain when I get home, I promise." But she knew this was not true. She would never see them again once they left—if they could leave.

"You're in danger," Richard replied. "I can't leave you." He crossed his arms and stared down at his wife.

Laura, demeanor unchanged, said, "Leave now."

Richard threw up his hands, closed the SUV's side door, and opened the driver's door. He looked at his wife. "The girls are in danger," he said. Laura nodded. "Bye, Laura." Richard slid into the driver's seat, closed the door, and left Laura alone.

Hearing the screen door behind her, Laura turned. Hank McCoy, bloodied and beaten, stepped out onto the porch.

26

Crystal Falls
Present Day

Jake rubbed the back of his head and tried to sit up. The train wreck between his ears throbbed tenaciously, and he wondered if he hadn't died and gone to headache hell. The last thing he remembered was a disagreement with Raven, which he had lost. The room—no, it wasn't a room, what was it—spun like a merry-go-round. The musty smell of stale air reminded him that he had been roaming underground.

"Whoa," Landon said and touched Jake's shoulder. He moved Jake against the tunnel wall and shined the flashlight in Jake's face. Jake swatted the light away. "Chill out," Landon said. "I didn't hit you that hard."

"You hit me?" Jake asked. He pressed his back against the smooth wall and pushed himself up, using the wall to secure his balance, relishing the cold wall's feel against his neck. He moved his tongue around his mouth and tasted his coppery blood.

"Laura?"

"Still missing," Raven confirmed.

"And you?" Jake said to Landon. "Where'd you come from? We thought you were dead."

Landon pointed down the tunnel from where he and Trish had come. "Trish and I came from that direction, heading the same direction as you and Raven. We saw your shadow and thought you were Hank McCoy."

Jake rubbed his head again, proving he was not Hank McCoy. "Trish?"

Landon explained finding Trish, leaving out the sex part, something he would never have left out before. Raven then explained how she and Landon convinced Trish that, because she was the only one who could leave the Falls, she should drive to Waverly Hills to see if the legends were true. Naturally, Trish had balked at the idea. However, Raven and Landon reminded her that this was her opportunity to escape the Falls, never having to return. That had been well over an hour ago.

"Trish said the church was less than a mile away," Landon said. "We should get moving."

Although neither Jake nor Landon gave the church much thought—or why they were heading there in the first place—Raven's research had forewarned her of the church's horrific past. Based on her findings, Raven had no desire to visit such a place. As almost a side thought, she remembered her family: Daniel, her husband, and Mathew, her teenage son. She would never see them again but thought that was okay. It was for their protection. She then considered all the sermons Daniel had preached about good and evil, her never giving either of the sides much thought, always accepting things as they are, not determined by the fallacy of these two ancient beliefs. But now, having been in the Falls for a few days, she believed in at least one side, the side of evil. However, she surmised, you can't have evil without good, so somewhere—soon, she hoped—good would have to rear its head.

"Look," Jake said. He pointed to the ceiling above and the wooden planks that stretched where the tunnel rock should have been. Attached to one of the planks was a rusty latch. Jake reached for the small metal device but fell short.

Landon stood next to Jake and bent down, cupping his hands to create a stirrup. "Come on, I'll boost you."

"Lift with your legs, not your back," Jake said jokingly. And, unfortunately, Landon did exactly that.

With Jake's foot resting in his hands, Landon pushed, with his legs, toward the ceiling. He heard the latch give but also heard the ligaments in his bad knee snap. Together, he and Jake dropped to the ground. Landon cried out, holding his knee as if shot. He pulled his hands away from his knee, and his lower leg dangled like it was on a puppet string.

"Damn," Landon said, working the leg to stretch across the ground. "Torn it to shreds." He moved back against the wall and clenched his fists. The pain was wavering, but the burning feeling made him sick.

"We've got to get him out of here," Jake pointed at the unlocked latch. "I'll lift you. Push open the door and climb into the church. Look around for rope or anything to help us get him up there."

Raven glanced at the wooden slats and then at Jake. "You want me to go up there alone?"

"I'll be right here."

"Yeah, right down here."

Jake pursed his lips.

"Okay, fine." Raven stepped over Landon.

Jake moved to his knees and patted Raven's shoulders. "Stand here."

"You're kidding."

"It's the only way you'll be able to reach high enough to crawl out."

"Fine." Raven placed a foot on Jake's shoulders, her legs trembling uncontrollably.

Jake rose, using his back instead of his knees as he watched Landon watch them.

Raven pushed back the latch and then forced the trapdoor door open. The door flopped to the side and disappeared. "I'm climbing up," she said. She grabbed the edge and pulled herself skyward, the shaking of muscles a signal that she needed to hit the gym. She laughed at this thought. She blew the dust off her shoulders and stepped away from the hole in the floor. The wooden door slammed shut, closing off Jake and Landon. Raven spun. Seeing Daniel and Mathew, Raven vomited what little food she had in her stomach.

Trish turned onto Parelee Lane and slowed, eventually pulling to the side of the road. To her right, a group of golfers was trying to get in the back nine, and the sun, setting, was splashing the horizon with a myriad of pastel colors, which, of course, meant that she would be entering Waverly Hills under darkness, not particularly something she cared to do. There was another option—leave. Get back on the highway and head west until the road ends. She had nothing to do with Crystal Falls, past or present. The others were paying for the sins of their Crystal Falls descendants.

She pulled from the roadside and started toward Waverly Hills, justifying in her mind why it would be okay to head west when she left Waverly. Find a waitressing job or a good man to take care of her. Really, for the first time in her life, she felt free of her past. She pulled to the front of the dilapidated hospital and immediately reconsidered going inside. Though going through remodeling, the menacing five-story building was clearly telling her to run.

Seeing that the main entrance was bolted shut, Trish continued around the building, remembering that somewhere in the back was a tunnel leading to the main building. She remembered names like the "death tunnel" and "body chute."

She parked at the tunnel's entrance and retrieved a flashlight from her trunk. There were miles of tunnels beneath Crystal Falls, all of which she had explored, but as she stared at the entrance in front of her—a blackened square of darkness—she was afraid. Was it the hundreds of bodies that had flowed through here almost eight decades ago? Was it that she was alone while the others had someone to protect them? She decided it was neither of these things. It was the presence of something unseen yet stronger than anything she had experienced in the Falls.

Trish took a step forward and felt like she was learning to walk for the first time. Her mind said retreat, but her body continued into darkness. She scaled the steps, deciding that the chute next to the steps, wet from the dripping ceiling, was too slick to traverse. Halfway down the tunnel, Trish stopped and closed her eyes. She let her hearing take over. The drip of water splashed against the cracked concrete and echoed in the tunnel and her mind's eye. The thin pattering of tiny feet approached and then passed on the left. The tunnel felt much colder than the tunnels beneath Crystal Falls. She pressed her hand against the wall and felt as if she were ten years old again, crawling inside the igloo her father had built that winter. Somewhere in the construction, she had lost her glove, her tiny hands numb. She pulled her hand away and continued her journey.

Whatever was pulling her deeper into the tunnel was gaining strength. As crazy as things were in Crystal Falls, Trish still questioned the existence of a woman trapped in a sanatorium for all these years without ever being discovered. At the end of the tunnel, where the tunnel met the basement, Trish opened the door and entered a darkness so deep that she felt a scream rising. She swallowed hard, pushing the scream down for another time.

The illumination of her flashlight stopped two feet in front of her. She placed a hand along the wall—so warm she quickly withdrew—and began her trek into the darkened abyss. She noticed that the further she moved, the more heat radiated from the walls. She took this as a sign she was moving in the right direction. Forty-eight steps in—scared she would get lost, she had been counting her steps—she felt a heat that reminded her of a beach in July. She lowered the light beam and found the doorknob to the door was beginning to glow red. The door trembled, threatening to burst from its hinges.

Trish backed away and covered her eyes, the glow blinding. She crouched against the opposite wall and covered her face. The door blew inward, sucking Trish and everything within ten feet into the room. Trish slammed violently against something in the middle of the room. The flashlight skittered away. But the light was no longer needed as the glow from the large crate in the middle of the room illuminated the crate and the mirror-lined walls. She looked up and saw reflections of her reflection created by the ceiling and floor lined with mirrors.

Trish walked around the box, looking for an opening. When she found none, the hallway outside the room suddenly glowed. She stepped back into the hallway, looking left and right down never-ending corridors. *Forty-eight steps*, she reminded herself. To her right, jammed beneath an old filing cabinet, Trish found a metal rod, one end split but flat. She shoved the cabinet away and retrieved the metal rod, hefting it in her hands as she returned to the crate. She slipped the smooth end of the rod between two boards and tried prying the boards apart—nothing. She tried two other boards, and still, the boards would not give.

She glanced around the room. *The mirrors*, she thought to herself. Trish stepped away from the crate. She stood in front of the mirrors lining the back wall.

Breaking the mirrors around the room only became a challenge when all that was left were the ones above. Each swing brought shattered glass crashing down on top of her head, shoulders, and arms. Dozens of small punctures bled but did nothing to stop her destruction. Trish turned back to the crate with the last mirror lying on the ground in a thousand pieces. She cautiously approached the wooden box, ensuring that her efforts had not gone unnoticed. She slipped the smooth end of the rod between two boards and pushed, applying the full weight of her body. The boards splintered and separated. She moved to the next two panels along the top. They came away in one fluid motion.

Trish examined the smooth grayness beneath the boards and then glanced at the thousands of broken mirror pieces; the backs of the pieces resembled the same smooth, gray texture. She would surely injure who or what was inside if she broke the glass.

"Hello," she whispered, lowering her ear to the crate. "I'm going to break the glass," she said a little louder. But, instead of taking a full swing as she had done around the room, she raised the metal rod six inches above the glass and let it drop under its own weight. The glass cracked but did not shatter. She raised the rod again, letting it drop. As the glass broke, Trish took several steps back.

The woman who stood inside the box—slumped shoulders, hair stretching to her feet, fingernails so long that they curled in small circles—appeared frail and incapable of saving herself, much less Crystal Falls. The woman brushed back her hair, raised her head, and glared at Trish. Trish took a step back toward the door. *Forty-eight steps*, she said to herself.

"Wait," the woman said.

Trish stopped backpedaling. "Catherine Rhodes," she said sheepishly.

Catherine lurched from the crate, her joints sounding like loose boards on a staircase. She stretched out her arms, her face straining as she reached for nothing. She turned her palms up and twisted them side-to-side before clenching them into fists. Her knuckles popped like firecrackers. She looked around the room at the broken mirrors and turned her attention to Trish, who had begun cowering against the wall. Catherine moved toward her. As she kneeled in front of Trish, her knees popped so loud that Trish looked to see if they had dislocated. Catherine slid her hand through Trish's hair, studying the fine dark threads.

Catherine turned her head to glance at the box. Her neck sounded as if a dozen balloons popped one after another. "Who sent you?" Catherine turned her head and then stretched it side-to-side.

Trish explained what was happening in Crystal Falls, especially what was happening to Trish's friends. "So we need you to come back and help," Trish added.

Catherine offered Trish a hand and then helped her up. As they returned to the hallway and eventually down the body chute, Catherine lit the way while practicing what she no longer called her gift. She now called it her power. Outside, Catherine gawked at Trish's car. She then gazed toward the sky and the large jet flying overhead. Things had changed in eighty years.

Trish opened Catherine's door and helped her onto the passenger seat. She didn't think Catherine needed any help, but Trish had been assigned a task: bringing Catherine back to Crystal Falls. She watched Waverly disappear in the rearview mirror as they drove away, securely secluded by a strand of trees. "How were you never found?" Trish asked. "I mean, it was so easy for me."

"How do you find what you're not looking for," Catherine replied.

27

Crystal Falls
Present Day

Raven started toward Daniel and Mathew but stopped when Daniel stepped in front of Mathew. She turned to the crunching sound coming from the opposite side of the church. "Aunt Mary," she said. Aunt Mary had a can of Pringles in one hand and a wad of chips in the other. The man sitting next to Aunt Mary had a look of amusement on his face.

"What's going on, Raven?" Daniel asked. He approached the eighteen-year-old Raven, confused and concerned about his family. He took her hand. "What happened to you?"

Raven pulled away. "It's okay, Mathew," she told her teenage son. "Why're you here, Daniel?"

"Someone called and said you were in trouble and that

we should come for you, so we did." Daniel glanced around the church. "You going to explain all this?" He held out his hands.

"Mom?" Mathew said.

Raven smiled despite the danger they were in. Mathew made a move to come to her. "Wait," she said. She held out her hand for him to stop. He took a step back. Raven approached Aunt Mary.

"You sent the reunion invitations," Raven said confidently. "And you called them to come here." She pointed back at her son and husband. Raven's hands trembled. "You brought all of us here. Why?"

Semia placed a hand on Aunt Mary's shoulder. He stood, his six-foot-six frame towering over the much shorter Raven. Raven sauntered toward him. Semia shook his head and laughed. "This has all gotten out of control," he said. "It's time to put this little town to rest."

"I don't think so," Laura said. She closed the church door and joined Raven.

"Raven, what's going on?" Daniel insisted.

"Shut up, Daniel," Raven retorted.

"Don't speak to me . . ."

Raven dropped her hands to her sides and clenched her fists. She turned from the immediate danger and faced Daniel. "You," she said and poked him in the chest. "Have done nothing but shove me in a corner for our entire marriage. I've stood by and taken a back seat to everything you've put ahead of me."

"I'm a preacher," he said.

"And I'm your wife," Raven replied. " You treat your congregation ten times better than you treat me. You tell me what to do and when to do it. You expect dinner on the table at six and breakfast every morning at nine. I'm not your slave, Daniel." Raven looked around at her son. "I don't want him growing up to be like you!"

"You're ill," Daniel said.

Raven screamed. She then took a deep breath and looked Daniel straight in the eyes. "You're going to do as I say. You and Mathew are going to get back in your car, and you're going to drive back home. I will be there when I'm finished here. Do you understand me?" Daniel nodded that he understood. "Then we'll discuss our future."

"If the happy couple is finished playing Family Feud, I would like to point out that none of you are leaving," Semia said.

"Laura?"

Laura's mouth fell agape. Standing in the church entrance were Richard and their two daughters. "What're you doing here? I told you to leave."

"The woman called again. Said you were in trouble at the church."

Laura's eyes fell heavily on Aunt Mary.

Aunt Mary shoved another chip into her mouth, speechless.

Richard crossed the church and joined Laura. He stared at Semia. He glanced at Laura.

"Don't, Richard," Laura said.

But Richard did. Having never been in a fight, Richard swung wildly, missing Semia's face by six inches.

Semia laughed hyena-like. He pushed his palm at Richard—never touching him—sending him flailing across the room into the old wooden pews lined against the opposite wall. Daniel charged forward, spewing a myriad of bible verses. But, like Richard, he was flung across the room. "It would be wise not to do that again," Semia said to the two men trying to regain their composure.

Raven advanced hard, attempting a punch, surprised that Semia allowed the swing to find purchase against his chin. The man did not move. Raven backed away and then caught Laura racing past her.

Semia caught Laura by the throat and tossed her like a dog's chew toy across the room. Laura skidded to a stop beside her two daughters, who were cowering beside their father. Laura glanced at them, unsure if the girls feared Semia or the change that Laura had gone through.

Laura was the first to hear people yelling outside. She was also the first to the church doors. She swung the doors open and almost cried for help.

As a child, Laura had once sat with her father in his favorite recliner, watching an old black and white Frankenstein movie. Near the movie's end, she recalled the crowd outside Frankenstein's castle. The people carried pitchforks, picks, axes, and a few held torches. The group in front of her was very similar, except that torches were lanterns, archaic weapons replaced by shotguns. Their clothing was not far from the old black and white movie as everyone in the crowd wore garbs from a long past.

Laura scanned the town. Old houses lined cobblestone streets, and plain wooden structures with large glass windows sparsely marked the main road stretching out of town. Although Laura and the others had been thrown back two decades, the town had relapsed nearly a dozen decades. The people in front of her barked obscenities and began marching up the church steps. Laura backed away and slammed the church doors. She turned the lock and then turned to the others.

"What?" Raven said.

Laura swallowed hard. She shook her head. "It's not possible," she said. She ignored Raven and looked at Semia. "What's happening?"

Semia walked to the vestibule, climbed the two steps, and stood behind the pulpit. He leaned forward, his elbows resting on the pulpit that was no longer old and worn. "They think they want justice," he said. Raven and Laura moved forward. Semia looked down his nose at the two young women.

Laura's daughters screamed when something banged against the church doors. Raven's son moved next to her.

"What do you want from us?" Laura questioned. "We don't know you or them, so why are you doing this?" Another thump against the door brought another scream from Laura's daughters. "Let my family go," Laura said calmly.

A slow smile developed across Semia's face. "I can't do that," he said. "Things are out of whack in the Falls and must be corrected." He opened his arms to the church. "You are the correction." He stepped from behind the pulpit and paced back and forth across the front of the church as he spoke. "You must pay for the sins of your father."

"Who're you to decide what happens to us?" Raven asked. She put her arms around her son as Semia descended the steps toward them.

"Who am I?" He said. He adjusted his tie and shrugged his shoulders beneath his suit coat. "I'm the monster under the bed, the thing that hides in the closet, the noise in the attic, the finger that pulls the trigger, the pilot error, cancer that fills the body of a child, the water that fills the lungs, the hands that spread fault lines, the wind that swirls across the plains, the disturbance that pushes winds across the waters onto land, the one who makes the water rise. I am everything he is not." Semia pointed upward. "I AM CHAOS. I have the say in your lives: what you do, where you live and work, how and when you die. I make the rules, you follow the rules, all because of humanity's need for free will." Semia rolled his head around his shoulders. "I am lust, greed, gluttony, wrath, slothfulness, pride, and envy. I AM EVERYTHING HE IS NOT!"

"Jealous much?" Raven said. "He's ultimately in charge," she pointed a finger toward the roof, "and you're just a temporary has been."

Enraged, Semia darted across the room and grabbed Daniel. Mathew yelled and raced for his dad. Semia swung with his free hand, knocking Mathew unconscious and sprawling across the room. Raven gasped and followed after her son.

"Why don't you kill us and get it over with?" Raven screamed. She raised Mathew's head and laid it on her leg. She brushed his sweaty hair away from his face.

"He can't," Laura said. "Can you?" Semia gazed at her and stopped moving. "We have to do it. That's where he gets his kicks. We all know right from wrong, but how often do we make the right choices? And when we make the wrong choice, this asshole is involved." Although Semia seemed to smirk at Laura's summation, Laura saw something in his eyes—fear. Really? She followed him with her eyes as he moved past her, heading for the doors. Was he leaving them?

Semia turned the lock and opened the doors, stepping aside so the fuming mob could fill the church. A dozen men cornered Laura and the others, herding them like cattle into the church's center platform. The crowd surrounded the platform. One of the men slinked forward and took his place behind the pulpit. Laura looked around for Semia—gone. To her left, Aunt Mary, still eating chips, stared aimlessly toward the front of the church, so unaware of her surroundings that Laura questioned if that were truly Aunt Mary.

"You," a man yelled. "The whore child of a demon."

Laura questioningly pointed at herself. She then recognized the man yelling at her. "Mr. Saddlebrook," she said.

Saddlebrook slammed his hand against the pulpit as if he were ready to preach hellfire and brimstone. "Silence! I warned you, told you not to stay here. And now look what you've done." He looked away from Laura and addressed the congregation. "Cornelius Miles is dead," he shouted. The people watching him raised their voices, demanding those standing on the platform die. "For what you've done," he said, "for what your father's did."

The crowd moved away from the small platform and made way for another man to enter the church. Laura turned and squinted, immediately recognizing Mr. Case, who had filled her gas tank. Except this, Mr. Case was much younger, dressed differently, and was carrying a large empty kerosene can. Case approached the pulpit and nodded his head. He placed the empty can next to the pulpit and exited the church, but not before grabbing a lantern from one of the men watching him.

The crowd slowly slinked from the church and down the stairs, standing at the foot of the steps and staring back into the church. Laura glanced over at Aunt Mary, who was nowhere to be seen. Upon exiting, Mr. Saddlebrook closed the church doors. A thump against the doors quieted the crowd outside.

"What's happening?" Daniel asked.

Richard stepped to one of the windows, opened it, and slammed his hand against the boards that blocked their way. He glanced around the church. "All of the windows are boarded?"

Laura nodded. "We've got to get out of the church," she said. Daniel grabbed her arm. She jerked her arm away and stepped back.

"What'd you do?" Daniel questioned.

Raven moved between Daniel and Laura, facing Daniel. "Find us a way out," she said and poked him in the chest. "Enough of your orders."

"Laura," Richard said. "We need to move the platform. We can get out through the hatch."

Laura moved to help but stopped when her daughters screamed again. "The church's on fire," she said as smoke rolled under the doors. "Hurry!"

They moved to the right side of the platform. In unison, they pushed against the platform. Muscles strained, veins bulged, and hearts pumped wildly, but the platform stayed in place.

"It's too heavy," Richard said. He pushed again and again, but the platform rested in place. "Girls," he said. The daughters moved to his side, the three staring at Laura like she'd just landed on Earth.

Laura felt the tears welling way before they began to pour. She moved to her knees in front of her daughters. "I'm so sorry," she said. "I didn't know." Richard kneeled next to her, the four now at eye level with each other. Laura placed her hand against Richard's cheek.

Raven sat on one of the pews next to Daniel and Mathew.

"I'm sorry," Daniel said.

"I'm the one who should be sorry," Raven said. "I put my family in danger."

"No," Daniel said, "I've been a complete asshole since day one."

Mathew looked up and cracked a smile. "Dad said 'asshole'."

"I should've never treated you the way I have," Daniel said, ignoring his son's intentional use of the word asshole.

Smoke filled the room as the doors burned. The roof crackled and popped before a loud snapping sound filled the room. They looked up as one of the large support beams fell from the ceiling, impaling the platform, half the beam disappearing below the ground. A ten-foot piece protruded into the air, the top three feet burning red and yellow.

"Laura!"

Laura looked toward the center of the room.

"Laura. Raven!"

"Jake," Laura said. She ran to the platform. Jake stood at the bottom of the hole created by the fallen beam. "Come on," she yelled.

One by one, they slid down the beam and into the tunnel beneath the church. Richard, the last one down, stepped beneath the mangled hole and found himself face-to-face with Jake. "Jake Simon," Richard said and held out his hand.

Jake glanced around at the others. He took Richard's hand. "And you are?"

"Richard Knox." Richard nodded at Laura. "Laura's husband."

Jake let go of the man's hand. His head twitched, and his neck stiffened. He glanced at Laura again. Another beam fell from the ceiling and landed across the smashed hatch. "I guess we should find a way out of here," Jake said robotically. "We'll head back toward the waterfall." He turned away from Richard and helped Landon, who had not said a word since Richard slid down the beam. "This way," Jake said, leading the way until their passage was blocked.

28

Crystal Falls
Present Day

Trish examined her hands and shook her head. When she left the Falls hours ago, she had returned to the thirty-eight-year-old woman who had lived in the Falls a few days ago. Now that she and Catherine had just crossed the county line, Trish returned to her eighteen-year-old troubled youth. But it was no big deal. Nothing surprised Trish anymore, especially not the ten-year-old Catherine Rhodes standing before her.

"I was ten years old when I left the Falls," Catherine explained. "And whatever's controlling the Falls is also controlling time. It'll make us what it wants."

Trish tossed the car keys in the seat. "Looks like we're hoofing it," she said.

"Hoofing it?"

"Walking," Trish replied. "It's about two miles to the church."

Catherine pointed. "Where that smoke's coming from?

"Shit," Trish said. "We need to hurry."

They walked fast as Catherine adjusted to her new body, only guessing that her gift still worked as a child. Trish had explained the last few days and the previous twenty years. Catherine surmised that this was the work of the man who had locked her away almost eighty years ago. He told her she had to set things right and fix what her parents had broken. But he, Semia, she remembered his name, was the cause, not her parents. She also thought about Alan Chesterfield, her husband, who would be dead by now. And there was Agatha. She didn't want to think about what those men had done to Agatha. Maybe it had gone fast when they had their way with her and not allowed her to suffer. She knew that wouldn't have been the case. Never was.

As they passed Hank McCoy's old property, Catherine stopped. "It's there," she said. "Where my parents were murdered." Turning, she crossed her arms and studied the bed and breakfast. "Who does that belong to?"

"Landon's Aunt Mary," Trish replied. "Doesn't look like she's returned yet." Trish noticed Catherine still staring at the house. "What's wrong?"

"Just a feeling," Catherine said. "There's something wrong with the house and Aunt Mary."

"She's obese and loves potato chips," Trish replied. "She said she's been watching the woods over there for the past twenty years."

Catherine nodded. Something felt wrong. She returned her attention to the woods. "Doesn't appear to have changed much."

Crystal Falls: A Witch's Revenge

"They're very different. Trust me," Trish said. "You can be walking in one direction, thinking you know where you're going, and then all of a sudden you're either lost or heading a direction you weren't meaning to go." She leaned against the fence. "There's darkness in there."

Catherine gazed down the road toward the church. "The church is gone," she said. "That's not the direction we need to head." She moved from the fence and started down the road leading into the woods.

"Wait a minute," Trish said. "My friends are back that way. They need our help."

Catherine slowed and waited for Trish. Trish moved in front of her. "Your friends are traveling through the tunnels right now. I can feel them. They're heading toward the woods, maybe to the falls."

Trish looked back toward the rising smoke and chewed her lip momentarily. She rubbed her hands together, trying to decide. Landon, that's who she was most concerned about. She had told him she would come back. She pressed her hands against her temples. "Okay, okay. Come on."

As they passed the old farmhouse that had once belonged to Hank McCoy, Trish stopped before entering the woods. "We need a flashlight. The woods change, and the trail switches back on itself, leading us where it chooses."

Catherine quickly stood at the tree line and rubbed her hands together, building pressure. Trish watched with child-like awe. Catherine opened her hands, and a softball-sized ball of light hovered over her right hand. The trees and ground twenty feet ahead glowed as if an afternoon sun was overhead. "This should help," Catherine said, keeping her eyes on the trees.

"Will you be able to stop the Falls? Stop the trail from

changing?" Trish asked. She had been in the Falls long enough to know that the Falls did what it pleased. She had no misconceptions that a ten-year-old girl had any such powers over an entity as large as what was controlling Crystal Falls.

"I think it's going to allow us to go where we want because where we want is exactly where *it* wants us," Catherine said. She smiled and glanced at Trish. "Clear as mud?"

Trish nodded. She couldn't help but keep her eyes on the ten-year-old Catherine. At Catherine's age, Trish had experienced something no one should ever have to experience. Almost twenty-eight years removed, for the life of her, she couldn't remember what had driven her to do such a thing. Kill her mother—why? What was so wrong with her mother? She stepped over a downed tree and massaged the back of her neck. She considered her arrival in the Falls, the death of her father, murdering Clark—killing all the others. And then she recalled her conversation in the car with Catherine about Catherine's stay in San Francisco.

Catherine had described this man named Babcock. Several hours before killing her mother, Trish had been approached at the playground by a man fitting the description of Babcock. He had given her a necklace and told her he had found it on the road and thought she should have it. She had turned to her dad sitting on the bench talking to another father, wanting to ask him if it was okay. She didn't want to interrupt, so she took the necklace from Babcock and placed it around her neck. When she looked up to thank the man, he was gone. She remembered feeling sick afterward, eventually asking her father if they could go home.

Trish stood in front of the bathroom mirror at home and

studied the necklace. She went to bed still wearing the necklace but woke around midnight from a terrible dream, her body dripping sweat. Looking back, she realized her father had never told her where he kept the family's only handgun. But that night, she entered her parents' bedroom, opened the closet door, and removed the small locked box holding the gun. The gun had not been in the desk drawer like she originally thought. She turned each of the small dials, landing on the proper numbers without knowing which were correct, opened the box, and removed the gun.

The carpet on the way to her mother's side of the bed had been soft, tickling the bottoms of her feet as if her feet were not pushing down on the carpet but hovering, only brushing against the soft fabric. And then the necklace hurt, she remembered. She had reached to take it off, but something stopped her. She raised the gun, looking at her mother. The necklace hurt more, so she lowered the gun to rip the necklace away. But then there was a hand on hers. She looked up, and the man from the playground stood beside her, holding her hand. He helped her raise the gun and wrapped his finger around hers, the one dancing around the gun's trigger. There was pressure against her finger and then a loud bang. She fell head-over-heels against the bedroom wall. She searched for the man, but he was gone. She reached for the necklace —gone.

Trish stopped walking.

"What's wrong?" Catherine asked.

Trish stood in silence, her eyes wide, jaw frozen in fear. She raised her eyes to Catherine. "I didn't do it," Trish said. "I didn't kill my mother." She tilted her head and intertwined her fingers. "It was that man."

"Who?" Catherine questioned.

"Babcock. He was there, in my mother's room." Trish held her hands out from her sides. "I didn't do it."

He stood before them, filling the tunnel, blocking their way. In the front pocket of his overalls rested a dirty, red bandana. His right hand held the butt of a shotgun, the barrel leaning against his right shoulder, pointing toward the ceiling. He spat a wad of blackness against the tunnel wall and smiled when the wad burst into flames. The three or four teeth at the front of his mouth threatened a quick exit. His hair, thin and gray, did little to hide the twelve-inch scar that started at his left temple, stretched high above his left ear, and then disappeared around the back of his head.

With all that had happened the past few days, Jake was still astonished to see Hank McCoy standing in front of him. Neither rock nor time had been able to take the man's life. "We don't want any trouble," Jake said, remembering that he had said something similar twenty years ago. He raised his hands chest level, keeping his eyes on McCoy and the gun. "We just want to leave this place and return home." Jake lowered his left hand, patting the air with his right. "Clark Hanson, the man, I mean boy, who did this to you is dead. So we should call things even."

McCoy spat against the wall again. The miniature fireball exploded, sending embers through the tunnel. "You still on my property, boy," McCoy replied, raspy-voiced. He looked around Jake at the others. "I seen that Clark boy die." He scratched an itch on his neck with the end of the shotgun. "Time for the rest of you to die."

Jake felt the rock breeze by his ear and saw the same rock crush McCoy's nose.

As he dropped to the ground, McCoy released the gun, attempting to steady his fall. The weapon bounced toward Jake, who immediately grabbed it and showed McCoy the end of the barrel. McCoy managed to heave himself to his knees. He spied Richard, who held a second rock, ready to finish what Clark couldn't twenty years ago. "This ain't the end," McCoy said. "It ain't never gonna be the end." He struggled to his feet.

"We can't let him leave," Laura said. "He'll follow us and try this again."

Raven grabbed the rock from Richard's hand and charged forward. McCoy threw up his arms a second too late. Raven's first of many blows caught McCoy in the temple. He dropped to his knees again. Raven beat McCoy's head into the rocky floor until his brains spilled outward. A hand squeezed her right shoulder, and then another squeezed her left. When she stopped scrambling McCoy's brains, she gazed at the blood and matter covering her arms and hands. She turned her head, her eyes catching her son's scared and confused face. She felt the hands slip under her arms and pull upward, settling her to her feet. She dropped the rock, which splashed against the mangled head of Hank McCoy. "He was never going to stop," she said. Her voice cracked, and the gush of tears sent her to the ground.

Laura moved between Raven and Daniel, who had helped Raven to her feet. "Let's go," Laura said softly, stepping over the bloody mass marking the tunnel floor. She took Raven's hand and guided her over McCoy's body.

The others followed silently. Jake, however, stood in the same spot, staring at what remained of Hank McCoy. McCoy had to be dead this time, right? He then stepped over the body and let McCoy fade into darkness.

They traveled for another twenty minutes before the sound of rushing water filled the tunnel. Landon rested on a rock, studying a second blown-out knee. All he could do now was hope that Trish had found Catherine Rhodes. Hope wasn't a strategy but something to lean on when no strategy seemed possible. None of them—those born in the Falls—believed they would ever leave Crystal Falls dead or alive. They would become a permanent fixture, like the waterfall before them. That was okay, he supposed, as long as Trish returned. But then Trish had a choice. She could leave them all here to die while she continued her merry way. Things could be worse, he figured as he looked at Jake, who unhappily watched an embrace between Laura and her husband. Yeah, things in the relationship area could be a lot worse.

"The water'll be freezing," Daniel said. He held a hand out beneath the water. He then glanced to each side. "No other way."

"Richard," Laura said. "I need you to do something for me." Richard had the look of *please, not again*. "The river marks the county line. Take the girls to the right. Twenty feet, and you're in the next county." Richard started to protest. Laura held a finger to his mouth. "Do it. It's the only way the girls are safe." He nodded his resignation.

Raven, only partially recovered from the Hank McCoy beat down, ordered Daniel to do the same with Mathew, assuring him that she would be safe—a lie they certainly all knew. "This is between us," she motioned toward Laura,

Landon, and Jake, "and the Falls." Daniel nodded his resignation as well, his lips whispering I love you. Raven nodded.

"I'll head out first," Landon offered. "My knee could use an icepack." He limped toward the falling water and then fell forward. And although the water soothed his knee, it also felt like someone had filled his underwear with snow. He waded to the left and crawled onto land, wishing Trish had been waiting for him.

Jake splashed into the water next, his body submerging. He came up shaking water from his hair. He glided toward Landon and crawled next to his best friend. He looked back at the waterfall. "Can you believe I'm going to lose the same woman twice?" He wiped his face with his wet hand. "If we do get out of this, I'm going to buy a new sign for my building: Shitty luck this way." Noticing Landon's eyes a million miles away, Jake said, "Trish?"

Landon, legs stretched out, half on his back, half on his elbows, sighed. "We finally did it, you know. Back there in the cave before I smacked you over the head." He let out a loud breath. "Damn it, I love that woman, and now she's gone. But you know, I don't blame her. I'd get as far away from this fucking place as I could and never look back."

They watched Laura splash into the water and then watched Richard and the girls follow. Richard held onto the girls, his footing firm against the rocks below. He kissed Laura on the cheek. On the cheek? Jake sat up straight. On the cheek? Really?

"Get them as far away as possible," Laura said. She hugged her two girls, knowing she would never see them again.

Daniel and Mathew followed, splashing Laura's family, who were still saying their goodbyes. Raven followed, kissed

Mathew on the forehead, hugged him, and then turned toward Jake and Landon.

Laura released her daughters and watched them follow their father across the water, Daniel and Mathew in tow. Richard stepped from the river and then reached for his daughters. Daniel also climbed the bank and then turned to grab Mathew.

At first, Raven thought her eyes were playing tricks, her chattering teeth blurring her vision. Mathew's hand reached for his father but only found a wall of darkness. She glanced at Laura's two daughters, darkness up to their elbows as they reached for their father.

Laura crossed the water, kicking her knees high, feeling as if something beneath the water was grabbing her feet. Tears swelled in her eyes. The look on Richard's face was pure loathing and hate. She watched him try to move toward the water, but it was as if he were working out on a treadmill.

Raven splashed toward Mathew. Daniel's head shook as he watched her and his son. "I'm sorry," she screamed. She grabbed Mathew and pulled his wet body against hers. "I'm sorry. I'm so sorry."

Mathew raised his head to look at his mother. "It's okay, Mom. I'll protect you. I promise." He wrapped his arms around his mother and gave her a reassuring hug. He took her hand and began leading her toward Jake and Landon. On land, he turned to his father and slowly waved. His dad waved back and said, "I love you."

Laura's girls reacted much differently. They screamed for their father, who looked on helplessly. Laura reached for their hands, but they pulled away. She glanced at Richard. The hate in his eyes reminded her of the hatred in Hank McCoy's eyes back in the tunnel. Laura spoke softly to her girls, telling them they would be safe and that she would help them get back to their father. None of which she thought was true. With no other options, the two girls followed their mother to the opposite side, joining Raven and Mathew.

Jake stepped forward. He wanted to hug Laura, tell her everything would be okay. But all four adults knew that would be a lie. "We need to get them somewhere warm," Jake said. He motioned toward the three kids.

"I can start a fire," Mathew offered and began foraging the bank of the river. "We need some dry twigs and a handful of dry grass." He scowled at Jake. "Come on, help me."

Jake considered laughing but also considered the situation. He moved to the line of trees to the left. He collected a handful of dead grass and then retrieved several twigs. Happy with his bounty, he turned to show Mathew.

Mathew gawked at the large man standing before him, remembering the man's clothes from his history books. Mathew slowly backed away, nearly tripping over a downed tree. He joined his mother and the others who gathered in a group. The large man moved forward.

Laura left the group and cautiously approached the man. She studied his face and saw something recognizable. "Arthur Rhodes," she said.

Arthur nodded.

29

Crystal Falls
Present Day

Trish stared at the overgrowth and wondered why Catherine found the ground in front of them so intriguing. Catherine was in a trance like she was studying a movie reel inside her head. On days she felt lost when she needed to get away from Fast Eddie's and become one with nature, Trish had strolled by this very spot a dozen times without ever giving it a second thought.

"We lived here," Catherine finally said, her face flexed into amusement, obviously reliving a magnanimous memory. "I always thought it strange when people from town visited, and my mother never invited them inside. My friends and I played outside; hide-and-seek was our favorite.
"I knew my parents were different from the other parents. I guess I didn't realize how different."

Trish placed a hand on Catherine's shoulder. "My

friends," she said, her voice filled with reluctance. She understood Catherine's grief, but Trish still had friends who were alive and needed Catherine's help.

Catherine nodded, and the two turned to leave.

"Catherine," Isabella Rhodes said.

Catherine stopped and grabbed Trish's arm. "Mother?"

"Yes."

"How?"

Isabella glanced at Trish. "You did well."

Trish nodded and moved away from Catherine.

"You're dead," Catherine said.

Isabella stepped forward, embracing Catherine, who stood board-still. Isabella moved to her knees and was at eye level with her daughter. "This town did nothing more than make me even stronger," she said. "But I needed you, my darling daughter, to leave this place." Isabella paused, her face hard. "Leave," she said to Trish.

"My friends need our help." Trish motioned toward Catherine. "I can't go without them."

Isabella pushed to her feet, and the ground beneath her trembled. "I suggest you leave, Trish."

"No, Mother," Catherine said.

Isabella ignored Catherine's plea, approaching Trish, fists clenched. "Do not tempt me," Isabella said. "You had one job to do. Bring me my daughter. Nothing here for you, and I won't tell you a third time to leave."

Trish stumbled back, catching her footing before falling over a log. *Landon. She couldn't leave without Landon.* Isabella caught her by the neck and raised her off the ground. Fire burned in Isabella's eyes. Trish struggled to breathe, Isabella's hand tightening. Isabella's face changed, and Trish tried to turn away.

Catherine grabbed her mother's arm, held it, and pulled

it toward the ground, lowering Trish. "Mother."

Isabella released Trish, and Trish dropped to her knees, coughed, and then vomited. Isabella turned to her daughter.

"I won't be like you," Catherine said. "I won't treat people the way you and father did. "Trish saved me. I won't let you harm her." Catherine shuffled toward Trish, standing between her mother and Trish. She glared at her mother questioningly. "What are we?"

Isabella stroked Catherine's cheek. "We're called the Dark Ones, the most ancient beings. We're also called the great equalizers." She locked her fingers together, a partial smile crossing her face. This was the mother-daughter talk she had always hoped for. "You," she said to Catherine, "were created to carry on what I started."

Catherine shook her head, afraid of how her mother might answer the question she'd had since speaking to Semia decades ago. "What is that you and I are supposed to do?" Catherine tensed as she awaited the answer she was sure she wouldn't like.

"It's very simple," Isabella replied. "Ensure that humanity meets its full potential. That it understands it has no limitations." She looked skyward. "Despite what anyone else may have suggested."

"I'm not interested."

"It matters not. You don't choose it. It chooses you." Isabella cupped Catherine's face in her hands. "It created you."

"And father?"

Isabella sighed, obviously frustrated with Arthur. "Your father is part human, part incubus. He's a very confused being," she said condescendingly. "He babbles on and on about switching sides, never quite understanding his role the way I understand mine."

"He's alive," Catherine replied.

"Yes, he's traipsing around these woods somewhere." Isabella released Catherine's face and stood, turning her attention to Trish. "You." She moved closer to Trish. "Have had many an opportunity to leave Crystal Falls, and you wander around here like a lost puppy dog."

"No, mother."

Isabella shrugged and threw back her head, releasing a stream of fire that instantly engulfed Trish, turning her into a clump of burning embers.

Catherine screamed and pushed Isabella away. She stood over the ashes of the woman who had rescued her, anger burning inside, pleading to be released. She turned on her mother, ready to surge forward, stopping as two men and a large woman sauntered from the woods.

"Mighty good show," Semia said. He gave Catherine a passing glance. "I would've liked to have thanked our friend there," he motioned toward the pile of ashes, "but you've already done my dirty work, Isabella." Seeing Isabella's surprise, Semia continued. "Oh yes, she was working for me as well. All of them were. They just didn't know it." He nudged the pile of ash with his foot. "Unfortunately, it all took much longer than I'd hoped, but then what's a few years when you've been around for millenniums?"

Catherine moved past Semia and the other man she recognized as Babcock. "Agatha," she said to Aunt Mary. "What're you doing here? No, how are you here?"

Agatha (Aunt Mary) waited for Semia's okay. He nodded. "I had a choice," Agatha said. "Help them and be given the gift of immortality, or die." She felt a tinge of regret. "I'm sorry," she said. "I didn't want to die."

Catherine laid her hand against Agatha's face but did not turn away from the bright light that consumed Agatha.

Incredible, Catherine thought to herself at the energy flowing through her body. Not only did she still have her gift, but it had become ten times what it was. When she removed her hand from Agatha's face, the brilliant light subsided, and the younger, much thinner Agatha stood before her. "Better," Catherine said.

"I hate to break up this lovely reunion, but we have matters that must be sorted out. You," Semia said to Isabella, "will return to the pit and eternal retribution immediately. And you," he said to Catherine. "I'm not quite sure what to do with you yet."

"I'm not going back again," Isabella said. "And if you try to send me back, I'll only escape again." She moved away, nervous.

"Looks like we have an old Mexican standoff," Semia said. "Babcock."

Babcock grabbed Catherine by the neck and wrestled her arms behind her back.

"Struggle all you want, but you'll be unable to harm Mr. Babcock. He's fought more challenging battles than a bratty ten-year-old." Semia paused but noticed Agatha on the move, "Don't," he said. "I won't feel bad about reneging on my promise of your immortality." He saw Isabella stepping back into the shadows from the corner of his eye. He placed his fist against his mouth and snapped his hand toward Isabella. She ducked to the right but not nearly in time. The fiery chain from his hand closed around her neck instantly. Though she was still in human form, she was also his dog on a flaming leash. He jerked her forward, and she rolled to his feet.

"Now all we lack is Arthur Rhodes. Shall we?" Semia said and started toward the river.

30

Crystal Falls
Present Day

Arthur Rhodes marveled over the small gathering in front of him. He had promised long ago to do away with every Crystal Falls descendent, but now he wasn't so sure. This was the human side of him that Isabella often complained about, informing him that people were here for the ancient ones' enjoyment. It was hard to argue with her summation, especially regarding creatures with so much disregard for one another. Murder, suicide, rape, crime, war. But then, didn't the ancient ones cause these things?

"This is not our fault," Laura said as she and the others followed Rhodes through the forest. "And now our children have to pay for something they knew nothing about." She grabbed Arthur by the arm and stopped him. "Your daughter is still alive."

"This is something only Isabella can fix," Arthur said. "We need to find her."

Landon, struggling to keep up, sighed in frustration. "What if she says no? Then what?"

Arthur shrugged. "Then you're stuck here."

"Stuck in Crystal Falls," Jake said. They were all still their eighteen-year-old selves. "As teenagers?"

Arthur started back down the path toward the river and the tree. "That's correct."

"We're not going to see Dad again, are we?" Mathew asked Raven.

Raven wasn't sure how to answer the question. Nothing they had experienced was possible, and yet here they were. "I will do everything I can to get us home, Mathew. I promise."

One of Laura's daughters tugged on her shorts. "I wanna go home."

Like Raven, Laura didn't know what to say. Deep down, Laura didn't think they would ever leave Crystal Falls. She didn't believe Arthur would allow Isabella to harm her, but she wasn't so sure he could control anything else regarding his wife.

"I don't get why you're helping us," Landon said. His foot hit a rock and twisted, sending him to the ground in pain. Everyone stopped and stared. His ankle instantly swelled, and his knee looked like a balloon filled with water. "I can't keep going."

"Stop!" Laura said, and Arthur turned. "We need to help him."

Arthur pointed at Laura. "You need to help him."

"I'll do it," Jake said and started toward Landon.

Rhodes grabbed Jake's arm. "No. Laura needs to do

this." He released Jake and stood over Laura, kneeling next to Landon. "Place your hands on his knee."

Landon smiled despite the pain.

"What can I do?" Laura asked and then remembered what her father had said. "And you stop smiling."

Rhodes saw the recognition on Laura's face. He held out one hand and placed his other hand over it. Everyone moved away when the space between his hands began to glow.

"Mommy," Laura's oldest daughter said, staring at her glowing hands.

"Put your hands on his knee," Arthur said again.

Laura complied.

Landon screamed.

"Get up, young man," Rhodes ordered.

Landon stared at his knee. The pain and swelling was gone. "How the hell did you do that?"

"Was it passed on to her from you?" Raven said to Arthur, and he nodded. "So she can get us out of here."

"It's possible," Rhodes said. "But she will need Isabella's help."

Landon stood and jogged in place. "Shit. Never felt better."

"My father said everyone from Crystal Falls has this power." Laura reached for Jake's hand. "Try it."

Rhodes began back on the path. "It's not that easy," he said. "It has to be believed. Your father made you believe."

"This is bullshit," Jake said, pulling his hand away.

"You know it's not," Laura said. She took her daughters by the hand and followed Arthur.

They followed Arthur Rhodes for nearly twenty minutes before finding the river, the familiar spot from twenty years ago, and a group of people only Arthur knew.

"Aunt Mary?" Landon asked and walked to Agatha. "What the hell?" She looked amazingly young and fit.

Agatha placed her hand against Landon's face. "Yes and no." She waited for Semia's approval. "Under orders, I came here long ago to watch things. I'm afraid we're not related at all."

"This from your whore child?" Isabella asked Arthur, nodding at Laura.

"Enough with the reunions," Semia said. "We have business to attend to." He shoved Isabella into the center of the group. She immediately turned on him, ready to cast a spell. Semia waved a lazy hand, and Isabella flew backward. He pointed at Arthur to stop when he started to attack. "You two are the cause of this mess."

"Then let us go," Raven said. "We did nothing wrong."

"Who're you?" Laura asked. She moved her daughters back.

"Semia. Head counsel for the Dispatch." He motioned toward Babcock, and Babcock shoved Catherine down next to Isabella.

Arthur broke from the group and went to his family. "You need to stop whatever it is you're doing."

"You lost control of her, Arthur," Semia said. "Our kind does not draw attention to ourselves by destroying an entire community."

"Because we're more human than that?" Arthur questioned.

Semia crossed his arms. "No. Because those are the rules, and rules are in place for a reason. It keeps the Ancient Ones safe and the rest of us in power." He grabbed Isabella by the hair and waved his hand at Arthur. For his troubles, Arthur stood in a cage made of vipers. "Remove the curse, Isabella."

"Do as he says, Isabella," Arthur said.

"Please, Mother." Catherine went to her side. "If she removes the curse, will you let her live?" Catherine turned her eyes to Semia.

Semia motioned for Babcock to move away. "Remove the curse, Isabella, and your family will be free." He dropped her to the ground and stepped away. "You have my word."

Agatha shuffled forward and tried to grab Catherine's hand. Catherine pulled away.

"No," Catherine said to Agatha.

"This isn't right." Agatha knelt in front of Semia. "Please let Catherine live."

Semia nodded. "She will be free, and the Dispatch will return to St. Louis. I've given my word."

"Your word doesn't mean shit," Agatha said, pushing to her feet. She backed away from Semia and stood between him and Catherine. "He's going to kill all of us. Don't do it, Isabella."

Semia sighed. He could reverse the curse himself, but the time and effort weren't worth expending energy over. Besides, he liked the cat and mouse game. "I won't tell you again, Isabella. The next time I do, you and your family will join the curse placed on Crystal Falls."

"Please, Isabella. Do as he says. We'll take Catherine and go." Arthur let his eyes look into Isabella's dark soul, reading her mind and heart. *Do it, my love. We'll leave here and start over. We can be the family we were.*

Using a stick, Isabella drew a pentagram in the dirt and stood in its center. She held her arms out and spoke to the Ancient Ones. She asked forgiveness for her selfishness and then asked that the curse on Crystal Falls be released. She brought her hands together, and her body shimmered, turning gold.

Catherine looked past her mother and into the eyes of Semia. He was a liar or liars. "No, Mother!"

The ground shook, and gray, bloated clouds sunk in the sky, washing over the trees. The river seemed to burp, and a wave of water washed over the bank. Everyone but she and Semia fell to the ground. Isabella turned to the liar of liars, realizing her mistake.

"Until eternity, witch!" Semia clapped his hands together, instantly turning Isabella, Arthur, and Catherine into ash. He laughed and nudged the ashes with his boot. "As I promised, you are all free."

Agatha screamed and went for Semia, pulled away by Babcock as she started a swing. "Demon Bastard!"

Semia grabbed Agatha by the throat and tossed her into the river.

"Why're you doing this?" Laura asked.

Semia leaned against the charred tree and lit a cigar. He blew gray smoke into the air and lazily shrugged.

"Isabella was a rogue who didn't know how to keep in step with the rest of her kind. Although all is chaos, there is also an order to things." He puffed harder on the cigar. "The time is coming for the Ancient Ones to be released and wreak havoc. Isabella got ahead of the game. She refused to turn back."

"Catherine was just a child," Raven said. "Is that what you're going to do to our children?"

"If necessary," Semia stared at the cigar's glowing end." Until then, I bid you adieu."

"Adieu?" Landon said. "What the fuck are you talking about? Where are you going?"

Semia and Babcock started through the trees.

"They left," Jake said. "What the hell are we supposed to do?"

Laura grabbed her daughters. "We take the path back."

The others followed Laura through the forest, keeping up to prevent the darkness from collapsing upon them. When they came to the tree line and where Hank McCoy's house should have been, Laura, terrified, stopped.

"It should be right here," Laura said.

Landon moved to the front. "Aunt Mary's, Agatha's, whoever the hell she was, house should be across a road that's not there."

"The streetlights are gone." Raven, Mathew in tow, continued forward.

"Shh," Jake said. "Everybody down."

As a group, they watched a wagon appear from the trees to the right, heading toward Crystal Falls. Chained, dirty, and lifeless, two women and a child were inside the wagon. The men laughed and drank, belching and singing songs none had heard before.

"Look at their clothes," Raven said.

"We weren't returned to our own time." Jake stood when the two men and wagon were gone. Jake started in the direction from where the wagon came.

"Jake," Landon called. "What're you doing?"

"Finding the truth."

The others followed Jake on his untold mission. The county line would have been a half-mile from Aunt Mary's house.

Jake counted his steps as he progressed toward the county line, telling himself none of this could be true. When he reached where the county line should be, he pressed his hand against an invisible wall. Just as he thought, they were trapped. He turned to the others and shook his head.

"There is no going home," Jake said.

Raven covered her mouth, and the scream surely making its way from her soul.

Laura pulled her daughters close and hugged them.

Landon stared at Jake.

"We're part of the Falls now," Jake said. He turned from the group and started back into the forest.

When they entered the forest, they heard the laugh of a madman—Semia.

"Welcome to Crystal Falls," Semia said, voice carrying through the trees. "The Dispatch is happy to have you."

About the Author

I'm an Indie writer born and raised in Lexington, Kentucky, where most of my stories are set. When not writing, I'm either traveling or spending time with family. I wrote my first story in eighth grade. It was my version of *Willy Wonka and The Chocolate Factory*. In 2008, I graduated with an MFA in Creative Writing and jumped into genre writing.

FOLLOW ME
www.markspearsauthor.com
Amazon
Facebook

Other Books By

MARK SPEARS

Finding Eve

Devondale

Madeline

My Father's Secrets

The Legend of Catfish Joe and Other Kentucky Stories

Who We Are

Bottom of The Ninth